RailRoaded

Books by J.L. Crafts

Will Toal Novels
RailRoaded

Coming Soon!
Will Toal Novels
Silver City Reckoning
Clear Cut Justice
Tahoe Destiny
Range War

For more information
visit: www.SpeakingVolumes.us

RailRoaded

J.L. Crafts

SPEAKING VOLUMES, LLC
NAPLES, FLORIDA
2023

RailRoaded

ISBN 978-1-64540-895-6

This book and all those in this series are
dedicated to William Jeffrey Crafts
October 28, 2003 to December 2, 2020.

Acknowledgments

Any acknowledgements must start with Colleen, my wife of over four decades, who has always been my first reader, my first critic, and my most ardent supporter. My life has been blessed with her presence.

I must also thank all those friends and family who have lent their names and personalities to the characters in the story. I hope I've done them justice.

Thanks also must go out to the wonderful group of friends and colleagues led by Wayne Purcell, Dan Frisch and Linda Crafts, who took the time to read early manuscripts and provide invaluable feedback. My initial readers also included Dale Paris, a true horse whisperer in the disguise of our farrier when he leaves his bowler hat at home who kept me in line and informed on all things equine.

Thanks also to my technical editor, Diane Davis-White. She spent hours adjusting my miserable grammar and keeping tabs on timelines and references. She has soft touch for guidance, backed by huge reserves of experience and know-how making her suggestions unassailable. Her professional attention is present on every page.

I also extend my gratitude to Jim and Nancy Harrell for their graphic skill creating the map of the not so fictional Carson Valley.

The construction of the Continental Railroad has been termed by some as the greatest engineering feat in history. It took priority over the lives of those who worked to build it, and those in its way.

As you can see in the Fact From Fiction section at the end of the book, I may have compressed the true historical timeline here and there to fit the story. Most importantly, though some of those you will read about in this and other books in the series did walk through history, and though many of the events did take place, the story within is mine and pure fiction.

J.L. Crafts

Foreword

The completion of the transcontinental railroad by the Central Pacific Railroad's construction crews coming from the west and the Union Pacific's crews building from the east was the major disruptive event of the nineteenth century. Before the railroad was completed it took the California immigrants five to six months to travel across the country. Once completed, one could ride the train the same distance in less than six days!

What if the Central Pacific Railroad's big four had to buy the right-of-way as the transcontinental railroad entered Nevada? Would Charles Crocker, Collis Huntington, Leland Stanford, and Mark Hopkins have to deal with reluctant ranchers and devious outlaws? This fictional work paints a story of how it might have been. It's a fast-moving tale of good-hearted ranchers dealing with railroad land agents and murderous outlaws. J.L. Crafts' fictional protagonist, Will Toal, is faced with gunfights and romance as he works to put together his life after the Civil War. The story is set in a carefully researched true historical setting of the railroad's construction weaving the real characters responsible for that monumental project into action with those of literary invention. The combination of real and fiction makes for a most interesting read of history.

—Jerry Blackwill

Jerry Blackwill is president of the Truckee Donner Railroad Society and the Museum of Track History. He has given numerous presentations about the construction of the transcontinental railroad to historical groups.

Carson Valley

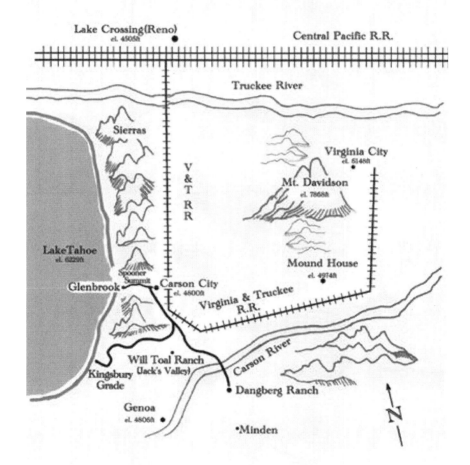

Prologue

1861
White House - Washington, D.C.

"Mr. Huntington, the President will see you now."

Collis Huntington sat in a rather narrow hallway of the White House. The pale walls were hung with portraits of prior presidents, a collection of eyes peering down on those seeking an audience with the head of the country's democracy. Their eyes seem to question those sitting below as if to evaluate the quality of the seat's occupant.

Huntington never imagined he would be in this building, awaiting access to the president. His palms were damp and the immaculately laundered pressed shirt he wore had begun to stick to his skin. He'd been in many varied business meetings, but nothing like this one. None that had this much riding on it.

Huntington was in Washington representing the investors who were staking their financial fortunes and futures on one of the riskiest projects ever conceived: a transcontinental railroad through the Sierra Nevada Mountains. His group knew the nation and the President wanted the railroad. But the costly war had run longer than anyone expected. It had ravaged the country's finances. No one had any real money and certainly not the enormous capital funds required to build a railroad across the unsettled west. However, Collis Huntington had an idea. The entire prospect hung on the balance of this meeting and what the President thought of his proposal. Huntington and his partners Leland Stanford, Charles Crocker and Mark Hopkins would have their financial fates decided today.

"Huntington have a seat. May I call you Collis? Can I offer you some type of refreshment?" Abraham Lincoln requested pleasantly.

"Thank you, Mr. President, but I will pass for the moment; maybe later," Huntington responded. The informality and openness of the welcome surprised him. *A good start. Now, can I build on the opening and get this done?*

"Collis, this is General Grenville Dodge." Lincoln lifted his hand in the direction of a well-dressed Union officer standing to the side of the president's desk. "General Dodge thought he had been summoned here for disciplinary reasons, but he is wrong. He is here to talk railroads."

Huntington could see the shock register ever so slightly on Dodge's face.

"You see, General Dodge has special knowledge as to a route for the transcontinental railroad from the Mississippi to the Rockies. But I want him to hear you speak to the western portion of the route. He doesn't know it, but he will be resigning his commission soon to work with Mr. Durant to build the eastern portion of the railroad."

Huntington watched as the earlier mild look of shock on the general's face now morphed into one of outright surprise.

Lincoln continued, "This war will end, and when it does, there will be a migration to the West larger than any military movement in the current conflict. Sit with me, General Dodge, and listen. After we hear from Collis, I want to talk about your observations for possible rail lines in Nebraska."

The President then turned, facing Huntington.

Huntington knew this was his opportunity. This was his stage. His financial future along with those of his partners hung in the balance of what would take place in the next few minutes.

"Mr. President, you and I both know that with the war going on neither you nor my investors have the money right now to finance a project of this magnitude. But I have an idea."

"Yes, your group while impressive with your investors and using the expertise and experience of Theodore Judah appears most impressive, this war demands every penny we collect. To have any hope at commencing construction of something so massive, I need some idea that I can present to Congress that makes sense in this most dire of times."

"Mr. President, my idea is summarized in a map."

"A map?"

"Yes sir, I'll spread it out on your desk."

Huntington unrolled a large length of paper and anchored the corners. He turned to the president as if to say, *come and take a look*.

The president did not move from his seat.

But General Dodge glanced to the president as if asking silent permission. Lincoln nodded. Grenville rose and walked to the desk to observe. It took but a moment for him to realize what he was looking at. He then turned to address Lincoln.

"I never thought the government would have the funds to pay for such an undertaking. But Mr. President, I think I understand what Mr. Huntington is going to suggest. If I am right, he has provided you with a very viable method of financing a huge project which could have immeasurable benefit to the country."

The president stood. "I think you both know I want this railroad built. I represented railroads throughout my years as an attorney in Illinois. They move materials and people more efficiently than anything else we have. The country needs this railroad to grow. Mr. Huntington, you think you have a viable solution for the financing?"

"I do, Mr. President. If you come take a look, I'll explain."

With the solemnity of another impending decision that could have momentous ramifications for the nation, Lincoln slowly rose and approached the map. "Show me."

Chapter One

1868 Late Winter
Toal Ranch near Carson Valley, Nevada

Will Toal had pulled up his boots and they had just hit the floor when he heard the shot. He stopped and held absolutely still. He knew the sound from the war—it was from a good distance. Sharp reverberations could bounce off the mountains for miles, but he could tell from the sound and direction it was still on his land. He had filed his homesteaded almost two years ago now. But the land agent in Carson City had held up the final paperwork. He had a meeting soon to try and finalize its purchase and get clear title. His ranch covered a full three thousand acres. It might take the better part of a day to get to the source, but guns going off on his land rarely signaled a good thing.

With that one simple sound, his day's plans changed. Now, instead of working new horses, he was going to head out and see what tracks he could find in the dirt. Hopefully, the dry soil would tell him a story of what had happened; it usually did.

He rose from his homemade cot and stretched. His bedroom was the second of the two rooms in the house. Little more than a log cabin, he'd built it by his own hand as his ranch house. While not much to look at, it kept the occupants out of the wind, rain, and occasional snow. Though small, the cabin had a wide wrap-around porch which made the structure look larger from the outside. When he had the time, Will usually sat under the ramada and faced east in the lee of the wind pattern. Here, unhampered by relentless wind, he spent his few moments of peace and thought. But not this morning.

The day promised to be brisk and windy. The sun was barely up. Cold mountain winds blew across the valley every afternoon this time of year, flashing down the eastern border of the High Sierras to be sucked like a magnet across the Carson Valley by the hot, high desert farther to the east.

The smell of breakfast wafted on the early breeze. María, the ranch cook, never disappointed the small crew, organizing a good breakfast before the day's work. He had to eat quickly then collect his gear for what could be a ride of one or two days. He would get to the site of the shooting sometime today, but it might take several days to chase down the shooter.

His crew consisted of two hands: a father, Raul, and his son Juan. They'd come north with him from New Mexico along with Juan's wife, María. Both had heard the shot. They looked up at Will as he crossed the yard to the barn. Their looks spoke without words. They, too, knew the source had to be checked. It was cause for concern. Both men knew their boss would head out. They looked to see if they would be going along.

His instructions were simple. "Do me a favor and saddle my horse while I eat and get packed up. Look to hold down the ranch and keep breaking the new horses while I find out what's going on."

Juan and Raúl both nodded understanding.

After gulping down a plate of beans mixed with eggs and rice, Will returned to the house to gather his gear. Strapping on his Colt, he grabbed his hat and shook off yesterday's dust. He buckled on his chaps and buttoned his winter jacket. Then he grabbed his canvas roll along with saddlebags which always held jerky and hardtack and headed back out the front door. He swung up on his late-gelded powder gray mustang, directing his gaze to Juan and Raúl.

He gave them one quick reassuring smile and a nod as he dipped the bill of his hat. No words were needed. He grazed the sides of the big gray with his spurs and headed east.

*****

Will Toal braced against the cold air of late March. He figured the temperature to be between 45°F to 50°F. The wind had only started to pick up, just a light breeze this early. It would come later in the day as it did each day. He set his horse to a steady trot, the kind good horses can travel at for an entire day. And Powder was a good horse. He could see the growing volume of moisture coming from Powder's nose as he warmed to the travel.

"Could be eight to ten miles, boy." He spoke to the horse as if to let him know to keep it steady for the duration.

Will had chased down killers before. His days as a deputy Texas Ranger had required many a long ride in pursuit of a lawbreaker. Now he owned his own ranch. Not a large parcel by comparison to some, but the world to Will. He was only twenty-three years old, yet he had packed a lifetime into those few years. He'd headed to war at the age of 16 only to return home two years later to be confronted with the loss of family and Georgia farm. Over the next five years he worked in Texas as a Ranger, then wrangled horses in New Mexico after which he headed to California only to stop here near Carson Valley. The migration west that had begun at age eighteen had taken a total of only five years. Life had moved fast.

Will had a feeling of foreboding as he headed out.

"Looks like rain." Though spoken to his horse, Will's comments were just for himself.

Maybe it was the clouds and no sun. Maybe it was the utter silence. Maybe it was just because he had other things to do on the ranch and riding out exploring was not one of them. But he felt he'd been pulled back to the work of a lawman, which he had left behind without any regrets whatsoever. Each of those early trips with the Rangers in Texas arose out of a duty, and none of them ended as originally predicted. He'd been an exceptional Ranger. The commander did his best to try to get him to stay. But Will was done. Too many bullets. Too many men who ended up dead. Just like the war. Today felt like another ride that would not end well.

Chapter Two

1868 Late Winter
Western Border of Toal Ranch

Will had ridden for a little over two hours. He figured he'd traveled at least six to seven miles. He approached the nearest base of the Eastern Sierra touching the edge of his property. The mountain slopes exploded out of the ground, rising quickly to the crest. This part of his spread was flat grassland until it met the scattered sparse foothills at the base of the granite walls rising up to cradle Lake Tahoe. There were only small stands of cottonwood and low scrub. A heavy mist hung in the air, reducing visibility to the crest of the Sierras. *May even be a storm coming.* Weather was unpredictable in the high country. Sometimes, it looked dark enough to make one think the world was about to end, but no rain came. Other times it could be clear, yet within a matter of minutes, the skies would erupt.

Then he heard a woman's scream, followed by "Stay back you monster."

Another shrill shriek followed.

Will looked toward a set of large rocks. Suddenly, there were multiple movements. Will pulled Powder to a quick stop and dismounted without taking his eyes off the unfolding events. He had a knack for slowing time in his own brain when most would let emotions get the best of them. It had happened quite a bit in his Ranger days.

Around a tall rock just outside the very base of the mountains appeared a blonde woman, or maybe just a girl. She looked no more than twenty. Running hard, though her steps were not steady, the young woman nearly stumbled with each stride, was crying and obviously terrified. Blood ran down the front lower part of her dress which also appeared ripped from the shoulder over her back.

"I tole you we needed that paper, and I aim to get it!" The angry male voice came from behind the same tall boulder. "An' that ain't all I brought you out here to get, an' you knows it."

A man of medium build strolled leisurely from behind the edge of granite obstruction into Will's view. He wore his hat pulled down low over his eyes and an old rag jacket over suspenders that held up cuffed jeans. The gun holster on his right sat at a level indicating that he made frequent use of it. He moved with a nonchalance.

"You got nowheres to go, and you knows it. Don't make me git mean agin'. You ain't gonna like..." The man stopped mid-sentence when he saw Will jump off Powder.

The girl spotted Will about the same time as the man with suspenders. But she was much closer and ran straight to the newcomer.

Will had no idea what had happened. He knew this was the general area from which the shot would have come. The girl looked to be in bad shape. Not only was her dress bloodied, but her lip was cut and her cheek badly bruised. Her eyes held a primal wildness, a fear. She continued her half stumble, half run, straight to Will and threw her arms around his neck, then went limp.

There was not much to her. She was surprisingly light for her height. Will wrapped his left arm around her waist but kept his right hand free.

"Don't touch her, partner," said Suspenders. "Let her go."

"Seems like she feels otherwise," Will tightened his grip on the girl.

"I'll give you one more chance. Let her go."

"She's doing the holding. Seems like she isn't interested in your company anymore. Besides, we also have to talk about the fact that you're on my land."

Suspenders reached for his holster.

10

Will never took his eyes off the man or his movements. Suspenders was smooth, but Will had faced others like him before. Will was quicker.

Will's shot hit the man in the middle of his chest, knocking him back two or three steps. Suspenders got off a shot, but after he'd been hit. His gun hand had angled up, and the shot went far right. Suspenders hit the dirt.

Will then looked down at the girl. Her long, matted, and gnarled hair had probably once been well kept. He felt her full feminine form flush against him, which caused a feeling he'd never felt before. His left hand still encircled her diminutive waist, effectively holding her up. His left hand touched skin, and it dawned on him her dress had been ripped off her shoulder entirely. When he glanced down over the top of her shoulder, he saw a series of raised ugly stripes running horizontally between the shoulders. *What had happened to her?*

He eased her face away from his chest to lay her on the ground. She was unconscious.

Chapter Three

No matter how many times he had faced down another gunman, the release of tension after shots were fired dropped through him from chest to feet. The fluids pumping through his system leading up to the shooting must have taken a toll as they coursed through his body. After the blasts were sounded, he always felt mildly exhausted.

When the smoke rose and dissipated, it took with it no small measure of his stored energy. He'd survived. While he tried his best to hide any outward evidence of anxiety or even fear, the pools of liquid gurgled deep within his body and told a different story. But at this moment, he was alone. No one was watching.

Will assessed the scene. The young girl lay flat on the ground where he'd laid her. He could see her breathing but still unconscious. The front of her dress was bloody from the waist down. She might have a wound to the stomach, but he'd not been able to check yet. Those could be bad. She had bruises and welts on her back. She looked a mess.

He stood over Suspenders. He was surely dead. *I will have to bury him, but it has to be quick and shallow. There may be others in the group with Suspenders.* Will knew he had to leave quick.

The smell of gun smoke still hung in the air. Both man and girl lay on the ground with blood all over them. Just like the war.

He'd gone to war thinking it was a family duty, a duty followed by his ancestral Scottish Clans for hundreds of years. But war was not what he'd expected. Those who'd fought on the front lines rarely talked about it later. He never spoke to anyone about his own time in battle. Only generals and politicians talked about war after it was over.

He thought back to how he'd argued with his father. How he'd pushed his Ma to let him join. He had finally prevailed on his Pa to let him go. Though his father had resisted, his family had a history of going to war to protect their homelands. It seemed the men in their family had always gone to war.

His grandfather's grandfather along with a brother had left Ireland. Their surname was O'Toole in Ireland. They were tough men in tough times. Quick with their fists they eventually took on the wrong people. Those two ancient ancestors were told they fought too much and could either take a boat to Scotland or go to jail. They took the boat. The brothers found a home in Scotland. O'Toole was soon changed to Toal, a Scottish version of the Gaelic. The brothers found an affinity with the land and the people. Being men over six feet tall and not afraid to fight, they joined the Black Watch. The Watch was a clan of special men. They policed the other clans.

His grandfather had come to America to escape the oppression of the Scots by England. As Catholics, they had fought on the losing side during the Battle of Culloden. Then came the American Revolution. Will's grandfather had fought in that war.

Next in the history of military commitments by a member of the Toal Clan was the Civil War. Will had argued his lineage had never shied away from taking up arms. His father had agreed. He bought Will an expensive rifle, an Enfield. Will had been an outstanding shot since he was ten years old. Decently armed, Will's father had reluctantly relented, giving him permission to enlist. At the time, Will thought he prevailed as it was the right thing to do. Both his parents had questioned joining a fight over slavery when they did not believe in it. Will argued he was joining to protect their farm.

But the farm had not been protected. His family had been killed by Union soldiers. Following the armistice, he'd ridden home to a burned out relic of what had been a family home. His father had buried coin money at the base of his grandfather's headstone. There was nothing left for Will but to dig up the money which was still there and leave. How he'd thought he knew better. How he'd been so wrong. How he'd never been able to tell them.

Now this. What was he going to do with this girl?

Chapter Four

1868 Late Winter
Western Border of Toal Ranch

Will came back to the young lady who had not moved. She had remained unconscious for a quarter of an hour. Dried blood covered the entire front of her dress from her waist down. The stain did not look fresh. He could see no new fluid pulsing through the fabric, so he scanned for other injuries. A dark, puffy bruise on her cheek looked painfully swollen. The cut on her lip was deep, and swollen, too. Her wrists had bruises, but they did not look serious.

He had pulled her dress back over her shoulders, re-covering the welts. There was no blood on her back, and he was more concerned with the areas that might be bleeding. He looked around the campsite, checking for signs of other men who could be involved. He found only two horses and two saddle rigs, leaving him feeling confident that no other men were in the immediate vicinity. But someone could return at any time. He needed to get this girl to wake up quickly so he could ask what the devil was going on.

Will knelt beside her again, needing to see how serious the wound was to her abdomen, but he hesitated to raise her dress. He'd seen hundreds of wounds during the war, but those were on men. When a fellow soldier went down close to him in a battle, he'd shoot back, trying to keep the enemy at bay and at the same time grab and stuff anything available into the wound to stem the bleeding.

Most often, you didn't have much time to assist. If you didn't get back to firing, you were going to be the next one wounded. Here under her dress, he couldn't see if there was an open wound. Kneeling beside her and about to lift up her dress, Will grabbed the lower hemline just as the blonde head raised looking down toward her feet. She immediately saw the current position of his hands. Depthless blue eyes opened panic wide immediately.

"What are you doing?" she yelled.

"Ma'am, I . . . I . . . I was worried about all the blood. I thought I needed to check your wounds," stammered Will. Obviously embarrassed by the timing and appearance, he tried to regain his composure. "If you are still bleeding, then we need to get a compress on the wound."

"The wound is not new. I was born with it. It comes with being female. It'll keep for now." Her face softened. The blue eyes relaxed. Her head lowered back to the ground along with a sigh of what Will took to be relief.

Will then pushed for information. "What's your name? Who is the guy who drew on me and why? Are there any others going to show up soon?"

"So many questions. One at a time," she uttered in a hushed, barely audible breath.

"Ma'am, I just need to know . . ."

"Please stop calling me 'Ma'am.' I am not a mother. My name is Elizabeth, Elizabeth Armstrong."

"Well, Elizabeth, I need to know what I'm dealin' with here, and we need to get you somewhere safe to take care of you. Where is your home? Where are your folks?"

"No one else is coming; at least, not right yet. My home is not near. I have no one left. They killed my entire family. I have no family, and I have no place to go."

He was taken aback by the directness of the statement. She showed little emotion. He half expected tears, but there were none. He had seen men act strangely unaffected by horrible things during the war. Some-

16

times the body and mind just shut down to emotions. Maybe it was better for some that way. Dealing with tragedy could outright overwhelm a person.

"By your comment, I take it that while no one may be on their way here, other men could be involved. We have to move."

"Yes," Elizabeth said. "At some point, I am sure that the other men who were also involved in all of this will return. The man you shot was supposed to take me to Genoa. The leader of the group has already gone to Genoa. His name is Drake Sutton. If the man over there does not get me to Genoa along with the rest, I am sure others will come. But I have no idea when."

Without a great deal of thought, Will then offered, "If you were to agree, I could take you back to my ranch. I have a Mexican lady who cooks for me, and she can tend to your wounds. You'll be safe while you recover."

Will was not sure why he was offering but couldn't come up with a better plan at the moment. He didn't want to admit it, but the soft magnetic blue eyes and body hug played a part, too.

"Do you think you can ride?"

She tried to rise on her elbow but did not get far before she collapsed flat again. While there was an obvious strain in her voice, she said, "I think I can ride if it is not too far."

Will admired the determination. "We can make it back to the house in a couple of hours of easy riding. Can you get that far?"

Elizabeth looked at him, "Did you say you have a ranch? You're a bit young to have a ranch, aren't you?"

"Long story. I own about three thousand acres and run about four hundred head of cattle and fifty horses." He surprised himself at his effort to impress. He'd never found himself doing that before.

"You're an awful young man for a long story," came the reply.

Feeling the need to change the topic as much out of embarrassment as strategic need to move to a position of defensible safety, Will said, "Let's try to get you up and moving. I will feel a good deal better if I can get you back to the house. Stay here for the moment. Let me check to see what we can use for a horse and rig so you can ride."

"They had me on a horse, the bay. Saddle and bridle are around behind the rocks by the campsite."

Then Beth raised up on one elbow with what appeared to be significant effort. "And I want you to go bring that monster's guns. Both rifle and handgun."

Will thought it a most interesting request from a woman, a young one at that. But he figured shock and fear welled up in the form of a desire for protection in the future. He nodded and set about getting the bay saddled.

After about twenty minutes, Will had assembled the essentials of what he thought they would need to make the ride back to the ranch house. He had also buried the man in suspenders in a very shallow grave.

"Are you ready? I have the bay saddled, and we are ready to go. Do you think you can mount and ride?"

"I can ride, but I might need some help getting up on top. Is there a rock or something that I can use as a mounting block?"

Will paused. "I could easily lift you."

"I'm sure you could, but I would prefer a gentler approach."

They found a knee-high rock, and Will offered his hand to help her step up and then into the saddle while he held the bay's bridle. As she turned away from him to lift into the saddle, he noticed that the back of her dress was covered with just as much blood as the front. She moved with slow, deliberate action, as if each step required extra concentration. And she winced with each step or lift upwards. He could only imagine what injuries she had sustained. He needed to get her back to the ranch soon.

Will then grabbed Powder's reins and swung into his own saddle. Elizabeth looked pale. He had seen the same color of skin on war injured who had lost large amounts of blood. He knew he had to get this lady back to a bed and some care.

"Are you sure you can ride?" he asked again.

"Let's go. The sooner we get there, the better I will feel. I don't want to be here when Drake Sutton gets back."

Will wondered what María would think of this wild looking filly when he brought her in.

Chapter Five

1868 Late Winter
Office of Patten Land & Investments

There were only two men in the office of Patten Land & Investments.

"Drake, did ya get the deed?" The question came from a middle-aged man in a tailored three-piece suit with two belly pockets, one of which held up a thick, solid gold watch chain. The man's name was Patten, Wes Patten. One of many immigrants who had initially come to California during the Gold Rush, Wes had made money by selling all manner of goods to the miners. Now he was looking at ways to increase his net worth by whatever means presented.

"We will get the deed. When have I ever failed to deliver?" Drake Sutton sounded confident to the point of arrogance.

"Then, *where* the hell is it?" The emphasis added a tinge of urgency. "You were recommended as a gun hand willin' to do anythin' necessary if the pay met the risk. Did I hire the wrong man?" Patten's question came with a derisive sneer.

Drake Sutton was indeed a hired gun. One might expect the gun hand to be the lesser educated of the two, but it was reversed here. His name was known among those of his fellow mercenaries as one of the quickest draws in the business. He was also one of the most temperamental. No one could predict when Sutton would go off the rails and do something utterly unpredictable. His demeanor would not change; it would not give a clue. But someone would end up dead in the flash of a second. Over their year of work together, Patten realized his reputation fit him. One needed to be really careful around Sutton.

Patten thought he had a good idea of what was running through Sutton's head. He was probably mad at the exchange, but for the moment, he remained under control. Still, Patten didn't like Sutton's tone. Though Patten needed the man's talents, it was important that Sutton know who was in charge and who took the orders.

But for the moment, Patten ignored Sutton's reputation for violence. Patten let his own temper overrule any thoughts of potential consequences.

"You think your fancy suit changes who you are? *Beware of a wolf in sheep's clothing.* That's Shakespeare." Patten's upper body shook as he pointed his finger at Sutton.

Sutton did have a hair trigger temper. His stance and manner all confirmed he would not hesitate to throw down a gauntlet. Patten's gesture would normally have resulted in Sutton's gun coming out of its holster. Instead, he shook his head, displaying a nasty grin with prominent canine teeth in his lower jaw. Patten could feel and sense Sutton's attitude of superiority despite his efforts to the contrary. Sutton then issued a challenge.

"As evidenced by the fact that you are more ignorant than you wish to appear, you quoted not Shakespeare but Aesop, an ancient Greek, who was far wiser than you. I may be a gun hand, but you are just a simple thief in fancy clothes." Gauntlet thrown.

"Well, if that ain't the '*pot calling the kettle black.*'" Patten's temper stewed warmer.

"That'd be a quote from my grandmother, who was a whole lot wiser than you. I know you think you're somethin' special because you spent time in some fancy school. No, I didn't go to any high and mighty college as you claim you did. But look at yourself. Black Stetson, black leather vest, black shirt, and a gun hanging halfway between your hip and knee. Seems to me your wolf fangs are out in plain sight for all to see." Gauntlet accepted.

Patten knew his temper had gotten the best of him but only briefly. He'd heard Sutton was formally educated, but for whatever reason had ended up as a gun hawk. However, this was neither the time nor place to let a confrontation get out of hand. He decided to back off a bit.

"Drake, listen. I'm the one who got the map. I know where the Central Pacific Railroad is goin' through the north end of this God-forsaken Carson Valley. These homesteaders are sittin' on land, which is by all measure useless to everyone except the railroad. We must grab what we can, as fast as we can, and do it before the railroad's land agents get there. Knowing the railroad's projected right of way gives us inside information to buy land in their path and then sell it to them after upping the price. It's a simple play."

*****

Sutton had heard it all before. He had no idea how Patten had gotten his hands on the map. He was sure it hadn't been done legally. At first, he'd been more than skeptical as to its authenticity. But Patten had identified ranch after ranch reaching up the Western Sierra that the railroad needed for its right of way. Each prediction proved accurate. Each property they had bought was eventually purchased by the railroad. Sutton no longer questioned the accuracy of the map. He sensed an easing of tensions.

"Look Wes, the only reason we're here is because we both know we need each other. You have the map and connections to the banks; I have the guns and the ability to *encourage* the homeowners to sell." The word encourage had the cunning sound of double meaning.

Sutton continued. "I can't work with the bankers. You can't handle the enforcement work with your hands."

"But Drake, this brings us back to where we started. Where's the deed? And where's the money I gave you to pay the old Mormon, Josiah Purcell, for his ranch? You told me you could close the deal for his spread."

Patten watched for any sign in Sutton's face indicating he'd gone too far. Seeing no sign of outright resistance, he persisted. "We need the deed to resell the property quick, so we can pay off our loan. You knew damn well we took out a loan so we could buy out Purcell. So, I'll say it again: Where'd the money go? Where's the deed? If we have the deed, we can sell the ranch to pay off the loan and get the cash we'll need for the next deal."

Sutton frowned. "Purcell took the money. I don't know where he hid it. Reynolds got the deed." This was a touchy part of Sutton's story.

Patten threw up his hands. "And where's Reynolds?"

Sutton was tired of being grilled. He pushed ahead with the story he hoped would deflect Patten from further questions.

"He'll be here soon. As I told you, one of Purcell's wives took sort of a shine to me. We leveraged her interest to deal with the Old Man himself. She wanted to come with us. She said she knew where her husband hid the deed, so we let her grab the deed before we rode off, but before we could get going all hell broke loose when they started shooting. We had to shoot back. The whole family died in the gunfire."

Sutton ran the risk of telling Patten more than he needed to know, but he had to explain the events at some level to keep Patten the other man from doing something drastic. The events had not happened quite like he relayed them now, but Patten didn't need to know that. The girl had taken a shine to Sutton, but in truth, Reynolds shot up the household before she got the deed. Sutton just created the story out of thin air to keep Patten from going to the authorities or getting too inquisitive.

Sutton remembered the actual truth. It all began at an earlier meeting pushed by Patten. While Patten had been at the Purcell Ranch talking with Old Man Purcell, Sutton had stood just outside the front door to observe. One of Purcell's wives was quite young, under twenty years by Sutton's estimation. He had seen her leave the house as Patten tried to negotiate a sale with the old man and his elder wife.

The young lady had walked around to the back of the family barn while Sutton watched, making sure he was out of sight. She pulled down the shoulder of her dress and dabbed some water from a wet rag on what appeared to be welts across her back. She then pulled up her dress and walked back toward the house. Sutton made sure he was standing on the porch outside as she approached.

"Where did you get those marks on your back?"

The young lady immediately looked embarrassed. "How did you see those?" Then it struck her. "You followed me."

Sutton nodded. "I did. However, I cannot help but wonder how such a young lady as yourself could have gotten them."

The girl had paused and looked to the ground. "First Wife, Sarah, says I have to pay because I have not given our husband a child. Each month when my flow starts, she says I must stand and accept judgement because I have failed my duty. The marks only last for a few days."

"That is barbaric," said Sutton. "Why do you stay?"

"How can I leave?"

Sutton hesitated. In that moment, a plan crystalized: a plan to get both Purcell's deed and Patten's purchase money.

"What if I could take you away from this place?"

She said nothing, but the look on her face told him all he needed to know.

"What is your name?"

Her head covered with a white cloth cap dipped forward which Sutton took for a continued struggle with her embarrassment at being seen wiping her welts. "My name is Beth, Elizabeth."

"I could take you to the biggest cities in the West. Places where you would be appreciated. You don't need to stay here."

She looked up. Sutton could see anticipation written across her face.

Sutton figured he had gone this far, so he had nothing to lose by continuing. "I'll be back in a week. We will come at noon. Find out where your husband keeps the deed to the ranch. Let us know where it is, and that's all you have to do."

"Will you take me away from here?"

"Of course." Their eyes locked. By the look on the girl's face, Sutton knew the deal was settled. The young girl had no idea, but Sutton had just figured a way to best Patten as well as her father. Her family would ultimately suffer, but he would finally have a stake and a path to live in a manner he aspired to.

*****

Sutton had been gazing out of the office window.

Patten had been watching. "Hey, you looked like you'd left the room while still standin' in front of me. Is there somethin' else that I need to know?" Patten's forehead lowered while his eyes remained fixed on Sutton, making the question sound as serious as he could.

Sutton drew his focus back to the cover story he'd created. He needed to deflect Patten again.

"She told us she could find the deed, but she kept it somewhere, insisting we take her with us. I think she had it stuffed down her dress or something. Reynolds stopped to camp and told me he would get the deed last night."

"Then why did you have to kill the entire family?"

Sutton sighed, thinking how to continue the tale. "The old man had a rifle stashed just inside his barn. When his young traitorous wife claimed she had his deed and was going with us, he went for it, and I had to shoot. The old Mormon had another wife back inside the house, and we couldn't leave any witnesses. So, we made it look like an Indian raid. We shot them both, burned the house, and let the stock go. When it was all over, Reynolds, Desmond, and I, rode off with the girl, the young wife."

Drake looked Patten directly in the eye. He had to close this inquiry. "In these situations, you have to do what is necessary. It's like a battle; nothing is ever predictable. You deal with the circumstances as they come up."

Sutton had provided more detail than he'd like. But by telling Patten, now he had a co-conspirator. Patten could not go to any sheriff. He was part of it, too. Sutton had shot the old man, but Reynolds shot the old wife. However, Sutton figured it was a detail not worth providing to Patten.

*****

Patten hesitated. He was taken aback at the blunt description of killing not only men but women. He backed away from Sutton. It was almost a physical reaction to the realization he was indeed working with a man who could kill without remorse. A predator presence. A lion looking to devour. *What a contrast. Educated, intelligent, composed, but lethal.* "Well, that's not what we'd have liked, but it's done. I suppose we can backdate the deed to look like the sale took place weeks ago, before the shootings. We can even tell the authorities to look for the people who damaged our asset. We could even file a claim."

Patten knew he'd stretched the possibilities, but he was trying to assert a measure of authority over Sutton. He wanted to throw off suspicion from Sutton and himself. Probably impossible, but he had to try. This was their first purchase in the Carson Valley, and hopefully, no one would make a connection between the death of the Purcell's and the later sale of their land to the railroad. With a little luck, they'd be long gone before anyone connected the dots.

Patten decided to bring this to a close. "Go get Reynolds, quick. We need to record the deal, and I need the deed to do it."

"I'll get him before the end of the day," Sutton responded as he moved toward the door and headed for his horse.

Chapter Six

1868 Late Winter
Placerville, California

The door opened, and a small bell tinkled its announcement. Suddenly, the door slammed shut as a rider covered in dust strode into the office of the Placerville Land agent. There were several loud footfalls on the wooden plank floor as the entrant looked about the office.

"Bran, where are you?" The man calling out the question was dressed in a woolen suit with vest that had seen better days. His boots and spurs had seen better days, too. A strange small hat of irregular shape carried a thick layer of dust while perched at an angle on his head. He had a satchel slung over his shoulder. The question had a tinge of exasperation in it, a sense of frustration after a long journey.

He heard a voice from within.

"Wyatt, is that ye?" The Scottish brogue was thick. "Where in God's holy name hae ye been?" The answer was from just outside the back end of the small office. "Ye should hae been back over two days ago."

Wyatt Richard was a buyer. His immediate employer was the Placerville Land and Title Office. His job was to buy land for the railroad before the construction arrived at the location of the purchase. But the real money behind the business was the Central Pacific Railroad. In using small outfits like Placerville Land, CPRR hoped to keep the sellers from thinking that they could double and triple their prices knowing the railroad was coming. That was the idea, but it didn't always work. Most people in these parts already knew about the coming of the railroad.

"Did ye get the Purcell deed?" asked his Scottish boss and current proprietor entering through the rear door.

"The Big Four be on me backside with telegrams every other day wanting to confirm the right-of-way is protected." Wyatt had been away from his bosses' Scottish brogue for over a week. It always took a little time to get used to the different cadence and lilt of each sentence.

The man issuing the question barely looked at Wyatt. His name was Brandon Stuart. He was a large wide man with a thick brogue who claimed to hail from Scotland itself, possessing a real kilt and Highlands claymore. While he had been in the country only a short time, he knew land title and purchase. A precise negotiator, he also had a knack for making money.

"I didn't get the deed," said Wyatt. "I spoke to Old Man Purcell two months ago, and he agreed to sell for the price we had negotiated. But when I arrived, no one was there, and the entire ranch house and barn were burned to the ground. I checked with the nearest sheriff. They heard that Indians had attacked the family, and all were lost."

"Damn the Crown and King! That'd mean we must process the sale in court, probate. That could take years. The money men in San Francisco are not a'goin' to be happy."

"But the sheriff added something more," Wyatt injected quickly. "He said he'd heard Old Man Purcell sold his property to the Millard Luce Cattle Co. He sold to them because they would keep the property as a ranch and not some railroad throughway. He had made the deal only two weeks ago, and money in the form of Millard script was to be exchanged shortly thereafter. Script from the Millard Cattle Company is like cash all across the West. They give out a piece of paper that banks honor just like money."

"Henry Millard the Cattle King?" asked Brandon. "The guy with hundreds o' thousands of acres all over California, Oregon, and Nevada?"

"Yep, one and the same."

"That will be a' drivin' the price up a bit, but the bosses say we must have it," said Brandon with a heavy shake of the head. "The San Francisco money says we simply must'a ha that deed. The Purcell Ranch is directly in line with the right-o-way set out by the engineers. They will nae take any result but possession o' the deed."

"Don't know what you can do now," responded Wyatt. "That cantankerous old Mormon had two wives, one old and one very young and very beautiful, but no one has seen either since the fire. Everyone believes they all died at the hands of the Paiutes."

Chapter Seven

Will and Elizabeth had ridden for about an hour in silence. She in front, he trailing. Her body moved with the rhythm of the horse's slow gait, but she swayed more than one would normally expect. The pain had to be part of the reason. Will was worried that she was going to pass out and fall off.

He trotted up alongside. Elizabeth glanced to her side, looking at Will through matted hair she seemed not to care about. The look confirmed she was in pain.

"How did you learn to shoot like that? That man you shot back there was named Reynolds. I saw his ability with a gun when he helped shoot my family. He was good. But he didn't even come close to getting his gun out of his holster on you."

"I had a lot of practice during the war and later," said Will, hoping to avoid talk of the past.

But Elizabeth pursued. "I need a distraction from how I feel right now. Tell me about the war. We only had bits and pieces of news about what happened in this territory."

Will did not like to talk about the war. In fact, he couldn't remember telling anyone in detail about his time with the Gray Army. But she had a persistent look. Again, the draw of the soft indigo eyes kept influencing his judgment. He thought it might be of benefit to deflect thoughts of her immediate discomfort, so he said, "Alright, but it's not a pretty story."

Will looked at the cattle grazing, his cattle. He was about to relate events he'd never spoken about to anyone. He took a deep breath and started.

I left home at the age of sixteen and headed west in 1864 knowing I would find someone who would direct me to the front. It didn't take long. Through a series of people providing information and direction, I found out where the armies were massing. I was eventually told to walk to a specific tent in a camp and told to speak to a man who they said dealt with new recruits.

I walked up to the man and said, "I want to join. I'm old enough and I'm here to fight."

The man wore a tattered gray uniform top and ragged pants of varied color. He did not question my statement. He simply looked at me holding my rifle.

"Where did you get that gun?" asked the recruiter.

"My Pa bought it for me."

"He bought you an Enfield rifle?"

"He did," came my reply.

"Can you shoot that thing?" he asked. "Ifin' you can't, someone who can is goin' to take it from you right away. We need good guns and don't have enough."

"I can shoot just fine," I said.

"Show me," came his skeptical retort.

"I readied the muzzle loader and pointed out a bough on a tree over four hundred yards away. The shot thundered, and the bough exploded. I then turned to look at the face of the recruiter. There was no change of expression in the man's face. I thought that was a pretty good shot. But the man simply didn't react."

Then the gray shirted man turned and said, "I have a special place for you. Follow me."

I was taken to a tent in which three men stood. "Captain," said the recruiter, "I have a good shot here who wants to sign up. He just hit a two-foot target at five hundred yards. He can shoot." He emphasized the last words, which caught the attention of the men in the tent. I thought the man had exaggerated the distance some but did not believe it to be the time nor the place to contradict.

A short man in a braided gray uniform looked at me carefully.

"You want to fight?" was all he said.

"Yes, sir," I responded.

After a pause, the Captain told the recruiter where to take me. When we arrived at the new location in camp, the recruiter then looked back at me and said, "Good luck young man, you'll need it." That was it. I never saw the man again.

I had met up with Johnston's army, which had been tasked to stop Sherman's March to the Sea. We would not be successful. However, new recruits were desperately welcome, especially those who were good with a gun.

Because I could shoot, I was attached to a sniper corps. It was a group of trained marksmen. I became pretty good at it, maybe one of their best. Not only did I train with long barreled weapons, I became particularly quick with a handgun. I was soon sent to the front lines of the Confederate defense trying to block Sherman. I was ordered to set up in front of the main lines and shoot at any Union officer I could hit. Not something I am proud of, but unfortunately, for those men I shot at, I did what I was ordered to do, and I did it well.

Will could not bring himself to look at Beth. He kept looking straight ahead. She had not taken her eyes from him since he started.

Will sighed and continued.

I thought the South really had a chance. But we just kept losing ground. There were dead and dying daily.

We snipers were set in pairs. I was teamed with James O'Connell. Jim was only a year older but had spent that year fighting. Jim's uniform, if you could call it that, was dirty and torn. His boots had holes, and his jacket was worn through at the elbows. I remember there was a strange calm about him. When I first met him, he looked me up and down and said, "How many Yanks have you killed?"

"None," I responded. "I just joined."

"I could tell that 'cause you ain't got no holes in yo're clothes. I was hopin' you just been transferred, but then yo're too young. How old are you anyway, more than sixteen?"

I just looked at Jim. I didn't know what to say. But in that unspoken confession there, a bond was created between the two of us. "Don't worry, I ain't goin' to tell no one. Just do as I tell you, and you'll survive."

Two days later, orders came for the sniper teams to move west, anticipating contact with Sherman's front lines as they headed east.

As we marched, Jim gazed at my gun with no small amount of envy. Jim was carrying a long-barreled smoothbore which had the look of long use. "How'd you get that gun?" Jim asked.

"My Pa bought it."

"Must've wanted to get you killed, 'cause as soon as the recruiters seen you with that gun and found out if you could even passably use it, they was goin' to put you right here with us," Jim said.

"Why does that mean my Pa wanted me killed?"

"You'll see once the day is done," Jim sighed. "Here's how it works. We get set up in the absolute most forward positions to try to pick off Yankee officers, wait for the troops to move up to and beyond us, but if their lines collapse, then we must stay right where we are while they retreat to cover their backsides. That leaves us as the last ones to run, dodgin' bullets all the way."

"But what if our troops break the Union's lines," I asked.

"That don't happen too often anymore in this army."

"Then I guess I'll just shoot as many Blue Coats as I can before they get me first."

Jim just smiled at me that day. Something very knowing in that smile. "What do you want to do after the war?"

I told him with a grin, a grin that probably told him of my innocence. "I'm goin' West."

Jim looked at me with an expressionless face. "Sounds like you been readin' fairy tales."

I felt as if I'd been punched. In the few days with Jim, I'd already come to the notion that Jim carried a world of knowledge I could never match. "I heard there's land big as Georgia waitin' for those who can take it," I spoke as if rising to a challenge.

"Wishful thinkin'," smiled Jim.

I didn't answer. I knew Jim might be right, but if I ever got the chance, I'd head west to see for myself what the tales were all about.

Well, in the face of Sherman's Campaign, in some god-forsaken open field, we reached our forward position. Our Captain pointed out the area we were to cover. Jim and I were some three hundred yards off the main road at the edge of a clearing. There was a wide-open field before them. We got down flat with our rifles. At that point, I then knew why Jim's jacket had holes in his elbows. Many more days like this, and my elbows would look just like Jim's.

"Won't be long," said Jim. "You okay? Get ready."

At that moment, a small Union cavalry contingent came over the rise at the other end of the field. They came to a stop once they saw the wide expanse before them. Even I could tell they knew they had to be careful.

I said nothing, just aimed, thought of home and family, and pulled the trigger. The lead officer tumbled. The rest of the company hustled back where they'd come from.

"I'm ready," I said.

"Jesus, Mary, and Joseph. That had to be seven hundred yards," Jim said in a whisper. He then turned his head toward me just a tilt. "Keep it up. I might just get to like havin' you right here next to me."

Everything seemed to stop. No one entered the wide field after my shot. But after about twenty minutes, a huge thunder roared from behind the Union lines. Artillery. Explosions started erupting all around the forested area where Jim and I were positioned. I felt fine holding my rifle looking across the fields at the enemy, but artillery fire was something completely different. Sweat started dripping down my forehead and chest. My heart bounced around inside my chest.

"Just sit tight," said Jim. "Can't move now anyway. You never know where one o' those things is goin' to land, so you can get hit running around just as easy as layin' here."

I tried not to let Jim know how scared I was. But the drips of sweat told him the real story. He tried to keep me calm. "Hold on, our boys are comin' up."

Just then I heard sounds of men, horses, and mules. Our boys moved forward in crouched positions. Then, the artillery from behind them sounded off. The gray line seemed to gather. There was a tension you could almost touch. An energy built up second by second. Suddenly, there came an order.

"Charge!" All hell broke loose. I'd never seen anything like it. It was unbelievable that first time. The feeling didn't last as the war went on, but on that day when I saw it for the first time, it was something to behold. There were sounds everywhere. Bugles, screams, and Rebel Yells all broke out at once. Men ran, and men began to fall. The tide seemed to surge forward like a river of fabric and metal. Smoke was everywhere. The surge continued for what seemed like an hour, but I'm sure it added up to no more than twenty to thirty minutes. More and more smoke covered the path of the gray wave. Then, almost as if someone waved a huge magical wand, the river began to recede. Men began running back beyond the same positions from where they started.

"The Yanks got repeaters," came the cries. I didn't know a great deal about weaponry, but I had heard talk around camp of the new Spencer repeating rifles finding their way into the Union armies.

"Run now; the front line's been cut down right in their tracks. Yanks comin' on fast."

I looked at Jim, and he just looked calmly back. Jim said what we both were thinking.   "Orders are for us to cover any retreat. Stay put, start looking for the Grays to pass by, and start hittin' anything blue that follows. But be ready to get up and move back fast as we reload."

"How are we going to run while we reload?" I asked.

"Ya'll learn quick when the need is strong," snorted Jim.

The gray wave began to peter out, but a new wave of blue fabric and metal started to materialize through the smoke. Jim and I started shooting as soon as we could get clear shots. We each made sure every bullet hit a mark. But we had to begin the backward movement. Our snipers were set up in pairs. One pair would shoot while the other was running to the rear to stop in a spot where they could turn and get a shot. That pair would drop, load, and aim. The initial pair that had shot would then get up and run to the rear. The process went on and on until an order came to move back another stage, stop, and shoot from the new position. It was on our third move to the rear when Jim got hit as we were running. He crumpled face down, tumbling forward over a shoulder and coming to rest on his back.

"Ah! I'm hit."

"Lemme see where they got you," I said. I could not imagine losing my only guide and mentor here in the first battle. But I looked down and saw a hole in the right side of Jim's front chest as big as my fist. Blood and body fluids were flowing free everywhere. I had no idea what I should do.

"Don't bother, Will," said Jim. "It's bad 'cause I can't even see you." Jim was obviously in pain, and the words got weaker and weaker even as he finished the sentence.

"I'll pick you up and get you back to our lines," I blurted with growing desperation. "Drop your rifle, and I will get you up on my shoulder."

Jim's breathing slowed. The tense muscles in his face began to relax. "Nah, just leave me be. Run quick, and don't let the Yanks get ya."

"Ain't gonna leave you," I blubbered, trying to push down the emotions building from within.

By this time, Jim could barely speak. But he looked at me, closed his eyes, and slowly opened them again. "Go. And get yerself through this war so you can see that land out West. Keep yer wishful thinkin'." It was like he pushed the last wind out of his lungs. His chest just stopped all movement. His eyes were fixed.

It had all happened in less than sixty seconds. I knew he was gone. I grabbed his rifle and started running. Bullets flew by, but I did not care. Yet as I ran, the bullets got fewer and fewer as I got closer to the main body of gray soldiers. Soon, I was just another drop in the waters of receding gray tide.

One battle was much like the next. The South kept running out of supplies. Ammunition became so scarce that each of us soldiers had about five to ten shots entering a battle. No one could win with those limits. Time and time again, the gray tide went forward and then just came back. Time and time again, I'd be on the initial front taking long shots across longer and longer distances, only to see the opposing lines clash and then cover the inevitable retreat. Time and time again, I had to stand long after most of the troops had moved to the rear, facing the endless lines of blue uniforms.

It was not long before I really didn't need to be given orders. In this kind of war, you kill simply to survive. A soldier doesn't have time to think about what he does in the moment of battle. You just shoot. And many of my shots brought down a Blue Coat.

*****

Will looked out across the Valley as he spoke. He felt all of his twenty-three years as he heaved the sigh of a forty-year-old. He gazed out over the blowing green pastures here in the present knowing he carried a history that would never leave him. He looked across the little valley that cradled his ranch.

It was called Jack's Valley and clung to the side of a much larger set of grasses called Carson Valley. The winds and grasses fed his stock, paid his bills, claimed his time and effort. The walls of the Sierras drained the snowmelt right to his pastures, keeping them green almost all year around. It was his home, his refuge from the war and what followed.

"Turns out I was a boy when I went to war. But war builds calluses around the soul. Those calluses stick in your memory, never to be erased. Though I suppose it's better to have calluses around the soul than to go crazy. I guess that's why they call us veterans."

Beth had kept listening throughout the story. She let him continue.

"But then, the war was over. There were lots of people who were mighty sad we lost. I just wanted out. wanted to go home. I was eighteen."

39

Will glanced to his side. Elizabeth was still looking straight at him. He hadn't even thought about the time it took to tell the story. It had just come out.

"Sorry I went on there," he said.

"You are young and do have a long story. From what I just heard, it's a courageous story but too full of tragedy for one so young," was all she said. But she continued to study him as if the prolonged gaze could help her to understanding how important that story was to him.

"What happened after the war?"

"I'll tell you later; we'll have time."

Chapter Eight

The fire was nearly out and the chill in the office held the biting winter cold outside. The furnishings gave no evidence of comfort, just like its occupant. Two windows looked out onto one of the main streets in what served as the capital of the new state, yet the view and location were anything but ostentatious. The single desk, two simple wooden chairs and a small pot-bellied stove provided only a small taste of accommodation to comfort.

The spartan confines matched the focus and drive of the man who claimed this office, Collis P. Huntington. His sole purpose in life was to see this railroad built, to overcome each and every challenge thrown at them whether by nature, man or politician not necessarily in that order. He and his partners, now being called in the press, The Big Four, had attacked the project ever since its inception in 1863. Lincoln had been true to his word. Following Huntington's meeting with him in Washington back in 1861, Lincoln had pressed Congress to pass the Pacific Railroad Act in 1862. Construction had started the next year.

This small environment of focus had just been invaded by one of Huntington's partners interrupting his address of the myriad of demands created by those challenges. He did not welcome the interruption.

"Why can we not proceed beyond the Donner Pass?" Leland Stanford was upset. He had staked a considerable portion of his personal wealth on this railroad project. He was a very successful self-made man. When he set his mind to something, he'd see it through.

Huntington, the object of Stanford's question, was no business wall-flower himself. In fact, some had described him as one of the most focused, possibly ruthless, businessmen in the state of California. Though not enjoying this conversation, he was not going to run and hide, either. Partner or not, he needed to know exactly where Stanford planned to take this argument.

"Leland, you know good and well why we haven't progressed beyond Donner." Huntington did not hesitate to display a good deal of exasperation as he continued.

"First, we have to complete one of the most difficult tunnels ever engineered. We lost several souls drilling through the granite section of the tunnel. But it's close to completion. Now, we are waiting to secure title to a parcel that is directly in the path of the right of way, which, as you know, we have to follow to stay in compliance with the route agreed upon with Washington."

"Collis, we started this project six years ago. I have hundreds of thousands of dollars tied up in this and have seen precious few pennies of a return yet."

This was not the first time Stanford broached this topic. Huntington had long ago tired of Stanford's continued push for some return on investment . Huntington thought it obvious from the start this undertaking would take time. At the outset, the partners had carefully and thoroughly discussed details and the magnitude of the project. They were now being called the Big Four: Huntington, Mark Hopkins, Charles Crocker, and Stanford. Those discussions covered the entire plan for both construction as well as financing. Stanford had been adamant that Huntington be fully briefed and prepared before he traveled east to talk to Lincoln. From the moment the deal was struck with Washington, there had never been any secrets about how long it was going to take.

"Leland, you knew what you were getting into from the start. You act as if you are the only one who put his personal financial resources at risk. You are not the only one, and you know it. You have been kept apprised of every step, along with both progress and the hold ups. This continued charade of having *no idea* as to the time and expense involved is getting tiresome."

"We have gone six years without any substantial return on the monies we staked."

"But Leland, you know the story. I stood with Lincoln to show him the map you and I had created. That map depicted a checkerboard of ten-mile squares across the entire west. Lincoln reviewed it with General Dodge and agreed to the concept of swapping one ten-mile square of government owned land for each mile of track laid on flat ground and swapping three ten-mile squares for every mile laid in the mountains. The land transfers were backed by bonds to provide initial financing for construction. Lincoln held to his promise and pushed Congress to pass the Pacific Railroad Act."

Stanford continued to fume. "Yes, I know the story. You've told it many times. But there is another story you keep telling that is getting tiresome- the story of no profits."

Huntington was now getting irritated. "Can't you see, the railroad will soon have over four million acres of land courtesy of the United States. We can sell that land for $1.25 an acre at purchase with a $2.50 per acre charge five years after sale. Do the math." The volume level of Huntington's voice lifted. He had hoped the change in his tone would finally make the point and end the conversation. But Stanford persisted.

"That land isn't worth a penny now because there is no simple, easy way to access it. If we don't get this railroad built, it will never be worth a penny," Stanford glared. "Furthermore, we are supposed to see advances from bond sales tied to those land subsidies. We need cash and we need it now. If we take the lands offered by the government, I know we ultimately must reimburse those bond amounts which we will do as you say through the later sale of those lands once the value has increased. But we have not seen any advances pursuant to those bonds. Where is that money? We could sure use the two to three million dollars to pay for some of the capital costs now. I thought the purpose of the bonds being placed, was to provide immediate funding."

Huntington shook his head. This conversation was going nowhere. He was about to respond when Stanford took the argument one step further, maybe one step too far.

"I'm wondering if we have a viable enterprise?" Stanford was getting increasingly incensed. The man was not going to let up.

"I thought you were aware that we are building a railroad here," retorted Huntington.

"Don't get sarcastic," came Stanford's grave response, the severity in his voice also increasing.

Huntington responded with equal severity. "Then don't be petty. Start acting like the businessman you are supposed to be, a businessman who is involved in one of the biggest projects this country has ever seen,"

There was a knock at the door to the office, which then opened without invitation from within.

"Gentlemen, the staff outside can readily hear the two of you raising your voices. We all know conversations like this find their way into newsprint." The stern voice was that of Charles Crocker, another of the partners in the Big Four.

Stanford turned and directed his next blast at Crocker. "This thing is stalled and it's because the political and production sides are not doing what they are supposed to do. That production side is being handled by you, Charles. The political has been handled by Collis ever since I finished my term as governor in '63. Maybe we need someone else to get this thing moving again."

Huntington was now in full bristle mode but held his tongue for the moment.

"I didn't know I was walking into a boxing event," said Crocker, trying to use some levity in deflating the current state of emotions.

Stanford looked back and forth between Crocker and Huntington. "I didn't come into this office with the intention to joke and have fun. I came here to see if this is going to succeed. Right now, I have grave doubts not only that it will succeed but that Huntington can generate that success. Frankly, I am seriously considering approaching the board of trustees to make a change."

Huntington could control himself no longer. "Leland, you do that, and you will greatly regret it." The words were uttered in a slow, even delivery to accentuate the undeniable threat.

Stanford stared back at Huntington. He was not one to back down from any challenge.

"Then I guess we will see what the board thinks." With that, Stanford left the room.

"What brought all this on?" asked Crocker.

Huntington shrugged and shook his head, "I have no idea. Stanford is getting edgy. He has risked his entire personal fortune on this venture. So have we. Maybe he is tired of waiting. Aren't we all? Perhaps he just feels extra important since he became governor. Or it could be, he just doesn't have the stomach to see it through."

Huntington then stood and took a deep breath followed by a lengthy exhale. He could see Crocker watching his movements with care. Huntington used the brief silence to collect his thoughts.

"I will tell you this: I am done putting up with his complaints. Our job is tough enough without having internal backbiting. He may be the president of the company for now, but I control the board, and I agree it is time to see what they think. But I think the real question they might decide is a vote to remove Stanford."

Huntington made eye-contact with Crocker, as he was known to do, communicating resolve much better than words along could do. Crocker's reaction showed Huntington he knew to tread carefully at this point.

With Stanford gone, the two friends could deal with the business at hand.

"Charles, might I ask; what is the hold up of progress in the east?" Huntington looked expectantly at his colleague as he spoke.

"A simple deed to a small ranch. But that ranch lies directly in the path of the right of way," said Crocker. "We have no alternative route."

Now, Huntington could hear exasperation in Crocker's voice. The magnitude of the project weighed on all four of the CPRR investors in a special way for each.

Crocker continued. "Beyond the Donner Tunnel, we plan to follow the Truckee River. It sits at the bottom of a narrow pass leading to the east side of the Sierras. It is a gradual, amazingly level descent into the very north end of the Carson Valley, a part some call the Washoe Valley."

Again, a pause. "But there are a couple of challenges. Before we actually get to the riverbed, we have three to four more tunnels to drill and two major chasms to bridge."

Huntington detected resignation in Crocker's voice.

"Once we get to the Truckee, we hit Lake Crossing and then the real hard work is behind us. The desert is beyond to the east. Once we get through the north end of the Carson Valley, we can make good time to the Rockies. From the Carson Valley to Utah it is essentially flat. But the base of this valley pass near the departure from the Truckee is owned by some Mormon family named Purcell."

"I thought we had some land agent who was supposed to buy that property," said Huntington.

"True, but for some reason, there has been a holdup," responded Crocker.

Huntington could see that Crocker's body language displayed no small amount of unease moving to this part of his report. He surmised the unease stemmed from the fact Crocker did not have a solution to the problem.

"We opted to purchase the property rather than use the slow process of eminent domain. Eminent domain always leads to litigation. Our land agents were told the man who owned the ranch hoped to move back to Utah. A purchase sounded like the quicker solution."

Crocker tried to get his details correct, anticipating what he knew would be Huntington's predictable sharp questions to follow. Huntington's acute questions were legend. This highly developed trait helped him to effectively manage large operations.

Without more than a quick pause, Crocker continued. "The owner of the land and his Mormon family originally came out with the group that settled Genoa to the south and built the Mormon Station Trading Post. It was later a fort and the first settlement in this area of the territory. But the community didn't take hold. Most are returning to Utah."

Huntington still looked interested. Maybe Crocker does have some solution.

"Rather than filing suit, we took the advice of our local agent and pursued an outright purchase. They initially told us they thought the deal would be done. However, we received a wire from the agent in Placerville this morning indicating that the family had been killed, the ranch burned, and the stock stolen. Current assumption is Indians did this massacre. Now we are looking at a probate hearing that could take almost a year."

Huntington mused, "Stanford probably saw the same wire when it arrived. It probably prompted him to come to my office, and that would explain the show he put on here. You did not see the beginning, but you saw the result."

Huntington then asked, "Isn't the agent we have on this named Stuart out of Placerville? He has never failed us before."

"Yes, he's the agent involved," said Crocker. "But Stuart added in his wire that there was no apparent alternative to probate."

"What do you propose to do?" asked Huntington. "Have you had enough time to come up with an idea? As opposed to Leland, I know you, Charles. You always come up with a plan."

Hearing no immediate response from Crocker, Huntington continued.

"Right now, there are three things that need to happen. First, I am going to talk to the board members and set the wheels in motion to have Stanford removed as president. We cannot have resistance at the very top. The project is simply too big for that. He can keep his stock in CPRR, but he will no longer have any operational involvement."

Huntington paused while Crocker watched and did not interrupt.

"Second, Charles, you need to substantially increase the number of Chinese laborers. We are not getting enough hired men out of the East. They are drawn away by the promise of silver mining in Virginia City."

This topic had become more and more significant. Crocker had initially hesitated to hire Chinese labor, but the trial runs of hiring small groups had shown that the Chinese were cleaner, quicker to learn, and more diligent in their work habits than their white counterparts. They had worked wonderfully in groups of twenty or more as a natural team.

Huntington continued the outline of his plan.

"Third, I have a man named Dale Paris who has assisted me with difficult matters in the past. You should think about sending him to the

Carson Valley to do what he can to get us the deed without litigation. He is not cheap." Then came the predictable analytic comments. Huntington was the consummate strategist.

"We need to lay as many miles of track as we can. We need those ten-square-mile parcels given by the government for later sale to recoup our investment. We cannot let that crook Durant get too far ahead of our projected meeting point at the Rockies. We cannot let that perpetrator of the Crédit Mobilier scam take land that we need to pay off banks and investors. He's lucky he's not in jail."

There was no doubt of Huntington's distaste for the man.

"Can Paris get this done?" asked Crocker. "The way you used the word *assist* leads me to think I should not ask too many questions about his methods. But there is a lot riding on getting possession of the right of way."

"If there is a way, Paris will find it."

Chapter Nine

1868 Late Winter
Mormon Station (Genoa), Nevada

Sutton had just exited Patten's office after their discussion about securing the deed to the Purcell ranch. But he did not move to leave town as he had told Patten he would. Instead, he immediately headed around back. There was a rear entrance, and Sutton knew he could re-enter without anyone seeing him. He walked out the front door to put Patten at ease, thinking he would head off and bring back the deed. However, his anger with Patten generated during their discussion now boiled over from within. He'd had enough.

Sutton had no intention of bringing back any deed. Not right now, anyway.

The back door was unlocked. Sutton knew this because he did the unlocking before he left. Patten thought he'd been looking at the scenery, but Sutton made sure the lock to the rear door was open. He'd need it as both an entry and exit for what he intended now.

Sutton re-entered the office.

"Sutton, you're back. What, did you forget something?" taunted Patten.

"No, there was just a loose end I have to deal with before I leave."

"What's the loose end?"

"You."

Sutton held a long bladed knife he had pulled from its regular position concealed low on his right leg before he opened the door. Without any change in demeanor, he whipped his right hand up, throwing the blade at Patten. The motion was quick, almost quicker than drawing a gun. And it was quiet.

The knife embedded deep into Patten's chest just a little off center to the right. Directly into the heart. Patten slowly started sinking to the ground, eyes showing complete shock and a look as if to silently ask, "What did I do to you to deserve this?" Patten fully collapsed to the floor, crumpled in a contorted heap. Sutton stood over the now inert body. He felt no remorse, only the accomplishment of a task.

Sutton then bent down and withdrew his knife from Patten's chest. Red fluid oozed out of the wound once the blade was removed but not for long. *The heart must have stopped beating he thought. Good, there'd be less evidence should anyone look through a window.* He pulled the body into an office closet. No one would find Patten for at least a couple of days when the smell would draw someone to investigate.

He then left through the back door.

*****

It was dark when Will and Elizabeth arrived at the ranch house. For the last few miles,

Will had been riding side by side with Elizabeth's horse, keeping his hand out to hold her up

in her saddle. Juan came running out, half pulling up his trousers with one hand and reaching out for the bridles with the other.

"Jefe are you ok?" he asked.

"I'm fine," said Will, "but this lady is hurt bad. Not sure exactly how serious beyond the cuts and bruises I can see, but I think there is some injury to her stomach area."

Will swung down out of his saddle and dropped the rein, knowing instinctively that Powder wouldn't move from that spot as trained. But he didn't know if the bay Elizabeth was riding would hold still for a dismount.

"Juan, grab the bay's bridle," said Will. "I'm taking her to my room in the main house. Please tie up the horses and ask María to come and tend to her. She can stay in my room, and I'll sleep in the barn."

"*Sí padrone*. I will get María. Don't worry about the caballos. They have been ridden hard and look like they need food and a rub down."

Will appreciated the fact that both Juan and Raúl knew horses and what it took to care for them. The cattle generated the money but working with the horses is what all three really enjoyed. Horses were the main reason Will, Juan, and Raúl had stayed together from New Mexico to Nevada. It had been a long journey looking for a place they could raise and train good horseflesh. The journey had created a bond between the three.

Will carried Elizabeth to the house in his arms. This time, he didn't ask, he just grabbed her before she fell out of the saddle on her own. He didn't stop until he got to his room and laid her in his bed. The room had been cleaned. Must have been María. She had a knack of knowing when to clean up after the men around the ranch. She must have figured it was a good time to tidy up in his absence.

Elizabeth's breathing came evenly as María entered. Elizabeth looked up.

"Are we here?" she asked in a hushed tone.

"We made it to my ranch," said Will. "This is María; she is going to take care of you. You'll be safe. Let her help."

"I need to talk to you," came Beth's reply. "We need to find the man that killed my family and stole the script, the money."

Moonlight filtered through the window above his bed just enough for Will to see a crease in Beth's brow and the pain about her face.

"We will talk about that when you feel better. Maria is good with wounds and injuries. She will be a comfort. I promise you I will help in any way I can to get what is yours."

*****

Drake Sutton started his ride out of town from Patten's office in Genoa. He moved slowly so as not to raise any undue attention. Genoa was a small city. Had he ridden out fast, someone might notice. So, he started at a slow, leisurely walk, passing the only saloon in town. It had been the first saloon ever built in the Territory of Nevada. Funny, he thought, a saloon in a Mormon settlement.

As he walked his horse out of town, Sutton relaxed into the gentle ride. He let his mind wander a bit thinking about the hamlet he was leaving for the last time. He had no intention of ever returning. Genoa was small, barely thirty to forty souls. Patten had told Sutton the town was founded in 1851 by Mormons from Salt Lake. He figured they probably came to escape the desert. The Carson Valley had plenty of water and plenty of natural grass. The Mormons had opened a trading post on what they believed would be the main trail from the east over the Sierras to the gold fields of California. People called it Mormon Station.

"Mr. Sutton, fine evening." The comment came from an elderly man exiting the cemetery at the north of town.

Sutton tipped his hat.

Sutton did not think Genoa would survive much longer. The first wagon trails followed the original Kit Carson path taken way back in the 1840s with Lt. *Frémont* over the Kirkwood summit. It was a hard climb

53

to the top. Wagon rigs had to be hauled up to the final crest using a pulley system on well positioned trees.

The trail past Genoa had been the original wagon trail to California. But the cross-country wagon trains no longer came this way. The wagon masters ultimately found an easier route. It travelled further north following the Truckee River up through Donner Pass and then down to Placerville. This town would die just like Patten, quietly and without anyone noticing. Now, the land around here was only good for raising cows.

Sutton was not inclined to raise cows. He thought them stupid beasts. A rancher's life was consumed by the well-being of his stock. They staked their very fortune on these animals. In his mind, that made ranchers just as stupid as the beasts themselves.

Sutton had ideas and a plan to make money in a much simpler, if less legal, way. He had acted as a land agent for Patten, providing extra *motivation* for landowners who held title to property Patten knew sat along the railroads' proposed right of way. They had worked on three deals, and Sutton had seen the money Patten made on the subsequent transfer to the railroad.

Sutton felt good about how his plan was playing out. He believed the girl had the Purcell deed and Millard Luce script. Reynolds would get that soon enough. Sutton had Patten's money in his saddlebag. He'd lulled Patten into giving him the money with the story that the girl was going to help close the deal. With the Millard Luce script, Sutton had both sets of funds intended to buy out Purcell. All he had to do now was ride back to the camp where he left the girl and Reynolds and collect the script.

If the girl wanted to continue on with him, he'd think about it. Might be nice for a while, but Sutton had no intention of keeping her with him for long. Though she appeared beautiful at first take, Sutton sensed a caginess about her, too. There was a worldliness in her demeanor, unexpected for a girl from a sheltered family.

Sutton was looking forward to getting his hands on the script. The script functioned like money. Millard Luce Cattle Co. was a huge cattle operation with headquarters he'd heard to be south of San Francisco. Everyone and anyone in California, Oregon, and Nevada knew of this cattle company. Though nothing but a piece of paper on the surface, Millard Luce script could be cashed at any bank as if it were dollar bills.

After the shootings and burnings, they had headed south. Located along the Truckee River, the Purcell Ranch was a two-day ride from Genoa and dealing with Patten. Patten was a loose end who could identify Sutton and link him to the Purcell deaths. His plan entailed removal of any links back to him. He had taken care of the loose end. No one other than those in his immediate group knew about what had taken place. Their silence could be assured too if necessary.

Sutton did not see the girl get the deed nor the script. She had told him she knew the location of both and ran into the house to get them just as the fire started. They had been in a hurry to leave the ranch worried that someone would come soon because of the flames and smoke. He had not asked her to show him the two documents as she ran out to get on her horse, maybe a mistake. But Sutton had a strong feeling she had it on her rig somewhere.

On the way to Genoa, they'd decided to set up camp near the base of Kingsbury Grade at the bottom of the Eastern Sierra. He told Reynolds and a second accomplice, Patrick Desmond, to find out where the script was and get it from the girl. Reynolds smiled at the prospect. Meanwhile, he'd go into Genoa and deal with Patten. While he didn't care how they did it, he'd told them to find the money in whatever form it took but not injure the girl. He had plans for her. Reynolds' smile diminished a bit at the instruction not to harm the girl, but he nodded that he would get the money if she had it.

Sutton then left for Genoa.

He now rode leisurely back to the camp. He hoped Reynolds had found the script. He didn't really care about the Purcell deed. He only wanted the money.

Chapter Ten

1868 Late Winter
Toal Ranch

Will awoke with a sneeze. He'd slept in a section of the barn where they kept the feed. A piece of the hay had fallen on his face. He was going to roll over and head back off to sleep, but his eyes opened just a crack to see the beginning of daylight through the barn door as it came over the eastern part of the valley. The smell of grass feed and the select animals within permeated the entire barn. He liked the smell, felt at home as it surrounded him. He was comfortable with his horses. The straw underneath his bed roll provided additional separation from the cold hard dirt below. Outside the knife-edged frosty air waited to chill the unprepared to the bone. He had been displaced. She slept in his bed. He remembered the sense that drove right through him when she pressed against his chest. He'd never felt that before. Cold as he was, the thought brought a pleasant but uncomfortable sense of warmth. He needed to get up.

He hitched up his pants and pulled on his boots. He wondered if Juan was still awake. Because Elizabeth had said there were two other riders, Will figured it would not be long before they followed the tracks to the ranch. So, they agreed to split night guard. Will had taken the first watch, Raúl the next, and Juan had the last through morning. The last watch was always the hard one.

"Ah, my young jefe, you think you will find Juan asleep?" Will had walked around the back of the barn to the outlying corral fence where Juan had taken a position seated with his back against a fence post looking east.

"Juan no fall asleep. If you'se fall asleep, then you could be leaving the casa open for the desperados."

Will chuckled at the addition of the letter *s* in the word *you* along with the elongation as pronounced by his friend from the southern border.

"No compadre," said Will. "I had faith in you. Even if I heard you snoring twenty feet away."

"No, no, no," Juan responded, wagging his finger to and fro. "I only snore after a night of tequila. Ask María. She will testify."

Will smiled. He loved the comfort in talking to his two hands, Juan and Raúl.

"Has it been quiet all night?"

"*Sí*, quiet all night."

"I just have a bad feelin' that they will be a comin' after the girl. Right now, I have no idea what the situation is. I only know that they had the girl, and the guy who drew down on me was pretty good. If he has others ridin' with him who are cut from the same cloth, then they will undoubtedly be lookin' to retrieve the girl."

"Cut from the same cloth? I no understand that one, jefe."

"The man I shot obviously rode on the wrong side of the law. If he had partners, I figure they'll be the same. The man I killed drew on me way too quick. He appeared overly concerned that anyone should happen on his camp. He just seemed to want me dead, like someone who had somethin' to hide."

"Ah, *sí*. Now I *entiendo*, understand. So, you think we will see the others soon?"

"Hard to tell," said Will. "I won't know much more until the girl gets better and I can talk to her about what happened out there."

"What did you do with the body?"

Will looked out over the still dimly lit grasses. He had thought on the way back with the girl about how many men he had killed. He had talked to Father John Cecconi in Carson City about the war and the need he felt to confess. His mother would have pushed him to go to confession. Ultimately, he sought out the only Catholic priest in what was probably one hundred miles. Father John had listened to his account of the war and his own deeds that were a part of it. Father John said God would understand that bad things happen in battle. Will wasn't sure it was so simple. Will wondered what Father Cecconi would say about the guy out on the far reach of his ranch now lying in a shallow grave.

He had often wondered how a good Catholic could live out here in this world without killing someone. In his short life, soldiers had shot at him, rustlers on the run had shot at him, and now, abusers of a woman had shot at him. He kept finding himself in situations where he had to pull his trigger or get shot. Will had pulled a lot of triggers.

Will turned to finally answer Juan. "I buried him but didn't have time to make it real deep. The girl was unconscious, and I hurried so we could get back to the ranch as soon as possible."

"Jefe, what kind of men would do that to a woman?"

"Juan, you know the answer to that. Bad men. And that is more 'n likely the same kind who are gonna come lookin' for the girl."

*****

Dale Paris arrived at the toll bridge at Lake Crossing. He'd been in town for three days now. Charles Crocker had given him a simple and clear directive: *"Get the Purcell property so we can continue laying track east of the newly completed Donner Tunnel."* The directive was delivered with a pair of piercing eyes that confirmed what came next:

"And I don't care a great deal as to how you get it done, as long as it doesn't reflect poorly on CPRR."

Lake Crossing consisted of a small collection of buildings not far from the path of gradual descent the Truckee River made from Lake Tahoe to the west. The town originally grew up around a toll barge across the river. Paris had spoken briefly with Mr. Crocker before he left to see if he could get any further useful information and background. The problem for the railroad involved a ranch owned by Josiah Purcell, a parcel near the town. While not a metropolis, Lake Crossing had its own sheriff. Crocker said he had been to the town and spoken to the sheriff personally on earlier travels for the railroad. Crocker suggested that Paris start his investigation there.

Crocker also told him that Lake Crossing had been named for Myron Lake, who had purchased a toll barge across the river. He later built a bridge over the same spot still charging for passage over the deep churning waters. Lake also built a mill, a hotel, and livery stable. He essentially built his own town. Crocker had talked to Mr. Lake on those earlier travels up the right of way, personally discussing a deal to ultimately build a depot here. Crocker told Paris he thought this would be a fair-sized town in the future. It would be the last real stop before the train headed across a large uninterrupted desert expanse stretching all the way to Salt Lake. Crocker said he suggested a new name for the town to Lake. He suggested naming the new town and depot after General Jesse Lee Reno, a Union officer killed at the battle of South Mountain. Paris was going to ask what Crocker's connection was to General Reno, but someone else came into the office at that moment, and Crocker had to leave.

Paris planned on talking to the bridge master, the man who took in the toll payments. Bridge masters were a source of information, seeing everyone who crossed the river. The Purcell property laid west of Lake

Crossing. Traveling south would require traveling through town to the east and using the toll bridge on the other side. The bridge was the best and safest way to cross the Truckee. Paris figured most traffic would use the toll crossing, thus the master would have seen them.

Paris had spoken to the sheriff earlier. The sheriff initially thought Paris was a Pinkerton man. Probably because Paris wore a bowler hat, suit, and vest like most of the Pinkerton men. He had used the likeness to his advantage many times. Though not a Pinkerton man, he did not disabuse the sheriff of his misapprehension.

The sheriff told him people had seen smoke coming from the Purcell property. Folks in the surrounding thickly wooded area were always afraid of fire. So, the neighbors had ridden to see the cause of the smoke. They told the sheriff they'd come upon the grisly scene of the burned-out house and barn with blackened bodies in the rubble.

The sheriff investigated the scene himself. He told Paris it had to be Paiutes. Tensions between townsfolk and the local tribe had been ongoing since the 1850s.

Paris had ridden to the scene himself. He had taken the train with his horse to the construction terminus just past the Donner Tunnel. Though he rode directly to Lake Crossing and then to the Purcell Ranch, he arrived long after the fire. The sheriff said the bodies had been buried, but the rest of the scene had been left as they found it. Paris thought it amusing that he saw not one sign of Indians. No arrows, no spears, no indication of multiple unshod horses riding onto the scene, no less surrounding the barn. Paris concluded the sheriff would never qualify as a Pinkerton man.

Luckily, Paris got a decent picture of horse traffic to and from the ranch. There had been no rain since the fire. While winter could bring regular showers at this elevation, it had been dry for a spell.

At the scene, while Paris did not find any real sign of Indians, he did see lots of tracks left by shod horses. He saw none heading west; all were heading east. The only thing east was the town of Lake Crossing.

So, he had first asked people in Lake Crossing if anyone had seen a group in town that just passed through quickly. No one had seen anything out of the ordinary.

Paris then thought maybe a group of riders would have used the toll bridge. That brought him here.

"Morning," said Paris to the bridge master. "A little cold today."

"Pretty much the way it is this time of year. You interested in the weather or just startin' a conversation?"

Paris thought the comment a bit caustic. This job had to be lonely. Not much traffic.

"People who ask about the weather are usually not from around these parts," said the bridge master.

The middle-aged man standing in front of Paris wore dungarees and a shirt rolled at the sleeves revealing the not uncommon Union suit underneath. Tobacco stains were splattered in various places on the shirt. *Obviously, not a Mormon.* The conversation had started awkwardly, so Paris decided to come right to the point.

"I have been hired to find out what happened to the Purcell Ranch. I spoke to the sheriff, and he thinks it was Paiutes. I found some tracks headed east from the Ranch and thought there might be a group of white men involved. From the signs left, I thought they might have ridden through here heading away from what they had done. See anything or anyone who might fit that description?"

"Nope, no groups of men on horseback." The man had to stop mid-thought and spit the ever-present welling of mucous from the tobacco plug sitting in his cheek.

"But I did have a group coming from the south, Carson City way, a day or two after the fire who said they saw three men and a young blonde woman heading south at a good clip. No group with a young blonde woman used the bridge. But there's a crossing some folks use over the Truckee about a mile east of the Purcell property. If folks got no money for the toll, they cross there."

Paris then asked, "Did you know the Purcell family?"

The bridge master responded, "I didn't know them, but they would use the bridge three to four times a year to head to special meetings at the Mormon Station near Genoa. That old man kept to himself, barely spoke to anyone. He kept his wife in his wagon. There was always a younger woman. I couldn't tell if she was a child or another wife. But each time they crossed, walking next to the wagon was a good lookin' younger woman. As I said, I don't know if that was a daughter or another wife. With them Mormons, you can't always tell."

Paris knew Purcell had a young wife and an older wife. That information had come from Stuart and his agent Wyatt Richard who had been negotiating with the Purcell's'. Now a thought struck Paris. *Maybe the young woman who the bridge master had seen with Purcell was the same woman with the men heading south. Under normal circumstances, riders that headed south from the Purcell's to Carson took the toll bridge. Everyone took the toll bridge unless they had just masqueraded as Indians in a massacre.*

Without saying anything more on the subject, Paris looked up and said, "Thank you very much. I might just head that way to see what I can find. You have been most helpful."

Paris headed across the Truckee. He had to stop in Carson City anyway to review the title records in the territorial land office. Genoa was another of his probable stops. If there were any Mormon relatives, they probably lived around Genoa. He hoped to speak to them in case there was a will that might prove useful.

Chapter Eleven

1868 Late Winter
Mormon Station (Genoa), Nevada

Drake Sutton was headed north at a leisurely pace along the base line road at the bottom of the Eastern Sierra. He had headed out of Genoa without raising any suspicion. Patten was no longer a problem.

Now all he had to do was get the Millard script from the girl and head west. He could stop in Carson City, cash that draft, and pay off Desmond and Reynolds. He knew Patten had a spread of over four hundred acres just east of Sacramento, which he obtained in one of the deals for property sold to the railroad. Sutton could easily contrive some recorded transfer and take it over. No one was left to contest whatever scheme he could come up with. He would wait for a few months, sell that spread, and then, with the combined funds, head to San Francisco. San Francisco was the only place in California holding any interest for an educated man.

In the middle of his thoughts, he saw dust rising further down the road. A rider was coming and coming hard. It did not take long for Sutton to make out the horse and rider. It was Pat Desmond.

Desmond was not hard to recognize. Though also educated, Desmond was short and as thick as any man he'd ever seen. Desmond's physique appeared like a bull improperly placed in human form. Sutton had never seen a man with lower legs as thick as Desmond's. Chest, thighs, arms, and shoulders were all the same. The man was almost as wide as he was tall and not an ounce of fat. Solid as a brick. He'd seen Desmond in bar fights take blows from much taller men without even coming close to losing his balance. All that weight and muscle stood so low to the ground that very few attackers could knock him off his stance. He'd seen Desmond absorb many blows only to then bull rush the opponent. Desmond would crush the soul, smash his opponent into whatever obstacle, and drive right through the man. Last time Sutton had seen it happen, Desmond ended up breaking the man's leg in three places. Very few ever got up after a Desmond rush.

But because of his stature, Desmond looked awkward on a horse. His thighs and calves were so thick that it made his legs stick out from the horse's body. They flapped as he rode at speed because he just didn't have the length to curl down and grip his heels along a horse's flanks.

Desmond saw Sutton and pulled up. His horse was seriously lathered. He had been riding hard.

"Reynolds is dead, and the girl's gone!" exclaimed the Irishman. The ever-present Irish lilt could not be suppressed in the unmistakable urgency.

"How?" Sutton stammered, shocked by the unexpected news.

"I 'av no idea. I 'av been up in the mountains huntin' as we needed food. I come back, Reynolds' horse was a'standin' free, the girl was gone, and there's a mound next to the camp. I dug back a bit on the mound and saw Reynolds' face. May the saints preserve us."

"No saints are going to intervene for us, and you know it." Sutton's demeanor was immediately charged by this news. His anger soon began to rise. The deed, the script, the entire plan hinged on Reynolds doing one simple thing: get the script. Now this.

"Show me where," demanded Sutton.

They both headed north, back to the camp.

*****

Sutton looked around the camp. It was just as Desmond had described it. Nothing but a lone horse, saddle on the ground, and a mound nearby with Reynolds' dead body in it. No girl.

Sutton checked Reynolds' saddlebags. No script, no money. The rest of the camp yielded no further clues.

Sutton looked for tracks. Though not an Indian guide, he had followed trails all his adult life. He easily found a pair of tracks from two horses heading off to the southeast.

"Let's follow the tracks and see where they go," said Sutton. He and Desmond re-mounted and moved slowly, in order to keep track of the trail.

Chapter Twelve

1868 Late Winter
Carson City, Nevada

It was late morning but vapor still puffed out from his lungs with each breath. His bandana was pulled high on the back of his neck and tight. His jacket was buttoned tight. The sky was a high one, no clouds, only crisp blue everywhere he could see. No clouds meant no moisture and no moisture meant a sharp coolness. The stab of the cold bit through his trousers. He should have worn chaps.

Will had left the ranch early. As Elizabeth had yet to come out of the main house, he thought this might be a good day to finish something he had been meaning to do for some time now. Will wanted to be there when she finally arose. He needed to find out what led to the shootout with suspenders. The mystery ate at him. More than that, he had to get as much information as he could to assess what risk there might be to men riding in on his ranch shooting their way in to retake the girl. But he needed to finalize the purchase of his ranch. That purchase had been held up almost two years. It was time to do something about it.

Will had talked to other ranchers nearby about his problem. He'd been told to see a particular lawyer here in Carson City who should be able to help. He entered the office with a sign on the door that read S. Samuel Grande ⬯ Attorney at Law. Maybe the lawyer could tell him how he could get this done.

Will still had the money his father had buried at his Grandpa's grave. In Texas, he had exchanged the coins for a Western Union draft, which he could cash at any bank. That draft had been kept in a leather case underneath the front of his saddle. He'd saved that money all along, and

. en added a bit more, waiting until he found a piece of property he could ranch.

He had filed his homesteaded claim and paid the eighteen dollar fee required by the government. But that is as far as he had gotten. The government priced all homesteads at one dollar and twenty-five cents per acre. He had worked the land for over a year. That hard work produced what was now a herd of a thousand cattle and over forty horses of good breeding stock. He, Juan and Raúl had raised a barn, bunk house and small main house. He wanted to protect what he had built. However, he didn't have enough to completely pay for the entire spread even at the government's low price. While he had an idea as to how he could finalize a purchase, he needed advice.

He'd spoken with a nice family, Martin and Sue Johnson, who had homesteaded a parcel next to the open space he'd seen. He also talked to the owners of the ranch on the other side of the Johnsons, the Dangbergs. They were to the far south of the Carson Valley and had homesteaded a large piece of land running both sheep and cattle. They did some farming, too. Henry—or Heinrich—Dangberg had told him he'd come from a place in Germany called Minden. He now owned what appeared to be a well-run ranch.

Both families had been very nice and open to having him homestead the section he wanted. The parcel near both the Johnsons and the Dangbergs was in a small barely secluded area just off the main stretch of Carson Valley. He was told this tract had become called Jack's Valley. He had no idea where the name came from. The little valley butted up against the granite walls of the Sierras.

When Will first laid eyes on it, the massive mountains wore caps of snow beneath the bluest sky he'd ever seen. The grasses across the acres stood knee high even in late winter—a good sign. He knew immediately the snow melt must be the source for the green he gazed upon. He'd intended to travel all the way to California. But he'd looked at both Juan and Raúl sitting astride their horses next to him and nodded. All three knew this was a good place to start a ranch. It had the grasses and water they had been looking for. Not only that, the folks he'd talked to nearby would be good neighbors.

Sitting inside the office he had just entered was one of the tallest men he'd ever seen. When he stood up, the gentleman must have been six feet, five inches or more. The man had a barrel chest and an olive complexion. He'd been sitting alone in a room surrounded by books stacked in small towers all over the office, a castle of book stacks. Will had never seen so many books in one place.

He looked up and down the stacks of books both on the ground and on the wall shelves all around the office. Without thinking, Will uttered almost to himself, "I thought I was at a law office. This must be a library." A movement snapped Will's attention back to the man before him.

The only occupant of the office swiveled completely around, extending his arms as if to encompass the expanse of his office empire as he turned. "This is my office. I happen to be a lawyer who believes one should *read* the law before you presume to advise people on it. There are many lawyers who practice otherwise. If you must read the law, then you must obtain the books that contain those laws. These are books that contain the laws that I need to access."

The tall individual before Will had risen from a wooden chair with a half-circle spoked back that arched high behind his head. The man was so tall, the chair must have been made especially for him. He had an expression that was hard to read. Will couldn't tell if he was upset at the interruption or if he was happy to talk to someone.

Then, as if he'd seen Will's look of confusion, the gentleman started a blunt yet detailed introduction. As time passed, Will would come to appreciate the man's direct, immediately perceptive approach. "My name is S. Samuel Grande. That's Sicilian. Sicily is near Italy. That's in Europe. My friends call me Sam. My father came from the old country on a boat and landed in San Francisco. My father speaks almost no English at all, but he now owns multiple businesses. He wanted each of my brothers and I to run one of them. But I wanted to do something else.

"I wanted to get out of the city. People in the country are much more pleasant. For a few years after law school, I did represent several clients in that good city. While it may seem like a boast, I obtained what I thought were numerous beneficial results. But it seemed I couldn't please anyone. No matter how good the result, they didn't want to pay my fee.

"Clients never wanted to retain you unless they were in trouble or in need. But, if you got them out of trouble, or if you removed the need, they acted as if that should have been the result all along. I was just a facilitator of sorts making sure their vision of justice came to be."

Will wondered why the man felt so compelled to tell him what amounted to his life story. However, not knowing how to respond, he just kept listening.

Grande continued, "But the truth is, had I not done what I did, most of those clients would have ended up far worse off than what they feared would happen when they came to me in the first place. So, I moved here. People in the country have a much more widespread appreciation for a job well done. However, the pay is harder to come by."

Grande then looked Will up and down in a focused, obvious, and nearly hostile manner.

"So, are you in trouble, or are you here looking for work? I have no work, and I am really careful about taking on clients who are in trouble."

"I am not in trouble, and I am not looking for work. I rode as a Texas Ranger for almost a year and have no patience with people who break the law. I want to buy the property I am ranching on. I want to buy the homestead parcel of land near the Johnson Ranch. I have filed my claim and paid the fee. But the land agent has held up finalizing my purchase. I have money; I can easily pay for the 165 acres I tried to homestead, but I want to get more land. I ranch both cattle and horses."

"What makes you think you are limited to 165 acres?"

"I was told that the Homestead Act allows people to buy a parcel from the government at one dollar and twenty-five cents per acre, but that they can homestead only 165 acres. But to build a ranch that can sustain itself, I will need over two thousand acres. The land is there, and I am hoping you can help me buy it."

"You look awful young for ranching. Most of those who start raising cattle don't last long."

"I worked on a ranch in New Mexico after I left the Rangers. I have two hands who have traveled with me, both of whom know cattle and horses. I have looked over the land out there in the valley, and it has plenty of grass and water. I have spoken to both the Johnsons and Dangbergs, and they tell me that the grass grows pretty much year 'round. Winter is mild compared to most. Summer can be hot, but the snow runoff brings plenty of water.

"I looked at land in Colorado, Wyoming, and Utah on my way west. There was plenty of open space in each, but no matter where I looked, there was always one thing missing. It could be that the grass grew only part of the year. In Utah, water could be an issue. In Wyoming, they said that the winters are really hard. I planned on heading to Central California but, in taking the old California Trail, we stopped here in Carson City and decided to look around. The parcel I am looking at fits all three of my requirements. More 'n that, the folks around seem outright nice."

Will could see the change in Grande's expression.

"I must admit I'm pleasantly surprised at the story I just heard. My initial impression was that you were in trouble with the law. I don't take criminal cases unless I can count on getting paid upfront."

"I can pay."

"I am now pretty sure you can. I am glad my first impression was incorrect."

Will relaxed just a bit. He felt as if he'd overcome something, though he was unsure what that might be yet hoping it was good as the feeling he had about this man. He was here with a purpose, and he wanted to get this homestead. It was his turn to be blunt now.

"I want to buy that land. Can you help?"

"I prefer to help clients with business matters, so what you ask fits. I know the Johnsons and Dangbergs. They are both clients, and if they hold you in high esteem, that speaks well for your character."

Will waited, but patience was difficult. Such was the level of his desire to get the land he'd seen.

"So, you need help buying land? A land agent named Scott Fallar has an office down the street. He serves as both the local recording agent and the agent for sales of government land. What seems to be the hold up with Mr. Fallar?"

"I talked to Fallar. He's the one who told me I was going to be limited to 165 acres."

"Well, did you *read* the law? Did you *read* the Homestead Act? It's hard to discuss the law if you don't *read* it."

Each time he said the word *read* it came out with elongated emphasis. Will felt like a schoolboy being scolded by his teacher.

"Maybe the problem is that you can't *read*."

Grande continued to use the emphasis. Will was insulted.

"I can read. I don't have anywhere near the books you do, but I can read."

"You have an accent. Where are you from?"

Will had worked consciously to suppress the accent of people in his home state. He learned in the war that the more twang someone had in his accent, the less educated people thought he was. He thought he had done a good job of erasing Georgia from his normal speech. He was surprised this man could pick up his roots from this quick conversation.

"I'm from Georgia by way of Texas," came his reply.

"You fight in the war?"

"Yep, I did. How is that important?"

"Again, I can say it over and over. You need to *read* the law. If you really want to achieve what you are aiming at, then you have to know what legal weapons you have and what weapons your opponent intends to use against you."

Grande's demeanor had changed ever so slightly. His tone shifted from chastising to assisting.

"To continue, as a Confederate soldier, you would not have had any rights under the Homestead Act until 1867. However, Congress just recently passed an amendment to that Act allowing ex-Confederate soldiers to participate. But to qualify, you must sign an affidavit of allegiance to the U.S. government. Do you have any problems doing that?"

"No, I don't. I have done my best to leave the war behind me. My plan is to sell beef and maybe horses to the army at Fort Churchill. I have no problem dealing with the army or signing something that says I will follow the laws of the Union."

Grande responded, "Well, maybe I can help you. Fallar is from the North. He probably detected the same accent I did and just didn't feel he had to inform you of the change in the law. But I can draft an affidavit very quickly, which should do the trick. If you present that to him, he will have no choice but to honor your claim."

"But I want more than 165 acres."

"Do you intend to stay on the land and work it for more than six months and reside on it for more than five years?"

"Of course. I've already been there over a year." Will thought the question silly. "Any serious ranch needs to breed and upgrade its stock year after year. You can't even have a decent herd of new horses for a year or two at minimum."

Grande then responded, "There is a provision in the Homestead Act that says if you intend to remain on the land for more than five years, you can buy an unlimited amount of acreage. You just have to pay for it."

Will looked down.

"That's my second problem. I have enough to pay for about one thousand acres but not three thousand. My Pa told me once that people can take out a loan to buy land. He thought it foolhardy to do so, but some did. He thought taking out a loan somehow let other people have a claim to their land. But is there any way I can do that here?"

"Yes, there are bankers who are willing to lend money for the purchase of land. But they will take an interest in the land as collateral. It's called a deed of trust, and it basically says that they will give you the money, but if you do not pay the loan back according to the terms of a promissory note, they can foreclose and take the property. They remove you from the land in the process."

Will was completely attentive. Grande saw the obvious interest and so continued. "Give me two or three days. I will prepare the appropriate affidavit, and I will speak to Duane Bliss. He's an officer over at the Bank of California here in Carson. I will tell him what you would like to do. I will also tell him that although you are young, you have a solid plan, and you have given this a good deal of thought. You also appear to have people who will work with you to make it happen. I think he will listen, and there is a good chance he will loan you the necessary money. But there will be a deed of trust recorded against your property until you pay it off. You understand what that means?"

"I understand. But I have fifty to one hundred heifers and a bull. I can get five dollars for every steer I raise the next year."

Thinking out loud, Will continued with his mental calculations. "Sales could generate five hundred dollars this year, and I expect that it would be four times higher next year. I should be able to pay off the loan in three to four years at the worst."

"Yes, you might. But ranching can be unpredictable. Weather could change. Your herd could catch some disease. You could get hurt. Lots of things could prevent you from making a payment. If you miss one payment, that could be grounds for the bank to foreclose."

"I won't miss any payments."

Grande looked at this young man. He had seen many legal entanglements over contracts, agreements, loans, or business deals. All those had begun with the best of intentions. However, when business transactions went south, people lost a measure of their natural rationality. Things often got ugly. But this young man in front of him had a strong measure of commitment. Grande liked that. Will Toal could be a client to support and cultivate.

Chapter Thirteen

1868 Early Spring
Toal Ranch

María came out of the house carrying a bundle of clothes. Will could tell from the strands hanging down they were the clothes Elizabeth had been wearing.

"María, how is she doing?"

"*Señor* Toal, she sleeps a lot. She has, how you say, darkness on the skin in many places?"

"Bruises," interrupted Will.

"*Sí*, bruises. She also have many cuts of the skin."

"What about her stomach?"

"She has lots of blood, but I no see any cuts from the outside. There is a big darkness here." María spread her hand across her stomach. "*Mucho* blood."

"We will have to keep an eye on her. If she is bleeding from the inside, I will have to go get the doctor from Carson City."

"Sí, she is resting, but I will tell you if there is any more blood, *Señor* Toal."

"Thank you, María. And please tell me when she wakes up so I can talk to her. I need to find out what she was involved in."

*****

Will walked across the open area in front of the barn. He, Raúl, and Juan had set up the ranch in something of a square. The barn and main corral were on one side. The ranch house sat opposite. The cabin where

María, Juan, and Raúl lived stood to one side. The last side of the square was to have a bunk house. But that would come only if they got good prices for this year's horse sales.

Cattle would pay for the regular expenses and covered the loans. Horse sales would bring in the money to expand and improve. They had good breeding stock. They should have fifteen to twenty good mounts to interest the Captain at Fort Churchill. Fort Churchill had replaced the old Fort Haven in 1860, built to protect settlers from the Paiutes. The Paiute Wars of the 1850s had left many dead on both sides, and the government was forced to maintain a larger presence. Timing could not have been better for Will as the army needed horseflesh. He quickly overcame his hesitation in selling to the Union Army. The war was over for him. He left all that behind. Will needed the money. The army needed good horses, and Will, Juan, and Raúl produced very good horses.

Raúl was standing outside the main corral. Juan was inside getting a new colt to bend and eventually fall completely flat on the ground.

"Any horse has to feel the trust to get him fully down." Will made the statement knowing that for a prey animal to lie flat, it had to trust its human master to the fullest. It took time and patience to earn that trust.

Juan was concentrating and did not respond to Will other than a nod of his sombrero.

"The army likes to have horses already trained to fold flat. It can be the only defensive position they can take if they are out in open space." Again, Will was almost talking to himself as he knew both Juan and Raúl were already aware of the army's preference. They appreciated well-trained animals.

Juan and Raúl had taught Will a way of breaking horses that combined the best methods of both the Mexican vaquero and the Indian. Raúl had learned both methods from his father who had worked haciendas in New Mexico and passed them on to Juan and Will.

Juan and Raúl were born in Mexico. Will met up with the two men on a ranch just north of the border where the three had worked wrangling beef and horses for two years after Will quit the Rangers. They had been together ever since. They agreed to raise horses the right way in California. They made it to Nevada, liked what they saw, and now were content here in the Valley.

"He is a strong one, jefe. That colt, he replace Powder someday."

"Raúl, we have a lot of good horses, but I don't see a one who could replace Powder anytime soon."

Raúl smiled. He had offered the comment as a bit of a joke knowing how partial Will was to his horse. But Will did not joke about Powder. Such was the feeling he had for his regular mount. Will had become very good at breaking new colts himself using the old methods he'd learned from Raúl. But Powder held a special place with Will. The late-gelded gray mustang with white flecks had a wide set chest with solid legs that were longer than most mustangs. In fact, Powder stood larger than any of the mustangs ever rounded up on the ranch, almost sixteen hands high. Because he had been gelded late, Powder had a thicker neck, like a stallion, but it balanced well with his wide chest. His neck and head came out of his body tall, allowing for a high front action and smoother gate. The head was also straighter than most.

"You right, jefe. Powder special. He brings out the Andalusian left by the conquistadors."

Juan and Raúl had often said that Powder was a throwback to the Spanish horses that got loose from the conquistadors. The Spaniards brought horses from Andalusia bred to work bulls for the ring. It was those same blooded horses that formed the foundation herds of mustangs. According to Raul, the horse was not a natural species of America; the Spaniards had brought them. And the horse the Spaniards rode was the Andalusian, the same breed of horses started in the 13th century by monks in Spain and followed religiously ever since.

Raúl said, "Powder, he could work the bulls."

Raúl was not referring to the bulls in their Carson Valley herd. He was referring to the black bulls bred for the rings in Spain, stories relayed down the generations from one vaquero to an another. Raúl learned it from his father, and he passed those same lessons to his son, Juan and then Will.

"Powder, he has size, but also, he quick. Andalusians were bred by the monks to train easy and be quick. It was the horses that worked the bulls. No bulls bred for the ring in Spain were to see a man on foot until he met *de matador* in the ring."

"You've told me that before. But why would you ever keep those bulls away from a man on the ground? You never really explained that. What do they do with the bulls in the rings?"

"The matador, he fight de bull," said Raúl, rolling out the word bull as if it was pronounced twice as long as in English.

"That's the strangest thing I ever heard," came Will's response. "What's the point in that?"

"Ah, but it is a thing of beauty to see," mused Raúl, almost looking upward into space, obviously recalling some old memory.

"I see a bullfight in north Mexico as a *muchacho*. The fight is in a large ring with rows and rows of seats up to the sky. The matador enters with only a cape and sword. The bull charges and *de matador*, he steps away at the last moment barely avoiding the horns. But *de matador* does this with the grace of a ballerina. The bull keeps charging until he tires. Then, *de matador* goes in for the kill, running at de bull as de bull charges at him. He strikes the sword just behind the head to sever the spine just as the bull passes. It takes great courage and skill to kill the bull with nothing but a sword."

Will was forced to agree that anyone who ran at a charging bull had either a great deal of courage or a death wish. But he still thought the whole idea sounded strangely pointless. However, at the time, he did not say anything further. Will found the special horses working the bulls much more interesting.

All Will knew was that Powder was the quickest horse he had ever ridden and had the stamina to ride at a good pace day after day for weeks.

"We have to get these horses ready. The steers have fattened up just enough on the early season grass. They could use some more time eating the coming spring grass, but the army will be needing beef after the winter. We need to sell as much as we can, so I can pay off a good chunk of the loan on the ranch. And, if we can get them to buy all twenty horses, we might get enough to build the bunk house and have some money to hire a new hand."

"The horses, jefe; they will be ready."

*****

Will stood next to the main corral just after turning Powder out. The mid-day sun was high and bright. When standing in the direct sunlight he thought one could almost warm a bit, but the air was bone dry and crisp. Not a lot of warm to it. Pretty standard for this time of year. He watched as the gray gelding kicked up his heels feeling the freedom of movement without saddle or rider. It brought a smile to his face to see the spontaneous joy with every buck and kick. The dust rose in driven clouds pushed by each thrust of Powder's hind quarters just before the rear hooves raised up off the ground in a high kick to the side.

"Go on, stretch it out son. Have your fun here. Better than when I'm aboard."

Will then noticed movement to his left. It was Elizabeth. In one glance he could see that she looked far different than the last time they had been together on the ride back to the ranch. It had taken several days for Elizabeth to rise and come out of the house. This was the first he'd seen her since the day they met. Up to then, María had been the only person having any contact with her. Maria had told him there had been no indication of any further complications with the injury to her abdomen. The cuts were healing. The bruises had turned to different colors but were fading. The swelling around her face and jaw appeared to be subsiding. With her clothes all cleaned by María, she looked almost healed. But those clean clothes undoubtedly covered parts still injured beneath. He marveled at how her appearance of a few days ago changed so quickly.

"I understand I have put you out of your house," she said on approaching Will.

"Minor inconvenience; sometimes a change is good to remind you of the things you worked to get. I slept in the barn for more 'en a few months before we built the main house. We raised the barn and the cabin where Raúl, Juan, and María live first. The ranch house was last. Bein' in the barn kind of reminds me how things were when we struggled to get started."

"I will be happy to switch with you. I should not be putting my host out of his home."

"Wouldn't have it. You need to get well. That will take some time. The barn is fine. In fact, I suppose it sort of suits me."

Will took note of the clean dress drawn at the waist with a blouse underneath. There was no head covering. All the Mormon women he had seen around Genoa always had a skull cap that generally covered their hair. Elizabeth had a thick head of hair that was a bright blonde color, brighter than he had ever seen on a woman. Her hair hung much longer than he would have guessed based on the matted nature of a few day ago. There were natural waves running the length. He also noticed that, despite her long lanky limbs, she was a woman of full figure.

Elizabeth was obviously conscious of Will looking her over top to bottom.

"I don't have my apron or my cap," she said, self-consciously looking down at her front while running her hand through her hair. Her hair had certainly been brushed since he had last seen her. "Those men took both from me."

"I have to beg your pardon for looking at you like a schoolboy. It's just that when I saw you last . . . well, you look a might different today."

"Better I hope," she responded, opening her blue eyes and meeting his. A smile spread across her face. Will had sometimes heard men talk around campfires during the war about seeing women and getting weak in the knees. He wondered if that was why he reached out to grab a hold of the corral railing.

"Elizabeth, you do look mighty nice." He felt stupid for not coming up with something cleverer.

"Call me Beth. My mom always called me Beth."

"Okay, I will try to call you Beth." Struggling to keep his footing, he said, "Beth, we need to talk."

"I know you must have questions. Is there a place where we can sit? I will do my best to explain what has happened."

*****

Drake Sutton looked through a glass down at Toal's barn. Desmond was right next to him. Sutton brushed off the dust that had collected at the back of his elbows. Desmond and he had spent the better part of the last days on their bellies lying in the dirt and dust; just watching. He pulled back the surveyor's lens. He spat. The ever present breezes constantly blew fine particles of dust into his nose and mouth. Layin' flat on his belly left him all too close to the earth. The taste had been tough to bear, until now. He rolled onto his back and sat up with no small measure of satisfaction.

Sutton and Desmond had been watching from a stand of rocks about a half mile from the ranch. The tracks they followed led here, but they decided to wait and see what developed. Sutton had noticed the ranch hands alternating watch duty beginning each evening. Obviously, whoever ran the ranch had some training, probably military. Someone constantly stood lookout; obviously waiting for those who might follow those same tracks. But neither Sutton nor Desmond had known for sure if the girl was anywhere near. Now they knew.

"Well, it took a while, but there she is. No doubt about it. Long blond hair, tall with long legs. It's her alright."

Sutton uttered the words with almost a grimace. Elizabeth was out of his control along with the script money. He could give up on a large part of his plan and just leave with the Patten money, but that Millard Luce script had to be worth every bit as much, and he did not relish going away with half the prize.

"Do you think we can surprise them with just the two of us, grab the girl, and find out where the money is?" came the Irish brogue of Desmond.

"No, we don't have the numbers. They are obviously prepared for what they think will be men coming in. Even if we did that, there would be no guarantee we would find the money. We need to be patient. If we avoid Genoa and Patten's office, we can stay out here and wait for the girl to leave the ranch compound. That's when we make our move.

"If she has the money, she will try to steal away by herself and probably head west. She told me at one time that she always wanted to see

San Francisco. That would make it easy. We just overtake her and grab what we need. If she doesn't have it with her here, then she is going to have to make a play to go get it. We will just have to follow until we know where the script is. That girl looks all innocent, but I just have a feeling there is a conniving full-grown woman underneath the girlish garb. We need to make sure. So, we wait, and we watch."

*****

Will led Beth back to the front porch. He now puzzled over how to sit and talk. He only had a short bench attached to the front of the ranch house and a rocker. Originally meant to just hold a saddle or tack beneath the porch overhang, the bench was big enough to hold them both—but barely.

The only other seating outside on the porch was Will's rocker. If they were to sit on the bench together, they would be closer than on one of those fancy couches in some sitting room Will had seen in hotels on his way west. He wasn't sure if Elizabeth would agree with his selection of a spot to talk. But this spot had a roof over it and out of both the sun and wind.

Will removed his hat and stomped the dust off his boots. He let Beth sit first. He waited for some sign that she agreed with the choice. She looked up, wondering at first why he was still standing. She then patted the bench next to her. He took it as a positive sign and thankfully sat.

Beth looked out over the flat ranch grasses to the east.

"How did a man so young get so much land and cattle to run on it? Your family rich?"

Will had anticipated talking about the camp, the man he shot, and the reason they were here. He was taken aback a bit with a question about himself. But she had a look on her face that said she really wanted to know. Without much thought to it, he felt at ease. He also felt a strange push compelling him to answer.

He almost started without thinking about why he would give someone any information about his background. He had never done something like this in the past. It was as if he wanted to somehow impress her. He had no idea why; he just did. So, he started what he intended to be a quick story.

"I came back from the war riding a four-legged remnant from the Confederate Calvary. Sorry animal, but it got me home. I had gone to war in some measure to protect my family and farm. My parents farmed acres in Georgia."

"How far is that from here?" asked Beth.

Will had started his story looking at the barn and stumbled at the unexpected interruption.

"It, … it would take months of riding to get there from here," he stammered.

He started again.

"I had gone to war to protect the farm and family. When I returned, all I found was our home burned to the ground and no one near. I didn't know what to do. So, I camped. After a day or two, a free black family who had worked for us came out of the woods and told me Sherman's army had come through and a company of scavengers arrived, demanding all stock that could be eaten. Said it was requisitioned for the army. Apparently, Pa refused, and they shot him dead in his tracks. Ma ran for a gun we kept just inside the door to the house and shot one of the officer's horses. They then shot her and my sister. After burning the house and barn, they took all the stock. The hands didn't know what to do, so they retreated to the woods to do for themselves as best they could."

There was a look of pain on Beth's face. She did not immediately offer any words of sympathy. However, she silently reached out and covered Will's hand with her own. The touch alone was electric.

"What did you do?"

"Waited."

"Waited for what? What was there left to do? Did you think of starting to work the farm yourself?"

"No, I really never liked farming. I always knew I'd leave home and head west. I looked at the free folk who had worked for us and told them I had nothin' to offer. We had never kept slaves. Pa didn't believe in it. But the best advice I could give them was to just move on as I was not goin' to stay. Then I sat down to wait until I was sure the families and hands left."

"Why?"

"Because I knew I had to make it clear that everyone had to move on. Those were good folks, but they would have stayed out of duty, and I had to make sure they moved on."

"But just as important, my Pa kept the family money in a box behind my Grandpa's grave. He never trusted banks. He never trusted any government. I hoped it was all still there."

"I camped for two more days. Didn't see a soul. Then I dug around Grandpa's grave and sure enough found the box Pa had described. Inside was over a thousand dollars in gold coins along with some Confederate paper money. Pa tried to keep only coin of value, but he must have taken the Confederate money out of desperation. By the time I got there, that Confederate paper money couldn't buy an apple. I packed up the coin money in a special pouch and started west.

"When I could, I bought a decent horse, saddle, and rig. I made a special leather pouch and attached it under the cantle of the saddle. I kept that money there the entire time I traveled west. Worked as a dishwasher initially, then started helping a local sheriff in Natchez, Louisiana. From there I moved to San Antonio and applied to be a Texas Ranger but only for one year. By then I'd had enough.

"After I quit the Rangers, I moved farther west to New Mexico, and was hired on at a hacienda close to Taos. Heard story after story of ranch land in California. I met Juan, Raúl, and María at that hacienda. Juan and Raúl were good hands. We got to talking, and I told them I had enough money to stake a purchase of ranch land. We all agreed to come see if we could raise cattle and horses on our own. Here we are."

Beth had never taken her eyes off Will. But when he paused, she looked out again over the corral to the space beyond and said, "You lost your family, so did I."

Chapter Fourteen

1868 Early Spring
Toal Ranch

Will and Beth had not moved from his front porch. Will was completely fixated on this lady before him. He had just given her his life's
story. All she'd done was ask. Never before had he been confronted by
the question of who he really was, or where he had been. He had done
his best to be simple and straightforward with the story, but he couldn't
help but think he'd been boasting. There had been an immediate connection with this lady. It began on their ride back from the camp where
he'd originally found her. He couldn't explain it, he just opened up like
an old book.

But she had said she too was an orphan. Maybe she felt the connection as he did and the need to open up more about herself. Maybe she
intended to reveal more than just how she came to be pursued by the
man in suspenders. Fearing he might be overstepping his bounds, he
decided to ask in return.

"You said you are an orphan too?"

Beth took in a deep breath. "Since you have been so unguarded with
your past, I should do the same."

Fumbling to think of something to make her feel more at ease he
said, "Just tell me what you feel comfortable in saying."

That sounded stupid, he thought.

"We lived near Salt Lake, Utah. My father was Mormon. His name
was James Armstrong. My name at birth was Elizabeth Armstrong. My
mother was a convert. While she dutifully followed the Mormon beliefs,
she raised me different from other Mormon mothers. She would talk to

me about other places far off. Places she had been herself. She would talk to me about men and what it meant to be married. I always thought I would be given to a boy near my age, and I might convince him to someday travel to the places my mom had talked to me about. But I was given by the Bishop to a man in his fifties with a first wife close to his age."

"You were 'given'?" asked Will. "What does that mean?"

"In the Mormon Church, followers of the prophet Joseph Smith believe a man can take more than one wife. As long as he can support that woman and any children she might have, it is their way. Momma had told me this might happen, but I never thought it would.

"I was given to a man named Purcell. He had the local Bishop here in Genoa petition an elder in Salt Lake to take another wife. The elder, they call them Apostles, decided that the local Mormon outpost needed to be supported and further populated, so he ordered I be given in marriage. Josiah Purcell already had one wife. They were married late in life after he had started the ranch along the Truckee. They had no children. I guess I was supposed to fix that.

"So, I was sent west with another family in a wagon to Genoa. Josiah Purcell came down from Lake Crossing to get me. We were married by the local Bishop, and we went back to his home. I cried for days."

"How old were you?"

"I was sixteen when the Bishop talked to my parents. I was seventeen when I arrived in Genoa. That was three years ago."

"Did you have any children?"

"No. I don't know why, but I never did. It certainly wasn't because Old Man Purcell didn't try. It made him upset. But it made First Wife even more upset."

Will hesitated, but the question hit his lips before he had consciously thought whether he should interrupt. "Why did the first wife get upset?"

Beth paused. "I am not sure. Maybe it was that I was an interruption to the life she had built with Josiah. Maybe it was because she saw me as a simple means to produce children. But when I didn't get pregnant, she became more and more upset."

After another more extended hesitation, Beth added, "She would beat me."

Will stared in astonishment. "She would beat you? Why?"

"Every month when I would start my flow, it was obvious that I was not pregnant. First Wife said I would have to stand and accept judgment that I had failed in my duty as a wife."

Will shook his head. He couldn't think of anything to say that could even remotely sound appropriate.

Beth looked up and continued, "Josiah thought we would start having sons right away. But nothing. He eventually got so frustrated it changed his whole outlook. He thought the ranch would simply die when he did. So, he wanted to sell. Wanted to move back to Salt Lake and his own family. That's what started the whole mess that leaves me here."

Will simply listened. He could see she was now speaking slower and slower. Elizabeth's words seemed to come harder and harder. Will knew he only possessed the social skills of a ranch hand. Unable to think of something to say, he just listened.

"Josiah knew the railroad was coming. Men from Placerville came and offered to buy the ranch. He asked why, and they told him that they anticipated a lot of development because of the railroad, and they were buying property on speculation.

"Later, another group came, led by a man from Genoa; I think his name was Patten. He also approached Josiah to buy the ranch. Josiah said he already had a buyer. This man asked what he had been offered and then said he would beat it.

"Then there was a third offer. It came from a single man with a horse and buggy. He said his name was Henry Millard, and he ran cattle ranches all over the states of California and Oregon. He told Josiah he'd be interested in buying the ranch and would keep it as a cattle operation, just like the rest of his property. They talked a long time. Josiah liked this man. He said so many times after they met. Before Millard left, they shook hands on a sale.

"Millard wrote out a piece of paper and told him that eventually this could be taken to a bank and cashed just like money. However, he asked Josiah to hold on to the paper and to collect his deed to the property. He said he'd be back in two weeks. They could then travel to Carson City together and record the transfer. Mr. Millard told us that he was traveling to the South and East to look at other properties and would finalize the transfer of our property on his way back to San Francisco.

"The man who called himself Patten came back only a few days after Mr. Millard left. Josiah told him he was going to sell the ranch to Mr. Millard. Patten was quite upset and left in a huff. He couldn't understand why Josiah would not sell to him as he was offering more money. Josiah never told him the reason. He just asked him to leave.

"But Patten had several men come with him this second time. It was these men who later returned with guns and threats. Those were the men who killed Josiah and First Wife. They burned the house and barn.

"I didn't want to die. I told the men I would go with them and that I could find the deed to Josiah's ranch. They agreed to take me and then put me on a horse. I told them the deed was kept in the Mormon Church at Mormon Station in Genoa. I convinced them that all members of our faith made sure that all important papers were kept by the local Bishop. I told them I could enter the church and get the deed."

Elizabeth looked down. "But that was not the truth. I knew where Josiah's deed was in the house. I also knew where the paper was from

Mr. Millard. I ran into the house as they started the fire, telling the men I needed some of my special things. I grabbed both documents and put them in my temple garment."

Will looked puzzled. "I'm sorry, but what is a temple garment?"

"Mormons wear a special undergarment at all times. It carries certain markings that are supposed to remind them of their position in the faith and with the Lord. They wear them as a constant reminder of how we fit into the universe."

Will noticed that Beth referred to Mormons in a way that separated her from them.

"As I told you, my mother was different. She personally made my temple garments. That was not out of the ordinary, as most mothers made the garments for their entire family. But my mother had sewn a special pocket in mine. She told me that I could always use it to keep things that were personal treasures. She had drawn a picture of herself with my brothers and sisters. I kept the picture in the special pocket. Well, when I ran into the house, I picked up Josiah's deed and the paper from Mr. Millard and put them both in the special pocket.

"I thought the men would leave me alone as they wanted the paperwork and deed. I thought they would take me to the main Mormon community in Genoa, and then I could run to the Church and ask for help."

Pretty good thinking in the face of men with guns who had killed her family, thought Will. It added to a growing admiration of this lady.

"Did you get to Genoa and the Church?"

"No, the men set up camp where you found us. They said we had to camp because we couldn't make it all the way to Genoa that day. Next day, the leader, Drake Sutton, said he wanted to go into town alone first to check to see if anyone had heard about killings at the Purcell Ranch. Then we could continue to Mormon Station. The stocky man with a funny accent said he'd hunt for some food. They left me with the man who you ultimately shot. He began to beat me."

Elizabeth looked directly at Will. Her eyes had moistened. She was trying not to cry, but Will could see it was an effort. Will saw that Beth obviously had been through a lot in her short life, yet despite the trials in her own history, she was trying hard to remain composed. Another point of admiration for him.

Will stood. He was angered at the thought that a man would beat a woman. He had risen incensed at the story. But as soon as he lifted off the bench he knew it was a mistake. Something inside him said that at this moment, Beth needed someone close, someone to hold on to. He'd been sitting right next to her and should have stayed right there. Maybe even put his arm around her. But here he was, on the opposite side of the porch. He had to say something.

"No one should do that to a woman."

Beth looked at her hands in her lap and then up at Will.

"The man named Reynolds, the one in the suspenders, kept saying he wanted something called the script. At first, I didn't know what he was talking about. Then I came to understand he was looking for the paper Mr. Millard had given to Josiah. I told him I didn't have it. It had been taken to the church in Genoa like all important Mormon papers.

"He didn't believe me. He hit me across the face and said he thought I had it stuck somewhere in my dress. The first night, he left me alone. I had been crying steady ever since he'd struck me. I just curled up and acted really young.

"The next morning, I told him I had to go to the outhouse. He started to follow me, but I insisted I needed to be alone. While away from the camp, I buried the documents. I knew he would eventually find them in my dress, so I had to do something to keep them out of his hands. Those papers were my only way of making a new start. I had just returned from relieving myself when he pointed a gun at me. He threatened that he could just shoot me and then search everything I wore. I thought he really intended to do just that. Then he actually shot the gun. But he changed the aim at the last second so that it just missed me. It was still early morning."

Will thought that gunshot was probably the one he'd heard early on that same morning.

"I went to my knees and begged him not to hurt me. That's when he hit me in the face again. I fell flat, and he kicked me, after which he started ripping my dress. When he didn't find any papers, he kicked me again.

"I lay as still as I could for most of the day. I hurt everywhere. Later in the afternoon, I told him I had to go to the bathroom again. I got up to move out of camp, and that's when you arrived. You saw the rest."

Beth looked up at Will again. Her eyes were seriously wet now. Will sat down again beside her.

"Will, he touched me. Touched me in places no one has ever touched. Not that way. Not even Josiah did that. He was grabbing for the documents. He did everything but take me as a husband takes a wife."

Beth then leaned forward and buried her head in Will's chest. At that moment, he felt anger while at the same time humbled and stunned. Here in his arms was something to build a life for. Here was someone to protect, someone to hold.

Beth then pulled back just a bit and looked up into his face.

"Take me back to that camp and help me get what's mine. It's all I have."

Will nodded.

"So, you see Will, we both lost our families. We were both orphaned by men with guns. We both come from the same circumstance."

Then, through the tears, a look of anger took over her face. Will watched, mesmerized as she said: "I never want to be that vulnerable again. Teach me to shoot a gun."

Chapter Fifteen

1868 Early Spring
Carson City, Nevada

Dale Paris had trailed four horses from the Lake Crossing area heading south. The trail ran parallel to the main road between Lake Crossing and Carson City but stayed off the road itself. Paris had already planned to travel to Carson City as that was the Territorial Seat and where he would have to check for any formal transfer of the Purcell property since the massacre.

The trail he followed headed to Carson City anyway, so he kept up his steady pace, figuring to make his stop in Carson and then continue pursuit of the blonde girl. When he arrived outside of Carson City, he marked his spot and headed into town, planning to return and pick up the trail after he checked in the land office.

Paris entered the Carson City territorial land office around noon. There was no clerk at the counter, which ran the entire length of the office. Maybe the man was out to lunch. But the door was not locked, and the office by all accounts seemed open for business. He stood for several moments inside the door and heard nothing. No one came. Not a sound to be heard. A door was half-open on which hung a nameplate identifying Scott Fallar as the land agent.

"Does anyone work here?" Paris half-shouted. He figured he'd try to get things moving.

A man of average size but wide solid bearing came out around the corner of the office and looked directly at Paris. His fair facial complexion beyond the boundaries of the thick mutton chops appeared to be showing a rising red tinge of displeasure.

"You always avoid common manners or decency, or are you just feeling out of sorts today?"

The comment was sent directly back at Paris in the form of a challenge. Obviously, the speaker did not shrink in the face of confrontation.

Paris pushed the issue a bit further. "I thought this was a public office here to serve its customers."

But this man Fallar still did not back up. "Public or private, you have a choice to make. You can either become civil, or you can leave without whatever it is you seek from the only source nearby for information on a parcel of land, which, if you are here, must be the reason you came. That being so, do you want to go home empty-handed because I can close the office indefinitely anytime?"

Paris now figured he had gone as far as this approach was going to take him. He smiled and decided to take a different tack.

"Please accept my apologies for disturbing you. I hoped to run a title check on the property owned by the Purcell family. The property is situated north of here along the Truckee River."

The man from the office had not changed expressions. In fact, the flush of his cheeks was even deeper.

"I know that property. A full title run will take close to a week. There is also a five-dollar fee payable in advance." Again, it was more of a challenge than a statement of fact.

"Mr. Fallar, it appears I have caused you some consternation wholly unintended on my part. What say you to a proposal that we work more in unison rather than at odds. I had not planned to spend much time here in Carson City. I am due to head south in the direction of Genoa directly. What if I were to pay you forty-five dollars for the title run to be completed with all due haste?"

Fallar's face softened. Wheels turned. Most people balked at the five-dollar fee. It was not every day someone offered to double the fee, much less pay forty-five dollars. He looked out of the office window, trying to mask his thoughts.

"Bribery of a government official is a prosecutable offense," Fallar said, then paused and looked directly at Paris. "But a gratuity for a job well done has no such penalty."

"I think such a gratuity would be in high order if the search could be done beginning right away." Paris offered a smile of his own as if to extend an imaginary handshake on the bargain.

Fallar then said, "Go over to the saloon across from the office and come back in two hours. I think we might be able to get what you are looking for."

"Appreciated. See you in two hours." Paris tipped his bowler and turned to find the saloon. A drink might be a good idea.

Chapter Sixteen

The tin can flipped high into the air spinning through space as if launched by a spring loaded mechanism. Smoke drifted on the wind, rising slowly until it dissipated. The sound of a gunshot broke the silence in a blast of energy.

"That's three in a row," said Will. "You keep this up, and you could get real good. It's only been three days of shooting, and you are hitting the cans regularly at thirty feet."

Beth stood looking down the barrel at the next can. It was as if she almost did not hear Will. Her concentration was all encompassing. The next shot exploded, but none of the cans moved.

"See, I just missed. I've seen you hit six in a row."

"But I've been shooting handguns almost all my life. You just started."

"I don't need to be some gunslinger. I just want to be able to pick up a handgun and hit what I am aiming at." Beth stared down the remaining three cans as if they had beat her in some competition.

Will grinned at her resolve.

"It's not life or death if you miss a can," said Will.

"But I may have to shoot something other than cans someday."

"Maybe. Remember, you should never pick up a gun and aim it unless you intend to shoot. We talked about this. If you are going to keep a gun, keep it loaded, and keep it in good working order. You should do everything you can to avoid the use of guns. But, if the time comes and you need to, your gun had better be ready to use. Because if you ever pick up a gun in someone else's presence, they're gonna figure you intend to use it."

Beth turned to face Will, and her shoulders slumped just a touch. She almost looked defeated. Then she smiled.

"That face is less determined. It's a face that is a bit more like you," said Will. "For a while there, you had the face of a gun hawk. You looked like you could shoot someone right between the eyes. When I first laid eyes on you, I never would have thought you could look like you just did at a couple of cans. I do believe you could shoot someone, and that is not always as easy as one might think. You were so intent on those cans, I thought your eyes would pop them off the railing like the bullets themselves."

"I don't want to seem ungrateful. I really do thank you for showing me what you have. I just thought it would be easier, that's all. I just don't think I should miss after all the bullets and help you have given me."

"In the short amount of time you have practiced, I would say you have a knack. Not many can shoot as well as you can, and you just started."

Beth looked up directly at him. It was the same face that over the last couple of days had time and again looked at him with a softness, making him almost melt. But deep down in that same look lurked a hint of darkness coming from those blue eyes he liked so much.

"I never want to be vulnerable again. If anyone starts to shoot at someone I care about, I want to be able to shoot back."

"I believe you would, too."

Beth held his gaze. "Can we go out to the camp to dig up the papers soon?"

"Sure, if you feel well enough to ride, we can go tomorrow."

"I can ride, I'm ready."

Will hesitated with his next question, but before starting out on a full day ride he thought he had to ask. "The bleeding I saw on your dress, is that wound ok? It's not something that will open up again on the trail is it?"

Beth smiled. "That wasn't from a wound Will. That was just from my regular monthly flow."

Will's face reddened. Beth had not seemed the least bit embarrassed. He started to speak but held just for a moment, almost a stammer. When the next inquiry surfaced, it came from some unrestrained depth he could not explain. It just came out. "Then, did those men have their way with you… ah, with you as a woman?"

"No, the man in the suspenders hit and kicked me, but he did not attempt what you're asking about." Beth then grinned unabashedly then added, "As a woman."

Being raised on farms and ranches all her life, Beth found it easy to talk about the cycles of breeding whether the topic involved animals or humans. She thought it adoringly quaint that Will struggled with the subject.

In some measure of relief for reasons equally inexplicable, Will moved to change the topic. "As it turns out, I am glad I picked up both the rifle, handgun, and holster that belonged to the man I had to shoot. You can have the handgun and his holster rig to keep. That gun fits you well. It's a bit of a rarity. They call it a Pocket Navy."

"What a funny name," said Beth.

"Colt sold lots and lots of a larger revolvers during the war called the Colt Navy. We saw several of the larger Navy's in the South, but this Colt is smaller, lighter, and has a shorter barrel than the standard Navy. It also weighs a full pound less than the regular-size gun. The difference is that the Pocket Navy has a cylinder with only five rounds. The full-size Navy has six rounds.

Also, the barrel on the Pocket Navy is almost two inches shorter. That can make a big difference when you are pulling this gun out of a holster facing someone doing the same thing with a longer barreled weapon. The man who tried to use it on me must have specially sought this one out thinking it would be lighter and shorter to make his draw quicker. But it will be a perfect gun for you."

Chapter Seventeen

1868 Spring
Carson City, Nevada

Dale Paris left Carson City. The records Fallar had pulled showed the title to the Purcell Ranch still resided in Josiah Purcell's name. There had been no recorded official transfers. Paris had hope he could solve CPRR's right of way problem in some simple fashion. It all depended on whether the blonde girl seen traveling with the group headed south of the Lake Crossing toll bridge was the wife of Josiah Purcell.

If so, then chances were she would have the rights to any property which had been in her dead husband's name. Maybe he could make a deal with a desperate wife who had no idea how to run a ranch and needed money. That would be the best solution he could ever imagine.

Paris had headed out of Carson City to the east and picked up the trail he had followed all the way from Lake Crossing. He made his way following the trail slowly. He first came across what appeared to be an abandoned spot where horses and people had stopped. Something had happened here but he could not tell exactly what. Then he saw what looked like a shallow grave. He dismounted and checked digging with his hand through the soft covering. It contained a male, not a blonde woman. The signs in the dirt only became more confusing.

He remounted and circled the area ultimately finding two sets of trails leading further east. Each trail looked to have been made by two horses. Paris knew he was following the thinnest of threads hoping to locate the wife of Josiah Purcell. But he had no other decent options at this point. Soon, he found the paths of where the two sets of horses split. He kept a keen lookout for what might be ahead.

He eventually came upon a camp and two men. He decided to observe the pair from afar. He saw that each day, one would ride to a rise of rocks and use a viewing piece to watch what appeared to be a ranch. While one watched the ranch, the other was in camp. This went on for two days.

The second set of tracks looked like they went on to the ranch itself. On his second day of waiting and watching, Paris pulled a looking glass out of his pack and saw a young man and woman shooting in what looked like target practice. The woman had long blonde hair. He had no way of knowing for sure, but he thought this had to be the Purcell woman. She wore a simple prairie dress. Even though she was shooting, she did not have the look or bearing of someone who would ride with outlaws. The young man was obviously teaching the blonde how to shoot. Paris figured that out here in the open spaces women probably needed to be proficient with guns. A lady with her man way out on a ranch might be confronted by anything from bears to outlaws. Capability with a gun might be the difference for survival.

He thought the three men who were seen heading south from the Purcell's must be at the ranch. But why would they start a massacre of the Purcell family? If you had done something like that, you were more than likely going to get as far away as possible. You wouldn't be at a ranch less than forty miles away acting without concern of the law following you. The scene provided few clues.

On the other hand, the two men watching these same events *did* look like the types who could have carried out the massacre. One was dressed almost head to toe in black. Not only did his clothing send an immediate message as to his probable demeanor, all doubt was removed by his gun, which was hanging at a level informing anyone with the right experience this man could use it. In addition, the other man with him did not look like any rancher.

Right now, nothing much made sense. Paris thought it best to wait and watch to observe what might develop.

*****

Drake Sutton looked at Desmond. "She shooting again? What can she be thinking if she is working with a handgun? Most country women use rifles or shotguns."

Desmond responded, "I have no idea why she be workin' on her shootin' ability. Maybe she's gettin' ready to leave and wants to have a handgun when she sneaks away."

"You might be right. It just might be she is thinking of leaving soon. This whole gun practice thing is probably her way of hoping to protect herself when she takes off. But a woman out traveling alone between here and San Francisco would be an easy target for anyone watching the roads, gun or no gun."

Sutton then turned to Desmond. "Keep a good watch until the sun goes down. She could be leaving soon. She won't leave after dark, so I will see you back in camp then."

Chapter Eighteen

1868 Spring
Toal Ranch

Everything outside was black. Darkness beaconed only those familiar with navigating the vast spaces after the sun set. Night stood just outside the door to the main house left open while supper fires had burned. Dinner had been consumed. There was a pause in the activity of the meal, all had finished. It was if they had reached an end, a finality. And no suggestion for further events had yet been made. Juan, Raul and Maria had joined Beth and Will for a collective meal, their first.

María had cooked a large dinner, combining local western beef recipes with a Mexican flare. The dishes came with a bite to the tongue and color Will had become used to but Beth had never seen or tasted. All were quite full. Will was pleased when Beth complimented Maria for her work and wonderful food. This was his group, his home, his family of sorts. He thought Beth fit well in the mix.

Beth then turned to Will, "Want to take a walk?"

He was both taken aback and subtly excited at the proposition. "Sure."

Will and Beth stood up from the table. Will noted the look of approval from Maria and knew that tonight he would not have to help with cleaning chores. It was silent encouragement from Maria that he should accept Beth's request.

"Where should we walk to?" asked Beth.

"Let's head toward the river and see how far we get," suggested Will. They both stepped through the open door into the black anonymity outside.

Will explained that the Carson River ran through this section of his land and continued down the Valley through the ranches of his neighbors. It was fed by the mountain snow runoff mostly year around. The Carson River was one of the few rivers on this side of the Continental Divide that flowed east. The Sierras rose up just to the west of his property. He told her that it always amazed him how they did truly just raise up out of the ground. There were no real foothills here on the east side of the mountain range.

It was like a string of volcanoes just lifted out of the earth leaving a line of steep-sided pyramids tall enough to have snow on them seven to nine months of the year. During the day, they were more than impressive; they were majestic. At night, you could still feel the presence of the mountain wall, a barrier of sorts. Their position gave you a bearing or sense of immediate direction. You always just knew the mountains were to the west. Everything else referenced from that barrier, that wall. There was a comfort in always having those bearings.

But the snow-packs at the top provided more than just scenery. They provided water and plenty of it. There were dozens of small creeks branching off the main river supporting the spread of grassy range. His father had told him stories of the streams and bogs in Scotland, the land of his ancestors. Here the alpine creeks hit the flat valley floor and cut deep sharp banks in the grasslands. He had never seen Scotland, but he imagined the rivulets here on his ranch closely matched those of his father's stories.

"We have to follow the path down to the river. There are so many small creeks and swamps this time of year that if you leave the path, you could get really wet. We end up hauling steers out of bogs regularly. The grass looks like it is growing up from solid ground but suddenly, you are in a swamp. Cattle just cannot seem to figure it out."

They had walked far beyond the immediate compound. The moon above consisted of only a sliver, leaving them in close to complete darkness.

"As you make it out to be so dangerous, I will just hang on to you as we walk," said Beth.

She had a shy downward tilt to her head and sheepish smile as she moved closer and grabbed a hold of Will's arm. Without breaking their steady gait, Beth pulled herself next to Will and matched his stride step for step. They moved in unison.

Will focused so much on the sensation of Beth at his side he almost lost track of the path. With each step, the contact between the two became more pronounced. Will tensed in a way he had never experienced. Beth, on the other hand, appeared to him to be enjoying a simple moment, nothing all that special. There was an ease about her movement. She pressed against him with an easy familiarity as she held his arm.

"Have you ever married?"

Will marveled at Beth's ability to ask questions that seemed to come from some other time and space.

"What brought that on?"

"Just asking."

"No, I have never married."

"Ever been engaged?"

He felt somehow embarrassed for some reason he could not place.

"No, I have never asked a woman to marry me."

Beth then looked up at the moon.

"Just a sliver. Most people talk about a full moon as the sight to marvel. But I always liked to see the little sliver of the moon hanging up there. It is almost like the moon is winking at us. I have always thought that the moon like this knows something is going to happen."

"During the war, we would dread the dark moons. Lots of patrols and lots of probing took place on dark nights. If one weren't careful, those were the nights you could get shot. Even by your own army. That is exactly how Stonewall Jackson, the best tactical officer in the South had got killed. He'd returned to camp at night when pickets from his own line shot him. Dark nights were something to fear."

"Are you afraid of this dark night?"

"No, although you keep asking questions that do little to make one comfortable."

"Well, you should just relax, and take in the evening. Is that the river?"

"Yep. That is the Carson River. That is the main reason I settled here. The water table is so high we only had to sink a shallow well, and we never lack for water. More importantly, the beef and horses never lack for water. In New Mexico, it seemed we had to worry about water all year 'round. Here, you have to worry about stepping in the wrong place, or you get wet."

"Here, give me your jacket. I feel like sitting."

Will took off his jacket. Beth spread it out, knelt, and sat down, folding her legs to her side. She looked up at Will who was standing above her, watching her every movement and wondering what would come next.

"Will, have you ever slept with a woman?"

"You just keep getting more and more personal."

"That's not an answer."

"Who said it was a proper question?"

"Well, have you ever slept with a woman?"

Will shifted his weight. He tried to think of a way to avoid answering but could not come up with any decent excuse.

"I have slept with a woman, but none were what you would call a *lady*."

"Come sit down here next to me." Beth reached out and grabbed his hand, giving it a gentle tug.

"Beth, I . . . I'm not sure this is . . ."

"Will Toal, you know I have been married. You know what a married woman's duty is to her husband. But my husband was twice my age. I never felt anything natural about it. I never had a child over those three years. It's probably because I just cannot have children. I was then taken by men who wanted something I had and beat me for it. I was lucky they did not rape me. They probably would have had I stayed with them any longer. I feel so much better here. The bruises are healing. I'm beginning to feel alive again, like I did before I was given up for marriage. Tomorrow, we are going to travel out to find who knows what. The men who originally took me from my home might be out there waiting for us to head back to that camp. There is no telling how the day will end. Sit. Sit down beside me."

There was a gentle plea in the way she uttered what normally would be a command. He bent over, reached out for the ground, and tried to sit on his jacket in a way not requiring her to move. He sat angled to her position with his right shoulder almost touching her right shoulder. She softly placed her hand on the back of his neck and pulled the two together. She kissed him.

He reached out and gently clutched her fully to him. He pulled her across the front of his chest still embracing. They slowly fell flat amid the grasses which continued to sway to and fro as they seemed to do twenty-four hours a day. Not far below, the bank dropped to the water's edge which flowed silently along. The river moved ever so slowly, ever so constant. Along with the breeze and blowing grasses, there was a silent rhythm to the night.

Chapter Nineteen

1868 Spring
Toal Ranch

Will had just finished saddling Powder. Will could sense the excitement in the big gelding having not been ridden in several days. Normally, Powder would stand coolly and passively while being saddled. But today, he danced a bit back and forth, pulling at the halter. Will hoped his outlaw knot was going to hold. He usually paid little attention to getting the knot tight as Powder's ground manners were never a problem. But as Powder pulled on the lead rope more than usual this morning, Will thought it best to check his knot.

The outlaw knot, a fancy slip knot, held a horse but could easily be untied with one pull of the protruding tether. It probably came in handy if one had just robbed a bank and hastened to get mounted and ride out of town, hence the name. But if you did not set the pull tether tight enough, the knot could come completely undone all on its own. Will made sure he'd set his knot tight before Powder pulled it apart and really started dancing.

"Hey, son," Will said to Powder in a low calming tone. "We will be headed out soon enough, and then you can stretch your legs."

Will pulled the cinch. He knew he would have to walk Powder a bit before getting the cinch fully tight. An excited horse or one who knew how to suck in air and bloat his belly could deceive a novice rider into thinking the cinch was tight, only to have the saddle slip right underneath the horse when you stepped into the stirrups. Powder was excited, so Will would have to wait a bit and walk him out before a final setting of his cinch.

"He is a fine-looking horse. I can see why you are so partial to him. It's a good thing you don't ride a mare, as I might get jealous." Will turned to see Beth walking up with her head tilted a bit to the right and downward, bearing an intentionally fake frown. She looked at him out of her left eye, beaming with undisguised playfulness.

Will felt a flush starting low in his neck, a complete circle quickly rising all around, first into his jaw and then his ears like a bubble in lake water. Embarrassed, he immediately looked around to see if anyone was within earshot. Never had a woman focused her attention directly on him in such a way, especially after a night like the last one. Seeing no one near, he did not try to suppress a sheepish grin.

"If I recall correctly, a mare here in the vicinity seemed to enjoy a walk to the river last night."

"Oh, aren't we full of wit and wisdom this morning."

"I have been accused of being full of things in the past, but I don't think anyone has ever accused me of being full of wit." The ease in talking to this lady returned, something he marveled at based on the short time they had been together. They could and did talk about almost anything. It just felt natural, more so than he ever felt would have been possible with any woman in his lifetime.

Will had always thought women would go out of their way to avoid blunt conversations about a relationship with any man, no matter whether serious or not. But Beth could fire the most direct, blunt, personal questions or comments as if discussing the weather. She said it originated in conversations with her mother when she was younger. Whatever the origin, he was beginning to get used to it.

He looked away from those distracting blue eyes and noticed she wore a completely different outfit. As usual, his attention was drawn to Beth's eyes, and her smile. He had been taken off guard with her initial question. Now he looked up and down with a different kind of amazement. She wore a pair of trousers ungainly gathered at the waist by a belt too large for her. The trousers were a bit short in the leg, leaving a pair of slightly oversized boots mostly uncovered.

Below the belt hung Reynold's holster rig cradling the Pocket Navy revolver. The thick canvass shirt was obviously cut for a male. The shoulder seams hung halfway to her elbow, but her arms though elegantly proportioned to her body were so long, the rest of the sleeve still did not reach the wrists.

She was short from shoulder to waist. Will imagined the garment probably hung down to her knees, but she had tucked it into her trousers. The trousers were another anomaly. Beth's legs were long, almost as long as his own. The trousers did not make it all the way down to the top of her boots. Her slender legs swam in the short but oversized trousers.

The silhouette made her legs look even longer. In this getup she looked almost two thirds legs and one third torso. Her blonde waves were pinned up somehow—mostly underneath an old beat up hat he had never seen. In short, the outfit was terrible.

But she looked great.

"You do have a habit of looking a woman up and down. Are you going to do that every time we meet?"

Jolted out of his assessment, Will replied, "There are often things worth taking a very good look at, sometimes even fillies. I am quite partial to blonde ones."

"This outfit is not one I would think would catch the eye."

"Oh, it's an eye-catcher all right. A cross between that of a miner and a mountain hermit. But the occupant is pleasantly interesting."

She smiled. He took it as a sign he had prevailed in the conversational contest.

"Where in the world did you get that belt?"

"María brought me all the clothes. She did the best she could on short notice. I am told the belt is one of Raúl's old ones. María said he punched some extra holes in it, but it still didn't fit, and I had to ask him to punch some more. I hope it holds these britches up."

Will could see the extra number of punched holes. All ranch hands knew how to handle and adjust tack for working stock. A leather hole punch was one of the most basic tools. But he was amazed at how small Beth's waist was when finally cinched in the old belt. He could understand why Raúl had to do some extra punches. The other man probably had the same reaction as he had; no human could fit into a belt that small. Yet here she stood with the belt fitting in what looked like the last punch he'd made.

"Yes, I suppose it would be quite embarrassing to lose one's trousers." This he delivered with his own version of a devilish smile.

"Oh, you would like that, would you?"

"No, that would probably put me in some position to defend your honor."

"Sir, I am armed and can now defend my own honor."

"Might be tough to do without pants. I 'spect that could put a new meaning to getting the *drop* on someone."

Will accentuated his old Southern twang for mischievous emphasis.

"Not only is that in poor taste, it isn't funny. But you are becoming more formidable in your conversation."

He smiled, figuring he'd won this round.

Beth then looked over his shoulder, twirling on her heel left to right. "Did you saddle my horse, or does a girl have to do that herself?"

"No, your mount is rigged and ready."

"Then let me go back into the house and get my saddlebag, and I am ready to go."

His smile faded. He turned and looked at the mountains.

"Beth, do you really think those men who rode with you are still out there?"

Beth looked down, took a deep breath, and unloaded a heavy sigh.

"Yes, I definitely think they are still out there. They are not the kind of men to give up on what they thought was theirs, no matter how ill-gotten the gains."

The tone of the exchange had quickly turned serious, no longer fun.

"Then, let's go see how badly they want to take it all back again," said Will.

Chapter Twenty

Corliss Huntington stood at his window. The stained springtime Sacramento air draped unseasonably hot throughout the Central Pacific's offices. Sections were close in this, the railroad's understated headquarters. Huntington would not pay for upscale offices. All available monies were directed to the construction. Most of the men had removed their regular suit coats. The barons of the railroad were sticklers for appearances outside the offices, but not here where the work got done. While clothing requirements were relaxed, the demands for performance permeated the workplace. Movement and effort on the part of so many people in crammed confines fouled the lifeless air with body heat alone.

Huntington turned to Charles Crocker. "Johnson is going to be impeached."

Crocker looked up from the papers in his lap. "Will that be a good thing for us or a bad thing? He hasn't exactly been a big friend of the railroad enterprise since Lincoln's death."

"True, but he hasn't taken any steps to interrupt the funding, either. As long as the government keeps funding, we can stay on the move," came Huntington's reply.

"Speaking of staying on the move, I got a wire from Paris on our right of way issue out near Lake Crossing. He said he thinks he is getting close to finding an heir to the Purcell family who survived the massacre. If so, there might be a quick way to solve our current challenge to moving east into the Nevada desert. He says the survivor might be a young Mormon wife with little or no means of support. If he is successful in locating her, he thinks he could make a favorable offer and get a quick transfer."

"That would be nice, almost too easy. So far, nothing about this project moving over the Sierras has been easy. We spent so much time getting the Donner Tunnel done. One could argue we made a mistake using Theodore Judah's forty-first parallel approach. Stanford certainly used the same argument when he tried to convince the board to make some changes."

"But didn't the board say they were very happy with our progress?"

"They did. The work boring through the Donner Tunnel was a big delay. But in using the path Judah and Dr. Daniel Strong laid out from Roseville to Donner Pass, we saved a great deal of time just getting to the spot where the tunnel started. As a simple druggist from Dutch Flat, Strong was the most unlikely source of information for a better way over the Sierras. But that is exactly what he did for Judah. Stanford seemed to forget we all agreed to the Dutch Flat approach starting out."

Crocker now looked at Huntington warily, as if wondering how Collis would take his next comment.

"I thought the board reached a reasonable compromise when you suggested Leland be removed. Having him remain in place as president of Central Pacific Railroad while eliminated from any position of authority in the larger holding company sent him a clear message. The position of president is nothing but a figurehead and he knows it. With the board's moves, Stanford now is keenly aware everyone must get on with the work of construction without running up any red flags to either investors or Washington, D.C."

Huntington sat at his desk, not directly facing Crocker. He stopped writing the note he was working on, sighed, and looked straight out of the window. He did not meet Crocker's eyes. He appeared to be looking into the distance for some source which could be consulted before he replied.

"I suppose on a broad spectrum it was a good decision. Even-handed. Logical. Arguably practical and good business. However, Leland remains close to the entire operation, including construction. He still has access to information which could be a platform for future attempts at pursuing his own agenda, whatever that might end up being."

A small suppressed exhale exposed Crocker's relief that Huntington seemed to be working past the recent board fight. The group needed to move forward, and arguments like these could be an insidious mortal disease for a company. They were so close. The railroad had literally reached the summit just past the Donner Tunnel.

They had accomplished one of the most remarkable engineering feats in the history of mankind just to get there. Now if they could just get to the desert in eastern Nevada. The desert meant flat land on which to lay track. Almost as important, all of the desert to the east into Utah belonged to the U.S. government. There, CPRR would have no interruptions whatsoever to their progress because of right of way issues.

"Looking back, it's a good thing we separated the construction company from the railroad corporation. Remember how we got bogged down using subcontractors during the work over the American River outside of Sacramento? Our ability to use a single contractor, the Contract and Finance Company, allowed us to keep the entire flow of men and materials under one roof. We would have lost control and any hope of progress long ago if we were now dealing with fifty to a hundred subcontractors."

"Lost control and lost profits," said Huntington. "The consolidation of contracting entities was critical both to moving the project along and for increasing our profits. But you had to leave the board of CPRR yourself to maintain some semblance of propriety."

"I know," said Crocker, "but it was worth it. Stanford and Hopkins, while full partners, have little to do with the actual decisions on day-to-day construction. Between Chief Engineer Lewis Clement, Supervisor Jim Strobridge and myself, all the major decisions are totally consolidated."

Huntington turned and replied, "So, where are we? Give me the good news, but also give me the bad news. There is always bad news."

Huntington knew his friend Crocker well. Crocker had asked for this meeting, which in itself was out of the ordinary. The time for their regular progress review had not yet arrived. Huntington knew some problem needed to be addressed. He decided they might as well get to the issue at hand.

"Charles, give me a brief update, and then tell me why you really wanted to see me."

Crocker had effectively been the construction superintendent since 1863 when the contracting had been consolidated. He was kept intimately aware of the day-to-day progress. He did not need to look at any notes to provide a detailed report.

"We have new locomotives being delivered. As you know, all our equipment as well as Bessemer track must be delivered from the East Coast. We tried using the route over the Isthmus of Panama, but while it is a great deal quicker, it is about four times more expensive than sailing it all the way around the Horn. However, over time, our supply lines have now been clearly established, and I do not anticipate any interruption going forward there. We have two locomotives on steamers headed up to Sacramento, which should come online in about a week. They only cost us two thousand in transportation fees. It would have been over eight thousand each through Panama."

Crocker paused to gather his thoughts and continued.

"The good news is that we finished boring the Donner Tunnel, Tunnel #6. That tunnel ended up being over 1,650 feet long. For the first time, we used nitroglycerin."

Huntington looked up, interested on this point.

"Is that the new blasting material developed by some scientist from Europe?"

"Yes, an Italian named Ascanio Sorbrero actually invented it. We got our supply from a company owned by a man named Alfred Nobel who is marketing the explosive worldwide. The use almost doubled our daily tunnel rate when compared to the black powder we use. We used black powder in Tunnels #1-5 and, as you also know, lost several workers because of the dangers in setting fuses along sheer wall cliffs. But the use of nitroglycerine was especially effective in the later stages of the bore through Tunnel #6, the big Summit Tunnel near Donner."

"So, give me the bad news; I know you always save that for last."

"You are right; the good news is that we are over the top, over the crest of the Sierras. The bad news stems from the fact we must now go down the other side. The track from Donner Pass to Lake Crossing, which I am beginning to call Reno, will only run about fifty-five miles. However, we will have at least four more tunnels to bore, and we will have to build five bridges over the Truckee River at various places. We can initially build them in wood using Howe trusses, but ultimately our agreement with the government is to have all water settings done with stone and rock covered in Portland cement."

Huntington looked mildly confused.

"This is the material that comes in a powder and, with the addition of water, becomes as hard as stone?" he asked.

"Yes. Contrary to the thought of most locals, it was not developed in Oregon but actually in England. Its name comes from its similarity to Portland stone. The current mix required for all underground and underwater foundations in New York has become something of a standard. A man named William Aspdin invented cement some ten years ago in London. The government is allowing us to get the railroad operational using temporary specifications, even if that means we use wood supports initially. But, at some point, we will have to redo any foundations set in water using the cement."

"But we will have time to do that after construction is complete, right? If so, that will give us time to raise the funds for the structural replacements after we begin generating a revenue stream from train operations as well as begin selling the land we obtained for laying track. Am I correct?" interjected Huntington.

"Yes, we can both build and finance the cement structures later," replied Crocker.

"That all sounds quite manageable. So, what is the problem you are holding back?"

"Snow," said Crocker.

"Snow?" asked Huntington. "Why is that such a big problem? We've seen snow in all the Eastern Seaboard rail lines. We just bought ten brand new special snowplow locomotives, each built specially to clear the lines. What is so different here from Back East?"

"The Eastern Seaboard sees maybe two to three feet of snow in their worst blizzards. In the Sierras during the winter of 1866, we saw almost one hundred inches of rain at the base of the Sierras and over ten feet of snow collected in places along the right of way only halfway up to the summit. We thought 1866's snowfall was bad. Then the winter of 1867 hit this past year. We had over one hundred feet of snowfall throughout the winter at the summit and in many of the canyons. Collis, it was one hundred feet in places! The hard-packed drifts were over eighteen feet tall.

"You mentioned those new snowplows we had delivered in 1866. Well, those new snowplows could not break through the drifts. It took 2,500 men to keep the track operational up to and through the Summit Tunnel during the height of winter. We had to house the labor force in the Tunnel itself as it was more palatable there than outdoors in the blizzards under forty feet of snow. We cannot hope to run the regular rail service all year-round unless we solve the snow problem."

Huntington was taken aback. A transcontinental railroad that could not run during the winter season was not an option. He asked: "Do you have a solution? What do the engineers say? I assume you have run this by your chief engineer, Mr. Clement?"

"Yes, we realized the magnitude of the problem once we saw how deep the snow could get. Clement and Strobridge both have worked on a solution."

"Okay, I can now tell where this is going. What is the solution, and what is it going to cost?"

Crocker took a breath; this was not going to be easy to absorb.

"There is no way to avoid the hard truth. The only solution is to build what we are calling snow sheds over the most exposed stretches in the spots where the worst drifts occur. It will be like building a peaked roof over almost forty miles of track. Those roofs will have to be supported by the strongest of timbers as the weight of the snow we are holding off the track is tremendous.

"Further, we will also have to build what we are calling galleries, large wood walls in places off to the side of the track, to block the drifts upwind. The engineers tell me we can prevent some of the deepest drifts if we build what are effectively walls to hold the snow back away from the track over those same open spots. We can use timber from the local pine forests which will cut down some of the cost of getting lumber, but it's going to take a lot of manpower to tackle this."

"How many men does your point man Strobridge need?" Huntington asked.

"It's going to take over two thousand additional men to get the job done by the time we are hoping to lay track to Reno."

"And how much do you predict this will cost?"

Crocker sucked in another breath.

"Two million."

Here was another blow. CPRR did not have anything approaching such a sum available. Time and time again Huntington had to fight off the dread of defeat. The challenges kept coming from unpredicted places. It started with the first miles of construction. The land just east of Sacramento stretched over the lowlands of the American River, which regularly overflowed.

Each spring there were miles of virtual swamp. Much of the first miles of track had to be either elevated or raised to keep it out of the flood waters. Then they started laying track up the grade of the Sierras, a challenge they had always anticipated. Cuts of mountain slopes and fills in canyons made progress ever so slow. Lastly, the Donner Tunnel. Now this. The challenges just kept coming.

"I am going to need time to make arrangements for capital of that magnitude as you can readily imagine. Charles, we don't have those funds on hand and will not see enough revenue from the land sales quick enough. I'll have to go back to the investors."

Crocker noted a slump in Huntington's shoulders. He knew the pressure they were all under. They were in a race to the desert. Both the Union Pacific and Central Pacific knew they could lay multiple miles of track each day out on the flat stretches of desert. But each had to get through the mountains. CPRR had to climb the Sierras, and the Union Pacific had to breach the Rockies.

Timing was critical. Delays in CPRR's operations could result in the Union Pacific setting more track in the desert and getting more of the checkerboard ten-square-mile sections of U.S. land. Losing those sections to the Union Pacific could be financially devastating. CPRR would lose the ability to sell land which it needed to repay debt and produce profit for investors. It would go to the Union Pacific Railroad.

"I know, Collis. That's why I asked to meet with you now. At the moment, we have the ongoing problem with the right of way over the Purcell Ranch property east of Donner, so maybe we can coordinate the multiple delays while we get the snow sheds completed. Maybe we will have the right of way problem solved about the same time. We are going to be delayed by one or the other no matter what."

"What kind of delay are we looking at?"

Crocker considered, then answered. "Probably four months, five or six at the worst."

It was Huntington's turn to sigh. "Charles, you and your group have done an amazing job so far. I trust you implicitly. Strobridge saved us over a year with his idea of drilling the Summit Tunnel simultaneously from four different approaches. Do your best to keep the delay to a minimum. I will begin work arranging the financing so you can hire your workforce to build the snow sheds."

Chapter Twenty-One

1868 Spring
Toal Ranch

Will still could not quite get over the change in Beth's appearance. Mounted, the hat and trousers created another persona. She looked like a man. It would take a close look to detect the truth.

After their brief exchange in front of the barn, Will had caught and saddled the bay Beth originally rode to the ranch. Will could sense Beth's anticipation at looking for her papers. She talked almost nervously.

Will lead the way as they both headed out using the same trail back to what they had come to call the Reynolds camp. Beth said she had buried her pouch of personal items several yards up the grade in a stand of trees. She had used the ruse of needing to relieve herself to find some place close with a measure of cover while she hid the pouch. The trees had provided at least small sanctuary while she tried to bury it as deep as she could in a short amount of time using only her hands and shoes. She marked the spot at the base of a cottonwood tree with a double trunk. It was the only such tree in the vicinity. Beth felt confident she could get straight to the burial spot if Will could get her to the camp.

Will led the way, but he kept turning around in his saddle on a regular basis trying to look for dust rising behind them. The unusual dry spell had left the trails with a top covering of fine dirt which turned to dust under the hooves of a horse. Dust rose, and it usually was easy to see any rider at a distance. But there were two problems looking for dust today.

First, it was early morning. Dew and moisture spread across the Valley which would not burn off for another couple of hours. The dew prevented any dust from rising. Second, most of the Valley floor was flat and, at this time of year, almost swampy. If one knew how to parallel the main trails, one could travel just off those thruways riding in the deep grass and never leave a dust sign at all. He would just have to keep a keen lookout.

*****

Sutton had been on watch using the long-range looking glass early that morning. He had figured if the girl headed back to the camp, she would go along with the young rancher in the morning hours. If the girl had decided to bolt by herself, she would do so at night. He had Desmond watching in the late hours so he could sleep. Sutton had been taking the morning hours as he sensed the girl would try to use the rancher's help to get back to the camp. Any break for the coast would happen later. Sutton wanted to be on watch early each day, thinking the girl had to get back to the camp first. He wanted to see if the rancher brought any other hands.

Sutton saw the pair of riders head out. At first, he was puzzled. He recognized the rancher right off. He thought he could make out the rancher well enough through the small lens, and he had seen the big gray horse he rode which made that identification even easier. But the other rider was not someone he had observed during their stakeout. It looked like the skinniest man he had ever seen. But then, despite the shabby clothes, he could make out the figure of a woman. It was the girl. They were traveling away from the ranch. If she was dressed like this, it had to mean they were headed out for something other than a social ride. He had to get a move on. He jumped into his saddle and headed back to the spot where he and Desmond were camped.

"Desmond, put your whiskey away and saddle up. And make it quick! They're on the move. It looks like they are headed back to the camp. I told you she didn't have the script on her. If she did, she would have bolted. In riding out with the rancher, she must be hoping he can get her back to the camp. Otherwise, if she had the script, she would have left long ago. There is something back at that camp; I know it. But if that is true, we must get up there before they do. So, put a cork in it."

"Now, how could ya be thinkin' I would do such a thing? Whiskey' in the mornin'. There's a time and place."

"You don't fool me. How much did you have last night?"

"Ah, I did have a wee dram, only but a taste. I did no serious drinkin' a'tall."

Sutton looked him up and down. He could never be entirely sure whether Desmond was drunk, sober, or even hungover. This Irishman had the capacity to drink volumes of whiskey and not show any effect for hours. The only sign would come later if he either fell over or got into a fight. Often, Sutton could not tell Desmond's sobriety status if he had not been in his immediate presence for a couple of hours.

"You look sober enough. This is it. If we are going to get that script money, today's going to be the day. I can feel it. So, you better be really clearheaded."

"How many of 'em are there?" Desmond said, looking up from another cold breakfast of hardtack and military rations.

"Only the two: the girl and the rancher."

"That'd be the best we could'a hoped for, right?"

"Yes, between the two of us, we can take care of the rancher easy enough. The girl should not be a factor. I was concerned he would bring others. He is either foolhardy, or he is not the military planner I thought he was."

"I'll be in my saddle in a wink."

"Good, then we will head up to the camp riding through as much of the grasslands as we can. We need to get to cover before they get to the woods around the camp. We can hide the horses and wait to see what she does. She could have put something under a rock, behind a tree, or just threw it somewhere when Reynolds wasn't looking. We must wait until we absolutely know she has the script. We don't make a move until we are sure, you got that!"

"Jaysus, we've gone over the plan enough times. I know what we are to be up to."

"I hope so. Let's get a move on."

*****

Paris decided to ride out to the south once again to see if the two men continued their strange spying. He had not been able to gather any information as to the identity of the two men spending so much time watching this ranch. He had headed out every other day for over a week now. The men held to the same routine. It still made little sense.

He came to the regular spot where he had been watching the two men's camp. He calculated the distance to be about a half mile away. He had watched as the men switched off, riding out to watch the ranch in the valley while the other stayed in the camp. Paris had been very careful to maintain a good distance at all times. He always kept the man watching the ranch between his position and the ranch itself. He could not really understand what could be so interesting, so compelling. Other than what looked to be a little target practice, all Paris had seen was regular ranch life.

He had watched as the short stocky man rode periodically off toward Mormon Station near Genoa, probably for food. While there was plenty of fresh water, there was no immediate source of food unless you considered killing a steer. But shooting a steer would bring unwanted attention. These two appeared to be doing their best to remain unnoticed.

However, today, when he arrived at his viewpoint of the spy's camp, the camp was empty. He waited to make sure no one returned. He did not want to enter the area until he knew for sure they had abandoned it. He rode slowly around the camp at a distance, making sure no one lurked. When he was sure no one was in or near the where the men had slept, he walked his mount to the central part of the camp itself. His hand was on his revolver. He took another long look around. No sound, nothing in sight.

He stepped out of his saddle.

From the scraps of food on the ground, it looked to him like the two men had left recently. The particles of food would not have survived one evening out here on the range. Some varmint would have made off with them. He saw the trail heading east. Following this trail would not be difficult. The grass was matted down where the hooves of each horse had trampled through. Obviously, these two were not worried about someone following them.

He thought about heading to the ranch and talking to the folks there. But if these two men had been the ones to ride with the surviving Purcell wife, he had to stay on their trail. His best hope to solve the railroad's right of way problem would be to find the girl and make a deal. The only way he could be sure he had the right woman was to see these two men in her presence. So, he set off following the trampled grass.

*****

Will and Beth arrived at the Reynolds camp. Will had not dismounted. Beth jumped off and ran to a set of trees slightly uphill from the rock outcropping where he had first seen her.

129

"The twin trunk tree is over here."

Will still stayed on top of Powder. He thought they would be in the camp only a short while. He had looked the camp over after he had buried the man in the suspenders but saw nothing of note. There was no reason to look around again. He had left the horse he had assumed belonged to suspenders back on the day of the gunfight. But that horse was not here now. It could have run off, or the other men could have come back to collect it. It made him even more suspicious of others being close. They could be near. As soon as Beth found what she was looking for, his plan was to let her remount and ride straight back to the ranch. He had his hand on his gun, having released the safety just in case.

"I found it. It was still here," she yelled.

"Damn," he muttered under his breath. He had forgotten to tell her to be as quiet as possible. "Just grab it, and let's get back to the ranch."

"Will, come see. I think it says it's worth five thousand dollars. It fits with the price Josiah told me he had agreed to sell his ranch for."

"You can show me the document back at the ranch."

"Will, please come. I just have to know if this is what it appears to be."

Will got down off of Powder. He walked up to Beth who was now holding out a piece of very thick paper. At the top was a fancy printed name: Millard Luce Cattle Co. He looked further down the document to see a signature of one Henry Millard, vice president. In the middle of the page were the words, *"The bearer of this note is entitled to the sum of five thousand dollars payable in U.S. currency. Said sum shall be reimbursed to the issuing bank by the Millard Luce Cattle Co. in full upon presentation to the Wells Fargo Bank, San Francisco."*

Will looked up. "I don't know what this paper means legally, but it does seem that whoever walks into a bank can get five thousand dollars if they give them this note."

"Will, do you think that is my money? Do I have rights to the money as the wife of Josiah Purcell?"

"I don't know what your rights are to the property, but this note looks like it doesn't matter what land you owned; just give the bank the note, and you get the cash. But I know of a lawyer in Carson City, S. Samuel Grande, who is helping me get a loan to buy the ranch. If you have any questions, he can probably answer them."

Will then looked at Beth. Her face carried an expression of what he thought included amazement and something like relief.

"It's a lot of money, Beth. It would be good if you talked to the lawyer to make sure what it is before you go start making plans to use it."

Will then turned to head back to grab Powder's reins. Beth was behind him when a strong, clear voice coming from near the woods broke the good feelings of the moment.

"I wouldn't take another step. Why don't you throw down your gun?"

There was a pause. Then the same voice continued. "Let's keep this simple. We are going to take that piece of paper, and you don't have to get killed in the process. Or, you can try your luck. Your choice."

Will looked at the man uttering this challenge. Black from head to toe. Statement clothes. He had dealt with men who went out of their way to make an impression in the way they dressed before in Texas. A certain type of outfit could create a sense of apprehension or fear in the susceptible. Will was not one of those types of people. All too often a set of fancy clothes were worn to cover up a flaw. He hoped that was the case with the man in front of him now.

"We? I only see you."

"That's because my associate is standing to your immediate left. You didn't think we would both be standing here shoulder to shoulder giving you a false hope you could take down two against one as we were in the same field of fire? Do I strike you as having a serious lack of intelligence?"

Out of the corner of his left eye, Will caught movement. A man moved there. His gun was drawn. But the man directly in front of him still had his gun in his holster. In one of those instantaneous thoughts one has on a battlefield when your life is threatened, he felt the man in black to be his primary concern.

As a soldier, Will had been in situations before where multiple thoughts ran through his mind in what seemed to be extended minutes but, in reality, were milliseconds. Thoughts like that were coming hard and fast right now. The young rancher knew from experience that his conclusion as to who was the larger threat might be wrong, but some decisions you just made based on the feel, not any analysis. Most of his battlefield decisions had been almost instantaneous, more part of a single collective view. The man in black had not drawn his gun. His stance, attitude, voice, and the position of his holster all went into a millisecond conclusion.

"Why don't we do this man to man? Let the girl go, and just you and I can decide this as you seem to want. You haven't even pulled your weapon yet. Must be you want me to draw. I can see it in your face. Tell your man to the left he can live, and I won't kill him after I have finished with you."

Sutton grunted. "And why do you think I should provide you with any opportunities whatsoever?"

"Because you want to." Will was looking right at him and thought he had been right. This man almost wanted the confrontation to be decided on a quick draw. His stance and attitude all readily displayed an overabundance of confidence. But Will didn't want Beth exposed. Without taking his eyes off the black-jacketed aggressor, Will said to Beth, "Stay right behind me until he agrees."

"The girl is going nowhere except traveling with me after you are dead."

Will chuckled. "And why would she go anywhere with you? Seems like lately, she likes the company right here."

"Oh, how you are mistaken. Partner, she begged me to take her. Begged me. She couldn't get away from that old husband fast enough. How do you think I knew about the whereabouts of the script and the deed? She put the whole idea together to grab the documents in return for me taking her to see the cities of the world."

He paused for effect. Sutton oozed unsettling confidence when he said, "Must be disappointing to be so young and so deceived."

Will was trying to think the boast nothing more than an attempt at distraction. But Beth had told him she approached this man. She admitted she had taken Purcell's deed and the script, which led to the later confrontation. Was she really responsible for the death of her family? Couldn't be. He might be young, but his read on a person's character was usually good. The last couple of days with Beth were not a smokescreen on her part. Last night could not have been a blatant deception.

Will tried to shake off his doubts, maintaining an appearance of control. "I think you have played your cards. I don't happen to believe your bluff. So, I am calling. My gun stays right where it is."

Sutton smiled. "So be it. Your choice."

The man in black went for his gun. So did Will. Shots came quick. Contrary to common saloon talk, gunfights did not usually end with one shot or even two. Revolvers were not that accurate, especially when someone stands opposite trying to shoot you at the same time. Will knew from experience a battlefield shooter—as opposed to a gunfighter in a town's street—would not shoot once and then stand there admiring his handiwork. He would shoot and keep shooting. He would also move if he could. On a battlefield, you never knew where the next shots were going to come from. In war there were way too many people to keep track of. So, you moved, and you kept moving. He planned to quickly fire at the man wearing the black clothes and keep moving directly at him. His motion forward would present only a side shot for the man to his left, who was going to have to hit a moving target. Hopefully, he'd miss one or maybe two shots until Will could dispatch the guy in black and then turn to his left. At least, that was his plan.

The plan worked better than expected in the beginning but only the beginning.

Will hit the man in black with his first shot. He knew from the start his first shot would be the most important, and he had to make that one count. The dark suited man was fast, but the younger man was just a little faster. He got off his shot first, but in the rush, it went out low. Instead of hitting his challenger in the chest, it got him in his upper thigh. The dark outfit stumbled back, completely losing his balance, which he did not recover. Dark got off a shot, but it went wide of Will as the man fell to the ground. Will moved forward as planned and pulled his trigger for a second shot, but that missed as Black fell out of his aim.

Then came the problems. The man to his left got off two shots also. The first missed. But before Will could turn to face him, the side opponent got off a second shot, hitting Will in the shoulder. Just before being hit, Will had turned to his left, putting his left hand over the top of his right, which was holding his own revolver. He intended to use his left hand to fan the hammer of the gun while he pulled the trigger in his right hand. But just as he turned to face the second adversary, he was hit in the front of his left shoulder. The impact of a .44 caliber bullet was devastating. It hit the back of his shoulder and spun Will further to his left ninety degrees. Will ended up bent forward at the waist and 180 degrees away from the man in black. Essentially, he was now facing away from his original assailant and straight at Beth, who had been behind him at the start of gun play. But he was still on his feet. In another of those milli-second conclusions reached in life or death situations, Will knew the wound to his shoulder was not life threatening. The blow hit the meaty part of his shoulder outside the joint. But it hurt like hell, nonetheless.

Turned and bent over, Will could now see Beth from the waist down. He saw her raise the Pocket Navy in her hand. She fired at the man to the left. He heard a grunt, then silence, and then a body collapsing to the ground.

The thought ran through his head that it was done. He had survived. He was still bent over at the waist but tilted his head up just enough to look into Beth's face. He saw her raise the Pocket Navy, extending it over her head, and then pull it down, crashing it into the back of his skull.

He dropped. Nothing but darkness.

Chapter Twenty-Two

1868 Spring
Western Border Toal Ranch

The smell of gunpowder still hung in clouds over the old campground. Silence. Not even a moan. Just silence. The Pocket Navy handgun trembled in her grip. She'd shot someone. She'd killed a man. She had done it to save Will. But then she struck him with that same Pocket Navy, the gun he taught her to shoot. It was a gun they had worked together to master and now she had used it against him. Beth knew she had hurt Will bad. She hit him hard. But she could see that Sutton was not dead. If alive, he would want to kill the man who bested him at the draw. Her blow to Will's head was a quick reaction to save him. Now she had to get Sutton up on a horse and away from here as soon as possible. Far away. She had to keep him from going after Will.

Beth holstered the gun and move to help Sutton to his horse. It was not going to be easy. Beth could see Sutton was bleeding badly from his right hip. The wound to the upper leg was deep. Real deep. Moving him from where he fell to where his horse stood was not far, but it took all their combined effort to get him on his good leg to a standing position. Then, as she literally supported his weight, he lifted his good leg up to his stirrup. With a loud groan and grimace, he flopped belly first onto the top of his saddle and pulled his injured leg over the side of his horse with his hands. The movement caused him to cry out in anguish and sink down over the neck of his horse.

"Can you ride?" said Beth.

"Get me my gun. I want to walk this horse over and shoot that rancher dead."

"I already took care of that. Can't you see the blood? We need to get you to a doctor and quick. We need to stop the bleeding."

Shocked by her behavior, Beth trembled. *She'd hit Will. What was she doing? Originally she had planned to leave the Purcell Ranch with Sutton and just be gone. Sutton had said they would take the Millard Luce script and deed then leave. No one was to get hurt. He'd said he would take her to see San Francisco or even Sacramento.*

She had so wanted to see those big cities; to experience what it would be like to see the ocean. Then she met Will. She had wanted to see the world her mother had seen; longed to walk in the places of the books her mother would read to her. But then she met Will. She'd wanted to leave the ranch life.

Yet there was Will. I am leaving with a man dressed in black who says he can show me that outside world, but can he? Have I just ruined the best opportunity life has presented in my short time?

"Here, tie this around your leg. We must get you to a doctor. That wound is not something I can deal with. The only doctor nearby is in Carson City. Can you make it there?"

Sutton grunted; even talking increased the pain. "I am not going to Carson. I want to make sure that upstart is dead."

"Yes, you are going to Carson because I am taking you."

You are my only chance of a ticket to the outside world. I have come this far. Getting you well is my only hope of finishing this as planned.

"And no, you are not going to shoot that man. He beat you. Live with it. His living or dying will not matter if we get moving to the coast, which is what you said you would do. So, hang on."

Beth grabbed the reins to Sutton's horse and began walking off to the north. She remembered Will had heard the gunshots as far away as his ranch when Reynolds had fired into the air. If there was anyone within range of the sound, they, too, could be on their way to investigate this time. Either Juan or Raúl could be on their way. She had to move out of the immediate vicinity and get to Carson.

Chapter Twenty-Three

The day warmed, but warmth was relative this time of year at this elevation. Save the sound of his horse's hooves hitting the ground, a cool quiet surrounded him. The frost laden breezes cut into his woven wool pants. The multiple layers under his coat kept out the chill, but there was only one layer on his legs. He now knew why ranchers wore chaps. Not so much for protection from the horns of cattle, but for warmth. The sun battled the breezes for the control of the air. If the sun had its way, it would have been temperate, even pleasant. But the frigid mountain-born gusts were winning. He pulled his collar tight.

Paris had travelled about two to three miles from the when he heard several gunshots. He spurred his horse forward and maintained a heightened lookout. The blasts came from a place near the base of the mountain. From the sound of the gunfire, he guessed he was still four to five miles away. It might be the same abandoned campsite with the grave he'd seen earlier. The gunshots were coming from the same direction.

After about a half hour of riding, Paris thought he was getting close to where the gunshots originated. He had continued following the trail which had been left in the grasses of the Valley floor and began up what looked like a pass over the mountains. The pass had numerous switchbacks, obviously maintaining the slightest grade possible, on what was a long climb up over the Sierras.

His immediate thought was that it must be a teamster road up over the top. The horse tracks he was following eventually veered off the road and moved toward what looked like a wide but deep canyon. He was coming into the canyon from the south. As he entered, he could see there were several sets of large rocks blocking any view across the mouth of the canyon itself. He knew if he traveled north and kept the mountain to his left, then no one could see him from that vantage. He might not be able to see past the rocks to the north, but he could significantly cut down the chance of being seen by someone with an anxious trigger finger.

The ground was a mixture of soft dirt and small pebbles, probably rock which had fallen from the mountain over the centuries. The combination made for an easy track to follow. As he had done earlier in the day when riding into the spy's camp, he stopped often and listened. Again, it was quiet, real quiet. He was riding at a slow walk now, rounding one rock outcropping after another. He stopped again. He heard nothing. He unfastened the safety on his handgun. He chambered a round in his rifle and replaced it gently into its scabbard. The Sierras were starting to make their incredible rise almost straight up from the Valley floor.

He had climbed the grade for about a quarter mile and was approaching a stand of trees. He had been right. He was back in the camp with the grave. Something special kept drawing people back to this spot, and some of them died because of it. He saw a gray horse with his head bowed hovering over a prone body. Across the open space of about one hundred feet, there was a second body also lying flat on the ground. Neither man was moving. Seemed like more people had died in this strange place removed from the normal world. Paris waited. Questions mounted.

A prone body could be a dead body. It could also be a wounded body desperate enough to strike at anything nearby, thinking the original danger had returned. There could also be other people around. Just as he had done earlier in the day watching the camp of the two spies, he watched and waited. The prone men did not move. There was no sound.

He had learned to listen not only for human sound but animals, too. If one heard birds chirping, they could probably rest assured there was nothing lurking about. But if it was quiet, the birds had either been scared away by the earlier gunplay, or there were more men, another danger keeping them away. It was still silent. No birds chirping. The signs were telling him danger could still be near.

Paris then rode around the back of the rocks. His left hand was holding the reins, and his right hand held his revolver. He was tense. His horse could sense the tension, too, and was prancing even at a walk, which made it harder to both control the horse and to focus on his surroundings. The area looked as if it had once been a campsite. He gave it a wide berth until he was uphill from the bodies. He got to a thick stand of cottonwoods and saw no one. Slowly, he began descending toward the bodies.

He could see blood near the first body but not a tremendous amount. The gray horse was hovering over this man. The horse looked up at Paris as he approached and appeared unsettled. The animal probably stood over its master who was laying on the ground. The horse obviously did not know Paris. Depending on how strong of a relationship the horse had with his master, Paris could be facing an animal who would either fight him or run. He had seen both.

A horse's predators all had two eyes which looked straightforward out of their skulls. Mountain lions, bobcats, and humans had two eyes positioned straightforward. Prey animals like horses, cattle, and deer had eyes on the side of their heads, creating a field of vision that ran from just off the side of their nose almost 180 degrees to the side of their hindquarters, all the better to keep a lookout for hunters. When a prey animal saw a front facing hunter, it made the prey animal really nervous.

"Whoa there, boy," Paris said as he turned his head down and to the left, trying to present himself as something of a side-viewing prey animal. In this position, the horse saw a man with only one eye. Maybe not a hunter. Paris knew the approach to be the best way to look like another prey animal, putting the horse at ease.

The gray snorted a bit but held still until Paris could grab the split reins. Once he had ahold of the reins, the horse did not resist when Paris gently pulled him away and tied him off to a low branch.

Paris then turned to walk back to the two prone men. His path took him near what looked like a short, very stocky man. There was blood in the dirt around this body, too. Paris stood at a distance and watched. There was no movement. There was no breathing taking place. He walked up and poked the body. Nothing. He then used his foot to roll the man over on his back. Paris was careful to keep his revolver pointed at the man while using his foot to move him. The body flopped over, lifeless. There was a gaping bloody hole in his chest just below his heart. While not a direct hit to the heart itself, Paris figured the wound was mortal upon impact.

Paris then turned to the second man lying on the ground. This man was larger, probably over six feet tall if he'd been standing. Again, he stood and watched. He could see the chest rise and fall. This man was still breathing.

Chapter Twenty-Four

1868 Spring
Toal Ranch

Will awoke. He vaguely remembered a man helping him to his horse. He remembered the man, along with Juan and Raúl, helping to haul him down off Powder. He clearly remembered a stabbing pain in his shoulder. He had little or no memory as to how long he had been in his bed. Time seemed blank. He couldn't place any of his memory with his present surroundings. He knew he was in his own bed, but he was not completely sure how he got there.

But he vividly remembered the look on her face when she cracked him in the head.

At that moment just before she hit him, there had been pain in Beth's expression. There was maybe even some indecision. But there was no doubt it was Beth who knocked him out cold.

Why? What in the world had gone wrong? Aside from the lump on his head and massive headache that went with it, his first sentient thought was of confusion. But almost instantaneously after that confusion, another emotion exploded. Anger. Deep anger.

Will heard someone enter the main room of the house, sounding as if they had just come through the front door.

"How long have I been here?" Will was shocked at the lack of strength in his own voice. The words had come out at less than half his normal volume. Was he now going to have to consciously use an extraordinary effort just to talk?

Juan stepped to the threshold of his bedroom.

"Ah, my young jefe. You are awake? This is good. Very good. You have been in a deep sleep for three days. We did not know if you would ever wake. The doctor, he says you might be out for days or months. He did not know how bad you were hurt."

It was about this time that Will noticed two serious sources of pain. The first was his left shoulder. The second was his head. He reached over his body with his right hand to feel his shoulder, finding it to be heavily bandaged. He then touched his head, which also had some type of gauze wrapping all around his crown and down around his jaw. He was resting on his side.

He rolled onto his back but felt an immediate sharp pain to his head as it met the pillow. He had rolled onto a large swollen lump. To say it was tender would not do it justice. Pain filled his entire skull. Without any conscious thought, he rolled back to his side. Anything to get away from the agony.

"María, come see, he is awake!" Juan then turned to make sure María was on her way.

María had not been far behind. She entered the room full of anticipation.

"Ah, *Señor* Will. It is good to see your eyes. We worry a lot that you recover."

"María, the way I feel now is a long way from being recovered. My head hurts like nothing I have ever felt, and I haven't even tried to move my shoulder yet."

"You just lay still. Let your body rest. I am pleased the good Lord has answered our prayers to bring you back to us. Now you must relax."

"I don't think you have to worry about me jumping out of bed right now. I'm not going anywhere."

María then had a questioning look on her face. She hesitated. "*Señor* Will, the lady, she give me a letter and tell me that if you come back and she no come with you, then I was to give you the letter. I know you no feel well. But you want me to get the letter now, or should I wait? She said it was very important that if she no return that I give it to you right away."

Will considered this. *She cracks me on the head but leaves me a letter? Did she have this whole thing planned?* More confusion.

"Yes, María. Get me the letter. I have no idea what she would have to say to me, especially after what she did. I just want to close my eyes, but I won't be able to sleep now until I know what she said. So, go grab the letter."

Chapter Twenty-Five

1868 Spring
Mormon Station (Genoa), Nevada

After dropping off the injured Will Toal at his ranch, Paris left and traveled to Genoa. He still had only the barest of clues. He had no idea if the lady with the outlaws had been at the campsite with the grave. The young rancher with the gray gelding had not been able to tell him what had happened. After getting him into his house, he went completely unconscious. Clues just kept eluding him.

Paris thought the young Purcell wife, having been married to a Mormon, would probably head for Genoa to reconnect with someone from her church. So, he headed there after leaving the young man's ranch. Upon arrival at Mormon Station, he spoke to anyone who would listen. The small Mormon community was a tight one and reluctant to provide information about church members to any outsiders. All anyone would say is that he should talk to their Bishop. So, he went to the church compound, pounded on the gate, and asked to see the Bishop.

The Mormon Church looked more like a fort. Apparently, it was the original Mormon Station where settlers would stop and rest while traveling the California Trail. Paris gazed at the high walls and figured they built it as a fort because it had to act like one. Constructed at a time when no one had any relationship with the local Indians, any settlement would first have to provide a defense.

The walls of large upright logs formed an oblong enclosure. On opposite ends of the enclosure were two raised lookout posts. Between two lookouts, they could see down along all the enclosure's walls. A stream ran close to the rear. Paris figured the original settlers could have easily pulled trenching straight into the enclosure for a constant water supply, or if they dug a well, they probably hit water quickly.

But the need for a fort had passed. Indians were gone from this part of the Valley. Paris supposed that the church had originally been constructed inside for obvious reasons, and there it remained.

Paris rapped on the ten-foot high gate again, this time with his balled fist. "I am here to see the Bishop. Can somebody please open the gate?"

A man opened a viewing slot. He stood almost an arm's length back from the slot, and Paris thought he could see a bearded man in a black straight brim hat. "Stand back and in front of the slot so I can see you. What is your business?"

Paris replied, "I work for a land office, and I am here trying to locate a woman who was married to Josiah Purcell. I believe she is still alive and might be trying to get back here to her church. I have asked around town, and no one will talk to me. All anyone would say is that I should talk to the Bishop."

"Wait there. I will return shortly."

After about ten minutes, and without any comment, the gate opened. The man in the black hat pointed across the compound.

"Bishop Benton has an office there. He said you can knock on his door."

Paris walked over and tied off his horse. He stepped up onto the raised boardwalk, noting how clean and orderly everything looked. There was no dust on the boards. Nothing looked out of place. He knocked on the door. A middle-aged man of slender build in a white shirt, suspenders, and black pants opened the door.

"I am told you would like to see me. Please have a seat."

Paris had instinctively stomped his boots before entering the office, which was just as clean and orderly as the compound, if not more. He sat in a wooden chair offered by the man at the door.

"Bishop, sir, my name is Dale Paris. I am an investigator working with the Placerville Land and Title Office. Our company made an offer to Josiah Purcell to buy his ranch, which we believe he was going to accept. However, Mr. Purcell was unfortunately killed in an apparent attack of Indians. I believe there are indications that one of his wives, a younger woman, may have survived the massacre. I am looking for her, as we would like to complete the transaction."

"While I am the local Bishop of the Church of Jesus Christ of the Latter-day Saints, you may just call me John Benton." The man was a tall, very slender individual who exuded intelligence and reserve. As he was dressed simply, his small, spare office contained nothing which would not be regularly used.

"The Placerville Land and Title Office is just another storefront for the railroad, is it not?"

Paris assessed this man more carefully. Most definitely intelligent. No sense in trying to be circuitous.

"You are right, sir, my fees are generally paid by the Central Pacific. But my task now is to find this lady and restate what I have been led to believe was a generous offer to purchase the property. The family, this lady, would be obtaining more cash than if the government institutes eminent domain proceedings. One way or the other, the right of way will be granted."

Paris tried to gauge the man's reaction but could not read his expression. He had gone this far; he might as well push forward to the meat of his proposition.

"Our offer is far above what the ranch will sell for if the government takes it by legal proceeding and then auctions it off. The railroad does need the right of way, but it has made a very generous offer which I am prepared to renew."

Paris waited for a response. It did not come immediately. Benton did not look like he needed to collect his thoughts; he looked like he long ago knew what he would say.

"You're just trying to take someone's property at a rock bottom price through intimidation." The man smiled. The smile said this man is generally at least one step ahead of anyone he meets. "Mr. Paris, I realize the railroad is something we all perceive is being built for the greater good of the country. But often, what the politicians and courts perceive as the small, inconsequential problems turn out to be very large life challenges to real people. In this case, I cannot help you."

Benton then looked to his open door as if to say that Paris could use it to exit any time, a pleasant way of saying the conversation had ended. Paris turned to leave.

"However, I will tell you Elizabeth Purcell has not been seen by any of our church members here in Genoa for some time."

At least Paris got some information. He left the office and walked through the church grounds, intending to mount up and head back to Carson City.

Chapter Twenty-Six

1868 Spring
Carson City, Nevada

Beth and Sutton arrived in Carson. It was after dark. The two-hour ride seemed like it would never end. They had to walk their horses as Sutton could barely maintain his seat even at that slow pace. There were numerous stops. Beth had to dismount frequently and make sure Sutton had not slipped too far in his saddle. His upper frame had been constantly bent down over the neck of his horse, and it never looked like he had a great deal of control as to where his body would go. His head would bob up and down with the rhythm of the animal's regular movement. Any abnormal step over a hole, through a creek, or over something lying in the road resulted in another deep groan.

"We made it. It's a good thing it's late and dark. There are fewer people out on the main street. No one to ask questions."

Beth touched her shirt, grateful she had changed into the makeshift set of masculine clothes given to her by María. She was not dressed as the wife of Josiah Purcell. She hoped to be able to move around town unnoticed.

"I am going to take you straight to the doctor. We once took a relative of the first wife to this same doctor. The small girl hurt herself falling off a fence post. I just stayed in the buggy while First Wife and Josiah went in. The doctor never saw me. We then went to stay with some church members toward Genoa while the girl stayed with the doctor a few days. He shouldn't recognize me."

Sutton did not even acknowledge her comments. They arrived at the doctor's back door. Beth dismounted and tied up her horse and then Sutton's.

"Stay up on your horse. I'll get the doctor and ask if he can help you down."

As luck would have it, the doctor was home and came out the back to assist in getting Sutton off his horse and into his examination room. The muscles in Sutton's face grimaced so tightly upon sliding off his horse, his teeth showed. But he did not cry out.

After looking over the wound, the doctor turned to her.

"Young lady, I am not going to ask you how this man was shot. It's probably best I don't know. But I can tell you that while I can and will clean out the site and sew him up, it will take weeks, maybe months, before he will be able to walk."

The statement stunned Beth. She knew Sutton was hurt, but she had not thought it would be that serious.

"Months?" she asked.

"The bullet looks to me to have entered on a path headed for the hip. It might be deep enough to have even grazed or broken bones in that joint. There is going to be an infection. If he beats the infection, there is no telling how those bones surrounding the joint are going to heal. I will tell you that even if he survives the infection, I suspect he will have trouble walking for the rest of his life. He will have a permanent limp."

This information wasn't fitting into any of her anticipated plans. Today had not gone anything like she had envisioned. Beth thought she would locate the script, head back to the ranch with Will, and leave in the next day or so, slipping out unnoticed. While she thought there was a good chance Sutton was still in the area, she did not anticipate the confrontation and gunfight.

Trying to think on the fly, Beth remembered Sutton talking about a ranch he either owned or could use on the road to Sacramento. She looked up to the doctor.

"We have access to a ranch outside of Sacramento. I can take care of him there while he gets better. If I get a buggy, will he be able to travel if he can lay down flat?"

"Possibly," said the doctor. "I won't know for a few days. You should leave him here for at least two days, and then I will be able to give you a better answer. If the fever is not too bad, I could give you some laudanum to ease his discomfort on the ride. It might work."

"Is there a boarding house in town where I might get a room at this hour?"

"There is a lady who rents rooms in her large house named Larson, Cheryl Larson, about two blocks north of the Capitol building on Stewart Street. I think she has rooms available."

"I will come by each day to see how he is doing."

Beth walked out the back, gathered up the horses, and started for the boarding house. Her mind was full of thoughts. She could still get to San Francisco. But it all depended on Sutton making a recovery. She didn't need him to be able to run. If he could walk, he could still take her to the places he talked about in San Francisco. A limp wouldn't stop that.

Chapter Twenty-Seven

1868 Early Summer
Toal Ranch

Will sat in his rocker on his front porch, the letter from Beth laid in his lap. It had been cool since morning. The descending sun sucked away even more of the day's warmth. His east facing porch blocked the winds from the Sierras, but it also blocked view of the setting sun. He would have liked a regular view of the sun's daily departures, but the late afternoon winds here were too constant and too disruptive. He had been rocking for over an hour. He loved this rocker. He loved this location, sun behind him or not. Despite the multiple points of discomfort around his body, he did not feel like moving.

He had walked from his room to the porch, the farthest he had moved in the days since the gunfight. His head throbbed constantly. The pain in his shoulder didn't throb; it was ceaseless. Any movement of the arm away from his body made the pain even worse. The doctor had given María a piece of cloth he called a sling. When tied correctly around his neck, it supported his injured left arm. The sling felt better than having to hold the arm up on his own.

The rocker moved back and forth. He had fallen into a gentle motion so as to not hurt his head. The movement soothed. Only a gentle wind blew across the ranch this evening. On the rare occasions when only a breeze blew, the wind carried a soft smell of grass. To Will, it was a sweet smell. He came out intending to think and try to make sense of what he had read. While the rhythmic motion seemed to take his mind off the pain, it had not aided his effort in making sense of what had happened. The words were simple enough. He could almost remember all of them without even reading it a second time.

Will, If you are reading this, you know that I have left. I don't expect I will ever be able to explain why I had to leave. It is simply something I had to do. From my days as a child listening to my mother read to me about the places in the world, I have dreamt that I would see them. I was bound to a marriage and a working ranch. I never thought I would leave that property. Then the men came to discuss the sale. I saw an opportunity to leave. I never wanted or anticipated the family would be killed. I hope you believe that. I had planned on taking the script and leaving Carson Valley to see the world. Originally, the plan was to leave with a man in black who offered to go with me. I know this man is not a good one. Now, I plan to leave by myself. I fear the man who offered to take me to San Francisco is an outlaw. He's a dangerous man. I know that. A big part of my reason for leaving is that I want to make sure he never returns to cause you harm. I hope I never see that man again, but my decision to leave is made with the hope that I do not cause you any strife. The only way I can do that is to move away from you so the man in black never knows who you are.

I will always treasure the time I spent with you. This was the happiest I have been since I left my mother. You made me feel like a girl again. I was no longer a wife but a girl being courted by a boy. Yes, courted. You may have needed some encouragement here and there, but that's how I felt. I will remember the feeling forever.

I am not completely sure how you feel. It is my guess that you would have preferred I stay. But as much as I can see a wonderful life with you in it, I cannot simply trade one ranch life for another. Not now. Not while I am young enough to see the world.

María should have brought you the deed to the Purcell Ranch. I kept that from Reynolds and did not bury it at the camp. María found it when she went to wash my clothes and brought it back to me. Mr. Millard intended to buy the Purcell Ranch. I think he should get the deed as he paid for it.

I am sorry if I have caused you any loss. I had no way of knowing you would even come into my life. I had no way of knowing how close to you I would come to feel. I have decided to give you something. I have no idea if it is legal, but on the deed, there is a place on the paper where it looks like an owner can sign over the deed to another person. I have signed it over to Mr. Millard, but I have given you 25% of the property. I would ask that you contact Mr. Millard and explain my wish to him.

Will, please accept this as an indication of how I feel about you and the time we spent. I will never forget you.

Beth

Chapter Twenty-Eight

Wagons pulled by horses doomed to drag their loads behind them moved along the busy street. Riders meandered at a walk or an aimless trot that announced an entrance; a gait at which those mounted aimed not necessarily to see, but to be seen.

Beth did not want to be seen. She hugged the edge of the boardwalk away from the dirt thoroughfare referred to as main street in Carson City. Moving along the front walls of the businesses lining the board-walk as though she were one of the signs advertising the wares inside that everyone ignored, she wanted to be anonymous, overlooked, unrecognized.

Men and women walked in pairs passing as if their morning saunter corrected the world's issues. With palpable uncertainty, gentlemen belatedly reached for their hats in attempts at standard courtesy as they passed Beth having initially failed to realize this figure in men's clothes and a gun was female. Women grabbed their man's arm tighter not knowing what manner of species this woman might be. She did not return any gesture or smile. She wanted to be forgotten, an image not remembered. She just needed to get to her intended destination and return without someone connecting her current visage with a past recollection when she had been here with the Purcell's.

Beth walked through the entrance. The name on the door told her she had entered the office of the lawyer Will suggested she talk to. Her landlady, Cheryl Larson, had cleaned her pants and shirt since Beth insisted on wearing it as her sole mode of clothing. She did not want to chance moving about town in the dress Cheryl had offered her. The proprietor of the boarding house turned out to be a delightful hostess who welcomed her immediately. Miss Larson kept a clean house and provided good food. They had talked several times, mostly about the town and its inhabitants. Nothing serious. Beth found it a bit of an escape to talk about simple things. But now, she had to find out where she stood legally.

A large man sat at his desk reading a book so thick it must have a thousand pages. The man looked up upon hearing the door open. His face at first looked upset at the interruption. But the expression changed quickly.

Beth wondered if it had to do with the fact that she was female. He probably didn't see too many women in his regular day. The man was clothed in a suit with a vest. She had the immediate thought that he would wait and let her introduce herself.

But he began talking before he had fully stood up. "I don't handle marital cases."

In the household of Beth's early life, blunt openings to conversations were common. Beth's mother had been a lady possessed of blunt expression. Beth had always thought she carried that blunt gene in her own manner of asking questions. But this man took the idea of blunt to the border of obtuse.

"I am not here about any divorce. Whatever gave you that idea?"

"Well, this is Nevada. You are young. You walk into my office wearing old clothes, pants which are too short, and carrying a gun. A girl your age should be married. A young girl who carries a gun must be either attempting to avoid her husband or holding off men in general. You are too young to own a business. Your clothes tell me that you are short on funds. I added that all up and thought you were here to discuss some problem either with a husband or some other male."

The man then broke into a broad, warm smile. "And it seemed a good way to break the ice. My name is S. Samuel Grande. I assume you are here because you have a question. You can talk to me about any question you might have, even if it does not involve men."

Relieved at the change in demeanor, Beth now thought she might just get along with a personality like this one. Smiling in return, she said, "While I have had plenty of trouble with men in my short life, they are not the source of my immediate question or problem."

"Then, please have a seat and ask away. I was in court today in front of a judge possessed of an intelligence approaching a fence post. I believe he must also have serious hearing issues, because he completely disregarded anything and everything I said during my court appearance. Unfortunately, no matter how logical and legal the law is, there are some individuals wearing robes on the bench who can make a colossal mess of it. I hope you and I will have a much more pleasant discussion."

Beth sat. She did not take off her hat as she did not want her tresses to fall. She had thought long and hard about this conversation and how to approach it. She started with a question to gauge this man just a little bit further.

"If I tell you something, are you going to run down to the saloon and tell the town?"

Grande looked offended. But he immediately attempted to instruct and not rebuke.

"No, if we come to an agreement for representation, anything and everything you tell me is privileged. I cannot reveal it to anyone without your permission, including the court. If I do, I can lose my license to practice law."

Beth considered. Will seem to trust this man. Now she had no choice but to find out if that trust would apply to her and how far it would run.

"I was married, but my husband and family were killed. We were Mormons living up on the Truckee River. My husband owned a ranch and planned on selling his property to a man who made him an offer. I escaped the massacre."

Beth paused. She looked down. She hoped to get a feel for Grande's reaction, but right now, he said nothing.

"Before the men who raided the ranch killed everyone, I was able to get the deed and a paper I think the man gave my husband as payment."

Beth kept looking up at this man's face. What had been an open, inquisitive, even welcoming smile had now vanished. His face now looked dark and judgmental, as if a cloud had descended.

"You are Josiah Purcell's young wife, aren't you?"

Beth looked him right in the eye and said, "Yes."

Grande then sighed, looked to his left out his window, and back to Beth.

"Tell me what your question is. I will reserve my thoughts until I at least hear why you are here."

Beth then handed Grande the Millard Luce script.

"This document says it's worth five thousand dollars. Can I take it to the bank and cash it?"

"Is that your question? Is that the reason you are here?"

Beth was now a little intimidated. Grande's demeanor was no longer anything close to inviting or welcoming. Much the opposite. He again paused.

"You say this man came to buy your husband's property. What did he look like?"

"He was middle-aged, very slender. He said he owned many ranches throughout the West. He was balding a bit. He had intense eyes but a very matter of fact way of speaking to people, maybe because he spoke with a thick accent. This man told Josiah he was born in Germany and came to America with very little but had built up a ranching business with thousands of acres in several states. Josiah and he seemed to get along well once he told my late husband he intended to keep the property as a ranch."

"Well, that allays one fear. The paper you have shown me is from the Millard Luce Cattle Co. It is owned principally by Henry Millard. By showing me this document, you indicate you have met Mr. Millard. I needed to know if you could describe him. You are telling the truth about seeing Henry Millard. I have done legal work for clients dealing with Millard Luce Cattle Co. You have described Henry Millard accurately."

Grande leaned forward and with purpose, looked directly back at her. "Where's the deed to the property now?"

Beth was not sure why this was so important or even connected to her original question. But she felt she should tell Grande the truth. "I have made arrangements to have the deed transferred to Mr. Millard. He paid for it, and I felt he should get it."

At this point, Beth did not want to involve Will in this discussion and was trying to keep from having to identify him as the person currently in possession of the deed itself.

"I have given the deed to someone I trust, and I asked them to do everything they could to see that the deed is transferred to Mr. Millard."

Beth then inhaled before heading into what she knew was the part of her explanation that was the hardest to justify.

"I did leave with one of the men who raided the property. I admit I had asked this man to take me away. At the age of seventeen, I had been given in a Mormon marriage to a man over fifty years old. I admit I wanted to leave. But I had no idea there would be any shooting. The man who said he'd take me away shot and killed my husband. I thought they would just pay Josiah, and I'd leave with him.

159

"But he shot Josiah. First Wife came out of the house with a gun, and another man shot her. The men then ordered me to get the deed and get on a horse. They pointed guns at me. It was not a request. It was a command. I felt if I did not do what was asked, then I would die, too. Guns were pointed at me by that time. After I got the deed, I was led on a horse to a camp and then attacked.

"All they really wanted was to get the deed to the ranch. I was a fool, but I never thought anyone would get killed. I thought they would pay for the ranch just as they said and leave, and I could go with them and then get away somehow.

"Later, I was rescued by a local rancher." Though she had originally thought to avoid involving Will, the way things were going in the conversation, she now felt it might help her plea to the lawyer to say who helped her.

"His name is Will Toal. There was another confrontation. More shooting occurred. Will was wounded, but I think he will recover."

Beth left out the part she had actually killed one of them.

"Why is he not with you now?" Grande asked.

Beth hesitated as her quick decision to identify Will created an additional complication to her story. "I left Will and his ranch. Will is a wonderful, simple man. He has straightforward values. I don't think he could or would ever forgive me for what it looks like I have done."

Beth remembered her gift to Will and stumbled to interject.

"Oh, and I forgot to mention something. Because of what Will did, because he saved me from these men, I signed over the deed to both Mr. Millard and stated that Will should get 25%. I have no idea if that is legal, but it was the only thing I could do to thank Will for what he'd done. When I said earlier that I left the deed with someone that I trust— that person was Will Toal. I put my wishes in a letter to him and made sure it would be delivered after I left."

160

Grande could see the directness in her demeanor. He could see a young girl trying to come to grips with her mistakes and realizing now there were going to be consequences because of those bad decisions. He could see a measure of contriteness.

Grande leaned forward as if to lend more emphasis to his coming point.

"Ok, let me tell you what I think. First, I cannot represent you. You are walking a very fine line between legal and illegal. I cannot be part of formally advising you if you are involved in any criminal enterprise. If you were in collusion with the men who killed your family, then you committed a crime. You cannot benefit as a result of that crime. As a lawyer, I cannot undertake to represent you in furtherance of any criminal activity."

These comments came as blows to Beth. The dark cloud over Grande's face told her what he thought of her. She was being called a criminal. Though sitting, he stood in judgment of a sort. She thought the judgment harsh. People had died, but she had never intended to have anyone die. She just wanted to get away.

After a pause, Grande sat back. His face softened ever so slightly.

"But if there was any criminal activity, it seems there were two aims. First was to get the script. The second was to get the deed. However, you tell me that the man who paid for the property is going to get the deed. There is no crime there. You have the script. If you are indeed the sole heir of Josiah Purcell, then you would have the right to cash it. Again, no crime there. Millard Luce script is well known throughout the West. It is unique. It is the equivalent of a bearer bond or note. Anyone who has physical possession of it has rights to its value. If you are the lone survivor of Josiah Purcell, you would have legal rights to retain the money from the sale of the property. Anyone holding the script itself can cash it. Again, on the surface, no crime."

161

Beth was brightened by these comments.

"Millard Luce Cattle Co. has such a favorable reputation with banks throughout the West that anyone who holds a script such as what you have in your hands can enter the bank, and they will give you cash. Millard Luce Cattle Co. will reimburse the bank. It is the only entity I know of with such a reputation."

Grande then crossed his arms, looked up to the ceiling, and back to Beth.

"But the reason I cannot represent you is because you are walking too fine a line. If you were in any way a part of the reason for your family's demise, then you could be arrested on charges of collusion or as an accessory to murder. I cannot be a part of that."

There it was. In cold hard simplicity. Beth had her answers. She could be happy with some of those answers. She could now cash the script knowing the money would be hers. But the other answers hit her hard. She knew in her heart her wish to leave brought those bad men into confrontation with her husband. While she did not tell or even encourage anyone on either side to start shooting, she had a part in everyone being present when it happened. To hear she could be arrested was devastating. She probably should have known things would go bad in hindsight.

"You do not have to pay me. I do not want anyone thinking I even came close to representing you. Young lady, I would think long and hard about what you've done."

"Are you going to talk to the sheriff?" Beth bit her lip.

"No, I am not completely convinced a crime has been committed. I am not going to ask any more questions concerning the event to intentionally leave doubt in my mind. In such a circumstance, I must still protect any comments you have made here with confidence."

Grande then stood and walked to the door, obviously indicating their meeting had ended.

"However, I will give you some free advice. If you go to the Bank of California here in town to cash that script as I presume you will now do, I strongly recommend you set it up in an account in your own name and *only* your name. Do not give anyone else access."

Beth left the office and headed directly to the bank. The sooner she could get the script set up in a bank account, the sooner it would be protected. She felt both relief and embarrassment following the meeting. She now knew she had to leave as soon as Drake could travel. She could not stay anywhere near Carson City knowing S. Samuel Grande thought of her as he did.

Chapter Twenty-Nine

1868 Early Summer
Carson City, Nevada

Paris had arrived back in Carson City, having been gone four days. He was dusty, dirty, and disgusted. Though certain the young Purcell wife had survived the massacre, he had no idea as to her whereabouts. After he roused the rancher, Will Toal, he tried to speak with him as he took him back to his ranch. But the man never became completely lucid. He could barely keep himself in the saddle. He kept babbling words like, "Why did she do it?" He kept repeating that phrase.

Paris had asked, "Who is she?" But he never got a good answer. By the time they got back to the man's ranch, all they could do was lift him down from his saddle and get him to bed. He stayed for a couple of hours, but the man did not even move. He had fallen into unconsciousness again.

The stocky dead man had been one of the spies he had watched. But the taller man always dressed in black was not to be found. Did the girl leave with him? Maybe. Paris was left with a simple truth: he had no idea where the girl was.

He needed to send a message to Crocker and did not relish the duty. Could hear the response already. It was not going to be pleasant. He needed a plan. But right now he had none.

He walked his horse to the livery barn. Told the livery man that his mount had been ridden hard for four days and should given extra grain. He also said he had no idea when he would need him saddled again.

Paris then walked to the hotel and asked for his key. He was looking forward to a bath and a solid meal.

*****

After getting cleaned up, Paris decided to go talk to Fallar in the land office. He headed down the boardwalk and in through the door to the land office.

"Mr. Fallar, how are you doing this fine day? Are we in a good mood or a bad mood?"

Paris watched as Fallar looked at him closely but with question as if he could not really tell if he were being mocked or if Paris was just generally sarcastic.

"Depends."

Paris thought he would be a willing fish and rise to the bait.

"And upon what would it depend?"

A smile spread across Fallar's face. In an air of his own sarcasm, he looked across the counter and replied, "It would *depend* on how extensive an effort it is going to take in order to satisfy the request I know you are about to make of me. My day will also *depend* on what arrangement we can make in the way of a gratuity for a job well done."

Paris smiled in return. Their business had now become a beneficial working relationship.

"How about I take you to lunch? I hear there is great lunch in a café near the Capitol building. I would like to talk to you about keeping an eye out for any changes in the Purcell Ranch title. In short, if anyone records a formal change of ownership, I would like to know about it right away. I am staying at the Ormsby Hotel."

Fallar stood up and pulled his jacket from a hook on the back of his door.

"Lunch sounds like a good idea. I am sure we can further these discussions over a nice meal. I don't think it would be a problem at all to keep a close watch on any developments regarding the Purcell title. Those are public records, after all. It's been slow over the last couple of days, anyway. It would be nice to get out of the office for a bit."

"That sounds promising. Are you ready?"

Chapter Thirty

1868 Summer
Carson City, Nevada

It took four days for the doctor to give Beth any indication that Sutton could be moved.

"He can go. I won't guarantee he will make the trip, though. You said you are headed to Sacramento, right? Sacramento is over ninety miles away, and to get there you must travel over the Sierras."

Beth answered, trying to make the trip sound a bit less of a challenge.

"The ranch is a little outside of Sacramento, to the east, so we don't have to go the whole way to Sacramento."

The doctor was an older man. As most doctors on the frontiers, he had seen the worst the West could do to humans. He had not asked how a man came to have a bullet buried deep in his thigh. He had refrained from asking any questions as to how a man in his thirties traveled with a girl who did not look twenty. And the doctor did not even come close to asking why she was wearing pants and a gun belt. He appeared happy just to see them go.

"If you travel slow and try to minimize the bumps, it will go better for him. You said you were going to get a wagon, did you not?"

Beth replied, "I did buy a wagon. I bought a market wagon, so he can lay flat in the back. It's out front. My horse will do the pulling, and I will put the saddle in the back with Drake. I have put some blankets down to act as a cushion."

The doctor nodded. "The more cushion the better."

He then went over to some cabinets and pulled out three small glass vials with interesting lettering on them.

"This is laudanum. It is an opioid. It will deaden pain, but it will also make the person lose all semblance of their personality. It will be like they are drunk. If you give him one small sip in the morning, it should last until past noon. For the first few days, I would give him another at noon and another before he tries to sleep."

He handed the vials to Beth.

"But you should begin reducing the dosage as soon as he can stand it. He only needs one small sip. Don't let him gulp it because he will want to. The longer he continues to use it, the greater the chance he will come to depend on it. If he becomes dependent, he will never be able to do without it."

Beth then asked, "Would it be better if I gave it to him myself in something like a spoon?"

"By all means. Try to hide the stuff. When he begins to move around, he will have terrible pain, too. The bones have been damaged. It will take at least six to eight weeks for those bones to heal. It will hurt the entire time, and he will want to find the laudanum to relieve the pain."

"How do I care for the wound itself?" Beth asked.

"I will give you more than enough extra dressings. The leg seems to be fighting the infection quite well, and his fever has not been bad. All of that is good. Change the dressing every day. You should probably continue changing it daily for two weeks. After that, the wound should be closed. Let the wound drain. Don't try to clog it up. It will dry up on its own."

The doctor went on to describe in detail how Beth should keep the wound clean. He helped her load the extra dressings. The doctor also gave Beth a crutch. He said Sutton would need it soon enough.

They then went back into the office and helped Sutton out to the wagon. Market wagons were used to haul all manner of items, but generally, they were used for dry goods purchased in town to be hauled to where one lived. It had slightly raised wooden sides and a drop-down tailgate. The wagon Beth bought was well worn, but she did not have the luxury of time and took the only wagon available. They helped Sutton out of the office and sat him down on the tailgate. Beth climbed into the back of the wagon and half dragged him under the shoulders to get him all the way up into the front of as the doctor held up his bad leg so they could get the tailgate closed. Sutton laid down flat, his brow damp with sweat from the effort and pain.

The doctor said, "I gave him a good dose of the laudanum already. I knew moving out to the wagon would be bad. The next couple of days are going to be rough."

"Doctor, thank you for all you have done. I will do my best to see that he gets well."

"Thank you for the payment. You were very generous. When you brought the man into my office, I must confess I thought this was going to be a patient who could not pay. I have to say I was mighty surprised when I told you my fee was ten dollars, and you gave me twenty. You are most generous."

Beth untied a tall dark horse that had been tethered to a hitching rail. She took the halter and tied a good knot to the back of the wagon. The horse was saddled. There was a second saddle in the back of the wagon with the injured man. The doctor figured the second saddle normally went on the back of the horse in the harness.

As Beth climbed up into the driver's seat, the doctor asked, "Why do you have the horse behind saddled?"

Beth looked down at him with a frown, then a bit of a smile.

"I was always taught to have a horse saddled. Never know when you might need to ride."

"Probably a good thought. Well, hope the travels go well." The doctor flipped up his hand in a quick wave and then turned back to his office.

Beth snapped the reins and headed north out of town on Main Street. She turned on the driver's bench to the rear and looked down at Sutton. His eyes were open. He seemed to be waiting to see how bad this ride was going to be.

"Drake, I can get us to Lake Crossing. I've traveled that road to the toll bridge many times. But I am going to need your help when we turn west on the road along the Truckee. I have never been west of our ranch."

Sutton replied in between winces on each bump.

"Get us to Lake Crossing, and I will get us up over Donner and down to the Patten Ranch."

They left town at a walk.

*****

Dale Paris stepped out of the telegraph office. He had sent his report to Crocker. He tried to get right to the point, informing the man that he had not found the Purcell wife. He also confessed he had no good leads. He did tell Crocker he would stay here in Carson City for a few days to see if anyone tried to record a transfer of the deed. Remaining in town watching the recorder's office was the best idea he could come up with at the moment. Paris figured he would get a blistering response in the next couple of hours. He had left a good tip to make sure the telegraph man brought him the response right away.

As he stepped out of the office, he gazed to the north of Main Street and saw what looked like a slender man driving a horse and wagon. The man's back was to him, but he could see that the man's belt was way too large. It had a long tongue of extra leather hanging out to his side. Paris found it most curious that someone so thin would not find a belt that fit. He took note of the large dark horse tethered to the back of the wagon with a halter. He could not see anything in the back of the wagon except the top of an extra saddle visible over the short wooden side. It was one of those observations one makes hundreds of times each day that has no reference or relevance. He thought nothing more of it.

Chapter Thirty-One

Charles Crocker picked up the telegram. He shook his head. The news was not good. There had been real hope that Paris would locate the Purcell lady and negotiate a deal. Now they would have to come up with some other plan to get access to the right of way. But what?

He decided to walk down the hall to Huntington's office and give him the news.

Huntington looked up at Crocker as he entered.

"And to what do I owe the pleasure?"

Crocker moved across the office as he had done hundreds of times and sat in a chair opposite Huntington's desk.

"Collis, we don't have a good read on the Purcell property right of way situation. Paris cannot find the lady he thinks survived the massacre. From his report, he has been riding all over the Carson Valley and can confirm she did survive. He has followed up what looks like two gunfights in which she is somehow involved, but he cannot find her."

"So, what do we do now?" asked Huntington.

Crocker fidgeted. "I don't have a good idea. Wish I did, but I don't. Paris is going to remain in Carson City near the land office to wait a few days to see if anyone comes in to change the title. If so, then he will approach the new owners. Someone has to make a move to change the title from a man now deceased."

"Charles," Huntington started, "General Dodge is asking for a progress report. As President Johnson has now been impeached and no one is deferring to him, Dodge is taking on more and more responsibility to push the railroad ahead. He is military. He wants results, and he is not the type to tolerate failure. Another delay will be viewed as such a failure."

"Collis, I understand. But what would you have me do? The only other alternative is to arrange with the state of Nevada to file an eminent domain action. Not only will that take more than a year, it means we have to deal with a large group of state lawmakers who will each ask for some quid pro quo."

"We cannot go there. We don't have the time. Charles, you have to solve this, and solve it quick."

Huntington's voice had risen louder than Crocker had ever heard it. He took it as a measure of the financial pressure they were all under. He looked back over the top of the desk at his partner.

"Collis, I will do what I can. You always know I will."

Crocker walked out of Huntington's office angered at being upbraided. He was not used to it. Huntington and he had worked together now for years. They had an efficient, businesslike yet personable relationship. The two actually did like each other and admired the other's talents. But things were getting tense. He had to come up with some method of securing the right of way.

He started to plan his telegram back to Paris.

Chapter Thirty-Two

1868 Summer
West of Donner Pass, California

Though traveling through a forest, the teamster road was open and uncovered, untouched by the shade of the tall timbered pines so near. The temperature in the shade was cool, typical for this elevation and this time of year. But in the open road the climate was completely different. In the middle of the day the sun pierced uninterrupted in little spores of intense heat. Her clothes warmed at their outer shell baking her body inside. Beth turned to look at Sutton in the wagon. The sun had to be even worse for him. Lying flat below the sides of the wagon the breezes would pass over the top leaving him to broil as if he lay in the middle of a fry pan.

It had been several days since they left Carson City. Getting over Donner Pass had been the hardest part of the trip. Once they had crested the summit, riding down the western slope had been much easier on the horse in harness. Beth had used Sutton's horse to give hers a rest here and there, but Sutton's horse was not trained for harness.

They had made fairly good time under the circumstances. The road over Donner itself had been jammed with all kinds of men and equipment heading uphill to the railroad construction, making progress slow. It seemed like a steady stream of loaded wagons with oxen and mules hauling all manner of materials both for the railroad and to support the thousands of men working on the monumental project.

Beth had been happy for one good night of sleep away from the roadside camping they had done since Carson City. Sutton and Beth had spent one night in a small hotel. Other nights had been spent out in the open after pulling off the road at a safe distance from the constant traffic and potential passersby who might have an idea to accost what looked like a lone female. She found that the hotel had been small and remarkably comfortable in lieu of its location far from any town or city. It was run by a husband and wife team: Peter and Bobbie Martin. The Martins had named their lodge out on the frontier, Edenhouse. They had been such a help and asked no questions despite the unusual appearance of a young lady in pants with a seriously injured man in the back of a wagon. When camped off the road, sleep came in short spurts because of her constant concern someone would try to enter their camp. Sutton was not himself. With the laudanum, he would sleep, albeit fitfully. But he did not provide any help in keeping watch. But in the warm, welcoming environment of the Martin's hotel, Beth got more sleep in one night than she'd had in a week.

Beth had used her own money to pay for the hotel. With only limited awareness of his surroundings, Sutton had not asked how she paid the bill. He had enough trouble just getting in and out of the wagon. Proprietor Peter Martin had been of great assistance getting Sutton up into the room. Even with Sutton using his crutch, Beth thought she'd probably not have been able to get Sutton all the way in without a man's helping hand. By the time he got to the bed, Sutton was exhausted. He simply laid back and slept.

The next day, Beth cleaned out Sutton's wound with water from a jug provided by the hotel. The wound looked to be healing well. But now they were back on the road.

"How far do you think we have to travel?" she asked.

Sutton tried to lift his head above the wagon sidings to get his bearings. "Patten told me several times it was near a small place called Fiddletown. We are going to have to cut off the main road about ten miles ahead and begin heading south."

"What a crazy name, Fiddletown."

"I've never been there, but I have traveled up and down the road from Sacramento to Donner Pass many times and know where the cutoff is."

"You sound like you are feeling a bit better."

Sutton shook his head. "It's all in the bumps. This part of the road feels flatter. Must be all the teamsters heading the opposite way. They have smoothed out the roadway."

He then winced. "But as soon as you hit one, it hurts."

"Do you know if the ranch has any kind of shelter?"

Sutton looked to the side of the wagon. "Only a simple one room cabin. He used to go there to get away and plan his future as a cattle rancher. It's in the foothills, and he said it has a view across the entire middle of California."

"If true, it must be something to see."

Sutton then returned his gaze to Beth, who was twisted in her seat and looking back down in the wagon. "I just want to get out of this torture chamber and to a bed. Hopefully, the throbbing will stop."

"We can spend as much time there as we need until your leg mends. Then you can take me off to Sacramento and San Francisco."

"I can hear your anticipation, but right now I can't imagine anything other than getting out of this wagon and away from this pain."

Beth turned forward. She was concerned that Sutton seemed distracted and disinterested getting to the bigger cities: her goal. But, after a moment, she figured it was understandable because he was in serious pain.

"Hold on; it doesn't sound like it will be long."

Chapter Thirty-Three

1868 Summer
Carson City, Nevada

Grande heard the little bell on his door. He looked up to see Will Toal walk in.

"What's that on your arm?" he asked.

Will glanced down at his left arm, still in the sling. The sling had almost become a part of his body.

"I had a little run in with some folks who thought they had numbers on me and could take advantage of the situation."

"Looks to me like they won. You're the one wearing the bandage and carrying the wound," said Grande.

"The other guy is under dirt right now," came Will's retort. He took a measure of offense that he appeared to have lost whatever competition Grande imagined.

Grande was taken aback. He was not the kind of person who even considered life and death confrontations. That was out of his normal realm.

"Are you here to tell me that the sheriff is looking for you?"

Now it was Will's turn to stop, hesitate, and consider.

"Not that I know of." He really hadn't thought about the fact that the sheriff might have some interest in a shooting with a resulting death. "They drew on me and shot first," came his less than convincing reply.

"Any witnesses?" came Grande's next inquiry. "You know, as an officer of the court and member of the Bar, I might have a duty to report you to the authorities." Grande was not above playing a slight game with this young client for whom he had a developing affection.

Will had been looking away and did not see the slight smirk on the attorney's face. Will had not given thought to the fact he might have a problem with the sheriff. Even though he came to discuss another issue, maybe he should discuss the shooting with Grande.

Grande saw the consternation written on Will's face and decided to let his conversational prey off the hook. "I already know about the shooting, and I know you acted completely in self-defense."

Will had been half-turned from Grande and whipped around to face him directly.

"How on earth do you know that?"

Grande had no small amount of satisfaction obviously being in possession of superior knowledge on this small point.

"A young woman came into my office and provided a very interesting story. I believe you and she are acquaintances."

If he did not already have it, Grande now had Will's full attention.

"You saw Beth?"

"Yes, I did. That young lady relayed the details of a confrontation near Kingsbury Grade in which, I am told, you were involved."

"She shot the guy who shot me and then knocked me cold with her six-gun!" Will blurted.

Grande's head recoiled a bit. "She neglected to tell me that. The story as she told it led me to believe she had no small amount of affection for you."

"I was out cold for three days. Would you consider that affection?"

Grande replied with a sarcastic, impish smile, "In my business, I have heard stories of many a complicated rendezvous, but I must admit, assaulting one's suitor over the head with a handgun does strike me as a fairly strange courtship." Grande did his best to suppress an outright chuckle.

Will sighed. "At one point, I thought I knew her. I thought she had been dealt a bad hand in life and was trying to do her best in threatening surroundings. But after sitting on my porch with a large lump on my head, I think she just manipulated the entire thing."

Grande's lighthearted banter ended. He saw the conflict in the young man. Will's demeanor, if not his words, conveyed an obvious affection for the lady even if he wasn't going to admit it. Grande changed his tone to match his observations of Will's conflict.

"I will tell you that I did not admire a good deal of her story, most importantly, the details surrounding the loss of her immediate family."

Will said, "Maybe it took a whack on the head to make me see things straight. Maybe it's best she moved on. I thought I had a read on her. I thought she was trying to make things right in her life. But I must have been mistaken."

Grande at this point knew that Will was not here to talk about the shoot-out. In fact, he knew exactly why Will had walked in the door. He knew from the moment Will entered.

"She told me about the letter."

"Yep, another mystery."

"Did you bring the deed?"

Will looked up again. "You are well informed. I need to know what to do with this." He reached into his shirt and pulled out a document and handed it to the lawyer.

Grande quickly reviewed the document.

"This is exactly how she described it."

"She knocks me over the head, and then she tries to give me part of her husband's ranch. Is this legal? Should I even try to record this at the land office?"

Grande took a breath. "It is not technically legal but only because it is not complete. It needs to be signed by an official witness. Had you brought this in by yourself, I would say that it is a document of questionable validity. However, the young lady presented herself to me and personally made her wishes clear. Those wishes match what it looks like she was trying to do on the document."

Will listened to the emerging analysis. The sounds outside the office seemed to fade away as he fixed his attention on Grande.

"However, under these circumstances, I believe I would have a duty to verify as a legal witness myself. Elizabeth personally informed me of her intentions, and they match the document you have brought."

Will almost had not come to see the lawyer. When María brought him the letter and the deed, he did not think the deed would be valid. This was a surprise to say the least.

"There is one issue," Grande continued. "Henry Millard paid a certain amount, intending to obtain 100% of the property. The deed as signed over only gives him 75%. As your advisor, I would not record the deed until you can discuss this with Mr. Millard and obtain his consent or negotiate a resolution of the problem."

"How am I ever going to do that? I don't know that man and would have no idea where in the world to find him," said Will.

"Well..." Grande drew out the word and stood up as he held the thought. "I have done business with the Millard Luce Cattle Co. several times in my career. I have met Henry Millard and represented clients who have had business with him. I know him to be a very practical, even-handed, and fair businessman. However, if you cross him, he is not afraid to take you to court and pursue it to the ends of the earth. He has pursued cases to the highest courts in California involving significant water rights and won."

Will now thought the whole thing would lead to nothing but a dead end.

"But I think we should approach him and see what he has to say." Grande looked over to Will, pausing to see the reaction.

"Again, how am I ever going to do that? I wouldn't know how to find him."

Grande, now standing at his full height, looked down and, with one of his broadest smiles, said, "That's why you come to me, so I can solve your problems. Henry Millard is staying at the hotel across from the Capitol. I spoke with him on another matter for a different client yesterday."

Will, utterly amazed, said, "You knew that all along?"

"Yes, I did. In fact, knowing you would probably bring the deed to me at some point, I raised your situation with Mr. Millard on an informal basis at the end of my conversation with him. He seemed intrigued and wants to meet you."

"When can we talk?" asked Will.

"Let's walk over together to the hotel right now and see if he is available. But if we do, I want you to let me start the conversation. You keep your mouth shut until I give you a nod to go ahead. Understood?"

If someone threatened to pull a gun at Will, he would never let anyone do his talking, but in a legal morass, Will happily agreed to let someone else guide him through.

"I'd be happy to let you do the talking. Do you think he'd ever agree to this?"

"Based on my initial conversation, yes, I think he might agree. But he has an idea that you should hear first."

"Well, let's go over and hear what he has to say."

Chapter Thirty-Four

The Capitol Hotel was the best hotel in Carson City. It was the hotel of choice for all the legislators to meet their constituents and clientele. The rates were the highest in town, but it was where business was conducted. If there was serious business to be done, it happened in the dining room of the Capitol Hotel.

Though elegant by Western standards, the dining room would be plain in most large cities. Wooden floors were covered with multiple rectangular carpets. Lace curtains covered the lower half of the windows. The tables were spaced at far greater distances than in most eating establishments. The spacing was deliberate in order to make it difficult for someone sitting at an adjacent table to hear conversation at any other table in the vicinity. The proprietors understood the need to protect the political and legislative conversations which normally took place here.

Paris was sitting in the eating room, dining with Scott Fallar. He watched as Will Toal and a large man dressed in a full suit walked into the hotel. The pair approached a balding man of slender build who had been eating by himself. After shaking hands, the pair sat down to talk to the unaccompanied dining patron.

"Who is that large man in the suit?" Paris asked Fallar. "I know young Mr. Toal, as I helped him back to his ranch some days ago, but I do not know the man in the suit."

"That is S. Samuel Grande. He's a lawyer in town. He's a good one, too. He's careful who he represents, and he gets them results."

"And who is the man who had been eating at the table?" asked Paris.

Fallar looked over at the table and squinted before he answered. The man in question sat mostly with his back to Fallar, so it took him a moment to answer.

"I believe that is Henry Millard. Mr. Millard came into the office yesterday to record some land transactions he had completed here on his trip. He told me that he'd been down near Topaz Lake looking at cattle ranches. He recorded two transactions, deeding him some five thousand acres. Do you know who Henry Millard is?"

"No, who is he?" asked Paris.

Fallar now looked up from his plate, setting down his fork and knife.

"Henry Millard is one of the two partners in Millard Luce Cattle Co. They are without a doubt the largest cattle ranching business in California. He has property all over the state into Oregon and now here in Nevada. He is one of the most powerful men in the business."

Paris then mused out loud, "And what could he be talking to young Mr. Toal about…"

Fallar shrugged. "Maybe he is making Toal an offer on his ranch. That is what Millard does. And it looks as if Toal has done the smart thing and brought Grande with him to guide him on the deal."

"I'm not sure," said Paris. "I need you to let me know if anything develops in the near future. I just have a feeling they are not there to talk about young Toal's property. I have a feeling it has to do with the Purcell Ranch."

Paris had been looking at the Millard table. He now turned to Fallar to look him dead on.

"We still have a deal? You will tell me as soon as there is anything involving a transfer of the Purcell Ranch?"

The look on Paris' face made the significance of the question clear. Fallar immediately understood. "I have no problem providing you with that information. As I said before, it's public record. Anyone is entitled to see the transactions recorded."

"Good," said Paris. "Something has to develop."

Paris knew the chances of the conversation at the other table having some connection to the young Purcell wife were thin. But he was running out of options and, short of some change in the legal status of the Purcell Ranch, he had no idea how he could provide his boss with the solution they desperately wanted.

"Something has to develop."

*****

"Mr. Millard, why would you want me to run one of your ranches?"

Will had blurted out the question honestly but without giving it much thought before letting it escape.

"Will, may I call you that?" Millard looked for an approval. Will nodded his agreement, and Millard continued.

"I look all over the West for ranches which are well-run. My business is to deliver the best quality beef to the markets in San Francisco and Sacramento. My buyers now expect the highest quality from my ranches. I charge a premium, but those buyers pay that premium because they know what they are getting."

Henry Millard had a firm but straightforward delivery. He spoke with a distinct accent. Will had heard the same kind of accent when he talked to Mr. Dangberg. Must have been because they came from the same country. Millard's voice was also high, almost feminine. The strange tone had led other men to underestimate Henry Millard. But Grande had warned Will not to do any such thing. He told Will on the way across the street that he was about to sit down and deal with one of the most powerful yet forward-thinking businessmen in California. With animated arms swinging and flaying about, he made it very clear that Henry Millard was fair but one of the toughest businessmen he knew. Grande appreciated capability. And Grande said Henry Millard was one of the most capable men in business.

Explaining his company, but at the same time assessing Will, Millard continued. "I have to deliver the best beef on the market. I do so by insisting the beef raised on property I own or manage is handled in the best way possible. I spend a great deal of my time working regularly with my ranches, watching detail after detail."

Millard did not really move as opposed to Grande. Though the tone of his voice would rise or fall for emphasis, his hands remained still. Yet the delivery was just as effective. Will could see this man was serious about his business.

"Water, grass, facilities." Millard annunciated the word *facilities* precisely. The emphasis reminded Will of one of his teachers early in school telling his class how to say the word with accentuated movement of their mouth. "If you don't take care of your ranch, if you don't take care of your ranch hands, then you raise poor beef. It's as simple as that."

Millard paused, then drove the point home.

"I had a ranch manager who I asked to paint the barns and bunk-house. I also asked him to clean and fix up inside both structures. When I returned from checking some other ranches, this had not been done. When I asked why, he told me that he did not think fixing those struc-tures to be important. I fired him on the spot. I reminded him I had made it clear how I looked after my operations. If he was not up to the task, then I would replace him. And I did."

Millard opened his hands before him as he laid them on the table. With palms upright, he added, "When I was traveling north from Topaz, I made it a point to stop at your ranch. I then headed here to Carson for a bit of a rest. Entering your property, I saw good grass. I decided to stop and talk to the owner. But you were injured at the time. I spoke to one of your hands, a man of Mexican origin I believe, and he obviously knew you well. He seemed like he knew quite a lot about ranching. Good hands are critical."

"Both Juan and Raúl are experienced, good hands," Will interjected.

"What I saw looked to me like a well-run ranch: good stock, good people, good facilities." There was that word again. He pronounced it exactly as he did the first time.

Millard then chuckled. "I had planned on taking care of my business here in Carson and then riding out again to talk to you. However, Mr. Grande approached me yesterday after we had concluded our business on another matter and told me about the Purcell deed. We discussed it and came up with this idea."

Other than flipping his hands upright, the man had still not moved. Everything about him was efficient. If movement was needed, then he moved. If he was involved with only talking, no sense in wasting energy of another sort.

"Explain it to me again so I make sure I have it right," said Will.

"This is simple; you retain 25% of the interest in the Purcell Ranch. You run both your own ranch and the Purcell Ranch, the latter of which we would jointly own. Sell the beef here locally as you have been doing. I will take 75% of the profit from the Purcell beef, and you take 25% of that stock and 100% for any beef raised on your own ranch. It's like you have doubled the size of your ranch holdings without having to pay a purchase price, and I have a 75% interest in an operation I don't have to find someone to handle. I have expanded my holdings just as you have."

"What about the deed?" asked Will.

"We record it just as Miss Purcell wanted." This time it was Grande who answered the question.

"I would agree," said Millard.

"To try to change that deed would probably take legal proceedings," said Grande. "This way, the transfer fits with the intention of the only logical holder of the legal title without getting very complicated."

"So, Mr. Toal, do you agree?" asked Millard.

Will had not seen this coming as he had ridden into town. He had thought the deed would be left at Grande's office and never spoken of again. Worthless. Another of the mysteries Beth had created to make men jump. But this had an appeal. He liked the idea. He also thought Millard's approach to ranching matched his. Thank goodness he had painted his barn and bunkhouse after they were built.

Will reached across the table and offered his hand.

"I do agree."

Millard, for the first time, smiled and grasped Will's hand in agreement.

Will then asked Grande, "What should we do now?"

Grande looked at both and then said, "I draw up an agreement that you and Mr. Millard can sign tomorrow, and then we walk down to the land office and record the Purcell deed."

"Done," said Millard.

Will smiled. He looked out the window.

Grande noticed and thought he knew what Will was thinking. He was beginning to think he could read his young client's mind at times.

"She might not be all that bad," he said.

Chapter Thirty-Five

It had been two days since Fallar had lunch with Paris at the Capitol Hotel. He was walking back to that same eatery for another fine lunch. Two trips in one week had to be a record for Fallar, who, on his salary, did not often have such opportunities.

Fallar entered the eatery. Paris had been waiting. Fallar began relaying the news before he fully sat down.

"Well, you were right to wait here in town. I just recorded a change in the title of the Purcell Ranch into the names of the Millard Luce Cattle Co. and William Toal."

Paris felt brighter than he had in weeks. A change. An opportunity to get a result that would appeal to his employers. A resolution that could lead to a bonus. Paris knew the importance of securing the right of way. As the last real segment anywhere near privately owned land, solving the Purcell Ranch situation would be the last barrier to hitting open ground over U.S. government property.

If Paris could solve this last problem, Crocker would be immensely relieved, for which he had been known to be quite generous. Paris knew he had until November while waiting for the special construction on the snow sheds from Donner to Lake Crossing would be completed. He needed to get his own task finished before that work was done.

"That is good news and much appreciated."

Fallar asked, "What's for lunch?"

Paris smiled. "Pick anything you want from the menu. As soon as you are done, I think I will ride out to young Toal's ranch and see if I can make a deal."

*****

Will was out in front of his house. His arm was feeling slightly better. The wound itself had completely closed. He was slowly gaining flexibility and strength. The doctor had removed the stitches in his shoulder and taken a last look at the back of his head. The dizzy spells had subsided, and the headaches were less frequent.

The day was spectacular: high blue sky, billowing clouds, and only a slight breeze. The wind had the crisp smell of spring.

Will saw Juan in the round pen working a new colt.

"Are we going to keep that one?" asked Will.

Juan had the colt with a paint coat of black and white colors, at a soft lope in a tight circle. Without changing his focus on the horse's stride, he responded, "It is for you to decide, but if you are to ask me, this horse, he would be a horse Juan would like to ride. He have a smooth glide. See how he can reach forward already."

Will took note of the front action on the young horse. The two front legs would stretch out in an extra reach, causing a hesitation in the gait. A horse with a gait like this looked like it was almost floating. It would be a very soft, constant seat for any rider. Will easily saw why Juan liked the horse so much.

"He's yours," said Will. "What are you going to name him? How about Domino?"

"*Señor* Will, you have made Juan a happy man. This horse and Juan will be friends for a long time. I like the name. His name, it will be Domino."

Will then changed the topic.

"Are we ready to take some horses to Fort Churchill?

"Sí, we have about twenty horses that the Capitan should like. They are finished even better than the last herd we take, and he was much happy with them."

"Fine, then we should gather the group first thing tomorrow, and let's ride up to Churchill and talk to the Captain."

Will then added another thought.

"Once we sell the horses, we can stop by the Purcell Ranch and see how Raúl is doing. We all agreed Raúl should be the one to check out the stock and tell us if he thinks the three of us can round up what the Purcell's left or if we need to hire more hands to help. He should have an answer by now."

"Sí, I think Raúl, he ready by now to tell us."

Just as Juan finished his comment, a rider came up the road into the ranch with his horse at a short trot, the kind of pace that rider and horse can sustain over long distances. Will thought that horse and rider looked quite comfortable in their ground-covering gait. As if they had done this for many a mile.

The rider wore a bowler hat. His suit and vest looked like it was more fit to be worn in town. But there was a revolver at his hip. A tied down revolver. Between the gait and revolver, Will had the feeling this was not some businessman lost on the range.

"Good morning. Might I stop for a bit and water my horse?" came a request from the man in the bowler hat.

"Welcome," said Will. "Step down and rest your mount. The water trough is over next to the main barn."

Dale Paris watched Will carefully. So far, he had not given any indication he recognized him as the man who helped him back from the shoot-out at the Reynolds camp.

"I don't want to give him too much right away, so if it is agreeable, I will give him some water and let him stand for a bit and then let him have some more."

This impressed Will; he would have done the exact same thing. Experienced riders did not want their horses drinking too much after a long distance as they could belly cramp. This man knew how to take care of horseflesh.

"Sure, give him a sip, and then come on over to the corral."

After the short stop at the trough, the man in the bowler hat walked up to Will, who had turned his attention back to the paint Juan was riding.

"Nice gait," said the man in the round hat. "That is a very good-looking horse. Almost as good-looking as the gray you were riding when I last saw you."

The comment grabbed Will's attention.

"When did you see me riding my gray?"

"After you had been shot. I helped bring you back here to the ranch." He offered his hand. "The name is Dale Paris."

Will was caught. He had not been in any condition after the shootout and crack on his head to recognize anyone. Juan and Raúl had told him a man helped him back but never gave them his name. They had not described the man, either. Will had just assumed it was a passerby, and he'd never be able to thank the man for his help.

Will took his hand. "I never thought I would be able to thank the man who helped me. I was not in any condition to even know my whereabouts that day. I am not sure I ever would have made it back had you not made sure I got up on my gray. Thank you for what you did."

The man took his hand in a firm grip. Will sensed there was more to this person than the first impression.

"Let me get you something to drink. Come on over to the porch, and we can sit."

Will looked again at the man. He appeared quite relaxed. But he wondered what he could be doing back here at the ranch. Maybe just being social. Maybe more.

"What brings you back out this way?" asked Will as he offered Paris his rocker. Will leaned up against the hitching rail, facing Paris.

"Well, the first thing I wanted to do was to see how you were doing. When I was here last, you could barely sit on a horse. But I also wanted to hear the story of that day. I came upon the scene after the fact. Never could quite figure out what took place."

"You a lawman?" asked Will.

Will's guard had been down thinking this was someone who had helped him and asked for nothing in return. This man claiming to be Dale Paris hadn't even left his name when he'd dropped Will off that day. Will had never told anyone what had really happened in the clash at the camp. If he was now going to share any of those details, he had to be sure he wasn't sealing his fate with his own words.

"No, I am not with the law. Far from it," replied Paris.

With that, Will thought he owed the man an explanation. He started relaying the story satisfied there could be no ulterior motive in the man.

"It was a strange day. I had been taking care of a young woman who I came across at that same camp a week before, when I had heard a gunshot and rode out to investigate. When I arrived, she looked terrible. All bloodied up and scared to death."

Paris thought he'd take a chance. With an emphasis of extra interest as if he were enthralled with the story, he asked, "Was this by any chance a woman related to the Purcell family?"

"Yes. She told me so at the time, but I was not sure until later," Will replied.

Will had opened up. Again, not thinking that this man had any intent other than to hear the story, he continued.

"When I arrived, she ran to me in tears. She appeared distraught. There was a man with her who told me to leave her alone. When I tried to find out what was going on, he drew and so did I. He lost."

Paris kept his eyes on Will. Will felt the gaze but continued.

"For a week she rested and recovered. The lady said she had buried some documents near the camp to keep them from the man I shot, and she wanted to go get them. She said they were real important."

Will did not include the night next to the river in his story.

"I went with her just in case the men she had been with returned. As soon as she dug up the documents, two men appeared out of nowhere and said they were going to take what she had recovered. When we didn't give them back, they both drew. Shots were fired. I hit the man who seemed to be in charge. I was winged in the left shoulder. I think the girl shot the second man. But after she shot the second attacker, she hit me on the head with her gun."

"So, that's how you were knocked out?" asked Paris. "I didn't know how you came to be unconscious. The gun wound didn't look like that could have caused it."

"Right," said Will. "I will never understand why she did it."

"That is one strange story. Did she ever come back? Have you seen her since?"

"Nope, she left that day, and I have no idea where she is."

Paris shook his head. "No telling what might enter a female's mind at any given time."

"Well, it's all still a mystery to me," said Will.

"So, she never came back, did she?" Paris restated the question as if to make sure he heard the answer correctly the first time.

Will looked down and then back up.

"No, but she did something that made the mystery bigger. She gave me a part of her ranch."

"She *gave* you part?"

"Yep, she did. Don't ask me why. How do you crack a man on his head and then give him property?"

Paris hesitated, but he figured there was no better time than now to approach what he came for.

"Well, as the owner of the Purcell Ranch, I'd like to have another conversation with you. Are you interested in selling it?"

Will hesitated. He felt instant concern. Suddenly, Will regretted being so open with the story of how Beth had given him an interest in the Purcell Ranch. He felt flat stupid, disappointed in himself. He took pride in being careful with what he told people, and here he had just blurted out something he should have kept to himself. With that one question about selling, Will backed off completely. This man could be here to contest the deed which he had recorded. Asking about a sale could be a ploy. Multiple thoughts began to race through his head. He did not reply.

Seeing obvious consternation in Will's face, Paris thought he should further explain.

"I see I may have caught you a bit off guard. Please understand; I represent some investors who are quite interested in your property there by the Truckee River. I can substantiate my client's interest and my authority to represent them. We are fully prepared to make you a generous offer."

Will finally got his feet underneath him again.

"Why would I want to sell? I only just came into possession of the ranch. We've been looking over its grazing land and stock. So far, we like what we see."

"All the more reason to sell now. You might find any number of problems with the property or stock, leading you to regret taking it on.

Better to sell and take the sure cash. My clients have plans for the property that do not involve ranching, so those items would not be a risk for us."

"No ranching?" said Will. "The owner who sold did so because he wanted the Ranch to continue to run cattle. That's what we intend to do."

Will looked at the man directly in the eye. His resolve continued to build. This man now stood as an opponent in a competition.

"Mr. Toal, my clients intend to get possession of that ranch." Paris returned the hard look, adding a squint of the eye. Will took the boldness of the statement as more than just a challenge. It was a warning.

"You are going to have a hard time getting it while I have a say," came Will's reply. "I think it's about time you rode on."

Paris didn't move. He continued to look straight at Will. The niceties were completely gone. Finally, Paris got up, stepped to the side, and started toward his horse. After two or three strides, he turned.

"You will regret your decision today," he said.

Will never looked away. "We'll see," was all he said.

Chapter Thirty-Six

Will strode into the headquarters of Fort Churchill. He had done business with Captain Joseph Stewart several times before. Captain Stewart was something of a local hero in the Carson Valley. In 1860, a band comprised of Paiutes and Bannocks attacked the Williams Station General Store and Saloon. The Indians would later claim one of the three Williams brothers who collectively ran the Station had captured and enslaved two young Paiute girls.

The whites originally denied the accusation, claiming the attack was unprovoked. Later, the accusation proved accurate. The net result of the Indian attack left some twenty patrons dead and two of the Williams brothers as well. Major William Ormsby led a group of soldiers and volunteers in a retribution attack, but the natives defeated the force at the first battle of Pyramid Lake. Government forces called in Captain Stewart to quell the rising crisis. He led regular army forces successfully in the second battle of Pyramid Lake. There were no further problems with the Paiutes.

Following the battle, Captain Stewart established Fort Churchill, named for the then Inspector General of the Army, Sylvester Churchill. In addition to protecting local settlers, the fort also served as a depot and station stop for the Pony Express. But the Pony Express operations ended in October of 1861. Since that time, Fort Churchill had been an important supply depot for the Union Army during the Civil War through which tons of silver ore were processed for transport to San

Francisco and then to the East, ultimately providing much needed funds for the North's war expenses.

An orderly sat at a desk positioned in front of a hallway. Will knew from prior visits that the hallway led to Captain Stewart's door.

"Mr. Toal, good to see you again. Are you here to see the Captain?"

"Yes," answered Will. "I hope to sell him some horses and make arrangements to sell some beef in a month or two."

The orderly then stood and walked around the back of his desk. He looked solicitous, almost sorrowful. Will thought the demeanor strange as he had found this same orderly's communication usually clipped, bordering on disinterested. Today, the orderly almost seemed concerned for Will.

"I know the Captain is quite busy. We have received new orders for the fort. But let me see if he has the time to talk to you."

"I would appreciate it," said Will.

The orderly walked down a hall and opened a door at the end. Will could hear voices, but he could not make out the conversation. Will heard footsteps on the wooden floors returning to the orderly's desk.

"The Captain will see you now. Please follow me."

Will followed the orderly back down the hallway. The footfalls of both sets of boots bounced off the walls of the narrow hall. It sounded like a whole company was approaching.

They walked into a small plain office. About the only items that were not of immediate utilitarian use were two flags. One was the United States flag, and the other appeared to be a regimental flag. The Captain stood.

"Mr. Toal, good to see you. That last batch of horses you sold us were fine animals. The army appreciates good stock."

"Well, Captain, we traveled out here some fifty miles east into the desert again hoping to sell you another batch of horses. I have eighteen horses all started and broke. I think you will find this batch even better than the last."

"I would seriously consider that," said the Captain. "However, I cannot make any further purchases. Fort Churchill has been decommissioned. My orders are to tidy up, pack up this company of two hundred soldiers, and head west. We will be stationed at Fort Sutter outside Sacramento."

"Decommissioned? That means you are closing the fort?" Outright anguish could be heard in Will's voice.

"Yes, we will be closing the fort. The fort was originally built to deal with natives. That has been accomplished. Then we supported the Pony Express and acted as a supply depot during the war. But the war is over. This fort and many others around the country are no longer needed. The army and the government have to reduce their expenditures."

Will looked down to the floor.

"It takes us two days to drive the stock here to the fort. So, you are telling me I am just going to have to drive them back?"

"Precisely."

"Does this mean you are not going to be buying any more beef?" Will knew what the answer was going to be. But he thought he'd ask anyway, holding out an unrealistic hope the answer would be different from what he expected.

"I can purchase five head which will be used for the trip. Other than that, I would suggest you drive your cattle down to Sacramento, and the army might buy from you upon delivery there. However, to be honest, there might already be local ranchers providing beef to Fort Sutter."

"All the ranchers in the Carson Valley count on selling their stock to you. The Johnsons and Dangbergs are going to be just as disappointed as I am."

"Mr. Toal, I understand your predicament. However, it is out of my hands. I have my orders, and I must carry them out."

Will stood there doing his best to absorb the impact of what he had just been told. He had no way to drive herds of cattle down to Sacramento. Still, if he did, it didn't sound like he would be certain to sell the steers even after the expense of driving them down the Western Sierras. He had no idea how difficult such a trip might be. Most importantly, selling his horses and beef to the fort was the only way he generated funds to pay his mortgage. He now had no source of revenue.

"Mr. Toal, I have a thousand things I must do to get ready to close the fort. I apologize, but I must take my leave so I can get back to my duty."

"I understand," said Will. "I'll be leaving."

Will then walked out of the office and mounted Powder. He rode out to a draw next to the stream which provided Fort Churchill with the only source of water in what was a huge expanse of desert. Will and his hands had used the spot before, finding it to be a good place to hold horses or cattle while waiting for directions to drive them into the fort or surrounding pens. Will always thought this location a crazy place to build a fort. Too far from anything important. Apparently, the government had arrived at the exact same thought. The government simply did not need a fort way out here heading into the eastern desert.

Juan sat on his new horse, Domino, keeping an eye on the herd. He looked up at Will, expecting an order to round them up and push them into the fort's gate.

"The army will not be buying our horses. They are closing the fort."

Juan looked at Will. After an extended pause, he gazed out over the desert and back to Will. "Then, jefe, who will buy our beef? Who will buy our horses?"

"I don't know," said Will. "I don't know."

Chapter Thirty-Seven

1868 Late Summer
Patten Ranch near Fiddletown, California

The dry morning ether was so thin it levitated off the ground. Beth stood in the doorway to a one room cabin early in the morning just as she had each day since they'd arrived. Her lungs labored to draw in enough oxygen to satisfy the bodily need. The elevation was not as high as Donner Pass, but the still air felt twice as thin. She wondered why. The vista from the front door stretched endlessly out across the central valley of California, tantalizing her dreams to explore. But the cabin and the invalid inside fixed her like a stone outcropping. She drew another deep breath, this time more of a sorrowful sigh.

Halfway down the western side of the Sierras the pine trees had thinned out sparsely, replaced with spreading oaks. There were no pine needles here, no scent of a Tahoe forest. The day would move to an umbrella of summer heat spreading over open slopes burning the life out of any living organism in the ground not shaded by an oasis of oak. But for the creek that ran downhill near the cabin, she and her injured patient might look like the blanched stones.

Beth felt sick to her stomach. It was now five months since she'd left Will and Carson City. The doctor had said it would take about five to six months for Sutton's injury to heal. The doctor was right. She was making breakfast just as she had day after day. Sutton appeared to be getting better, but the recovery was slow.

Small increments seemed to occur but being with someone day after day made those changes almost imperceptible. If a friend or relative had come by periodically to visit or check in, not that there were any here, they might have seen the improvement as moving along in greater strides. But to Beth, it seemed like the recovery was taking forever. They had been here at Patten's ranch after the wagon ride over the Sierra passes. Sutton could now stand and move with his crutch, but he barely got out of their small cabin.

"Here's breakfast, Drake. Come sit down and eat."

Sutton limped over, holding the crutch under one arm and half sliding while mostly dragging his right leg. The pain seemed to be getting less and less, but his mobility was still very limited.

"Where's your plate?"

Beth looked up. "I don't feel much like eating. I think I am going to go outside."

And she *didn't* feel like eating. She didn't know why, but the smell of food just didn't make her hungry. Drawing a breath seemed to be more and more difficult, especially when she cooked. She struggled just to make the meals for Sutton.

Sutton finished the meager breakfast and stood to follow her outside.

"I'm going to kill Will Toal."

The tone was sinister. The demeanor was lethally sincere.

Sutton now stood in the doorway to the Patten Ranch house with his crutch under his arm and most, if not all, of his weight on his left foot. He tried to take a step without the support of the crutch but, while the right leg could now hold his weight, it still caused a stab of pain running from his hip up into his flank. He took another. Same result.

"He's going to pay for this."

Beth sensed Sutton to be talking to himself, but he knew she was well within hearing distance just outside. She stood still, a statue looking off to the west. She spent a great deal of time outside now. The smell of the cabin made her ill. Beth was more comfortable grasping for air outdoors. She turned to Drake and shook her head. Not wanting to aggravate what had become a recurring theme, she decided to try to change the topic.

"The air here doesn't smell like pine trees. Our ranch always had the smell of pine trees. It got to be comforting. You sort of knew you were home, in the right place, when you could smell the pine trees."

Sutton acted as if he didn't even hear her.

"As soon as I can ride, I am heading back there to get Toal."

"Drake stop it. We have much better things to do. We have places to see. You are getting more and more mobile. We should be talking about what we are going to see in San Francisco. We are here in Fiddletown. Went I went into the settlement last week to get more supplies, I asked the manager of the general store how far we are from Sacramento. He said we are only forty-five miles away. Forty-five miles to a city I have never seen. That's where I want to go, not backward. Leave Toal and Carson City behind."

"I can't leave it behind. Every step I take reminds me I need to go back and make him pay."

"Our plan was to head west."

Just then, Beth felt a queasiness in her stomach. The feelings had become frequent lately. She stood up and hurried off behind the cabin into a group of small trees Drake called madrone or mountain mesquite. She got sick to her stomach. This too had been happening with irritating regularity.

When she returned, Drake stood in the same position he had been in when she left. He had a casual, almost offhanded air.

"You're pregnant, and you don't even know it."

Beth was stunned. She'd never been around a pregnant woman. First Wife had never conceived. Yet with Sutton's blunt statement, her recent denials now evaporated. With a tinge of fear, she looked up at Sutton.

Sutton then posed a simple question, "Who's the father?"

Chapter Thirty-Eight

Dale Paris waited again in the telegraph office in Carson City. He had been doing his best to come up with a solution to the right of way problem for several months. Beginning to like Carson City more and more, he needed to finish the job he'd signed on to complete. Dale knew he had to satisfy Crocker's demands. But nothing had presented itself. However, he'd just heard the government intended to close Fort Churchill.

Beef prices in the Carson Valley would plummet. It gave him an idea. The snow sheds east of the Donner Tunnel would be finished by November. It was now late August. He didn't have much time until the railroad would absolutely need access to the ground through the Purcell Ranch for the right of way. If he could not deliver, then there would be another delay which would allow the Union Pacific to make more progress moving from east to west. He knew what Crocker would say about that, and it wouldn't be pretty.

Paris had already informed Crocker about the news from Fallar in the land office that Will Toal and the Millard Luce Cattle Co. now appeared on the title to the Purcell Ranch. The news of a title change into the hands of a young cattle rancher whose market for beef had just dried up led to an idea. Crocker's response should come any minute.

Paris heard the familiar tat, tat, tat of the telegraph indicating a message coming through. When the sound stopped, the operator tore off the piece of paper and handed it to Paris.

Millard Luce Cattle Co. is a large business. Stop. That could be a problem. Stop. Meet me in Placerville office in 10 days. Crocker. Well, at least he was going to get a chance to talk about the idea in person. Good sign.

Chapter Thirty-Nine

1868 Late Summer
Sacramento, California

Beth stood in downtown Sacramento. Drake would not come with her. His leg was not yet ready to ride a horse, and he had no desire to make the trip in the back of a wagon. So, Beth rode her horse west for two days down through the foothills of the Sierras to finally get her first look at a big city. Along the way, she reached a different impression of the sunbaked grasses covering the western slope of the range. As the sharp jagged mountains leveled, the smoother rolling hills were covered by a golden carpet of toasted grass everywhere she could see. The lack of seasonal rain created a glistening hue in a fading light. The oaks dotted the rounded dried out glades. September had now arrived. Despite the onset of fall, the sun scorched any exposed skin on her trip down the hill. The heat regularly caused shimmers in her line of vision over so much open space. It had been good-looking land for a ranch or farm, except water seemed scarce.

Entering the center of town, Beth still wore her riding outfit of trousers, hat, and gun belt. She had not put a dress on for a long time now. But in this town, she felt her riding outfit appropriate. She relished her look, a strange mix of male and female. These were heady times in Sacramento. There were men and women of all walks striding around the central portion of the city. There were boatmen, businessmen, women in dresses, and women in houses of questionable repute. It seemed the thrill of seeing a gold nugget in a pan or a strain of silver ore in a cave rock could attract people from any corner of the planet. They were all here. There were miners from south of the city who panned for gold. There were lumberjacks hired to fell trees and make railroad ties. There were storekeepers, hucksters, stragglers and drunks. There were plenty of drunks all of whom seemed lost in life. Beth rode by the dock, abutting the river. Men walked off carrying sacks of belongings. Most had the look of anticipation of things to come mixed with an apprehension of the unknown. The men seemed to arrive by the hundreds every other day, almost all looking for jobs on the railroad. But the railroad had been losing most of their new employees brought in to lay rails as soon as they were hired. Once they could, the prospective new hires headed up over Donner Pass to mine for silver. In fact, the proprietor of her hotel told her that he'd heard almost two thirds of the two thousand men Crocker had recently hired and transported with room and board from the East had arrived and, within days, breached their agreement to work for the railroad and headed up the hill to Virginia City to seek their fortunes in silver.

It had taken Beth two days to ride around and see the city. She stayed in what she thought was a rundown hotel off the main streets, only to be shocked when she learned the price of a room in Sacramento to be two to three times what someone would pay for the best hotel in Carson City. There were large buildings and impressive houses. But she quickly found a completely different world when she moved out of the central part of the city. Open air markets with all manner of beast or plant could be found hanging from racks for sale. There were rows and rows of buildings in which you could buy almost anything. But there were many more shanties and boarded up buildings of what must have been failed businesses. She even rode past a small wooden building with a large sign overhead indicating the home office of the Central Pacific Railroad. She thought it would have been one of the biggest buildings in Sacramento. But it wasn't impressive at all.

She made it to the river wharves, finding them to be covered with constant activity. Steamers came up the river from San Francisco, almost one each hour. Frantic activity would then occur while dozens of men and wooden cranes would offload the shipment. Men and animals sweated in the oppressive heat.

Most of all, the city was dirty. There were the people who just wandered. They looked lost without any place to be or job to work. With so much hiring, it was strange to see people who did not seem inclined to find work. Beth wondered if all big cities were the same. She overheard comments from the Eastern workers, most of whom said Sacramento looked like every other city they had been to, just a matter of how big.

Beth carefully avoided conversations. She just wanted to see what the city looked like. In the end, she was deeply disappointed. Without anyone to provide access by way of experience, she could only observe from a distance. She didn't like what she saw. Instead, Beth headed back up the hill to Patten Ranch, sorely disillusioned.

Riding had become more and more uncomfortable. Her stomach protruded to the point she barely fit into her saddle. The disappointment seemed to make the discomfort of her stomach even more distressing. The inches of excess leather on her gun belt were now almost gone. She purchased a dress anticipating the day when her trousers would no longer fit. The ride up the hill was going to be much harder and feel a lot longer. On her way down to Sacramento, she had been full of anticipation. She could barely contain her excitement of going to a big city. Now she was headed back up and filled with doubt as to what she should do. Her head had been bursting with hope of travels. Now those destinations had lost some luster. Her stomach told her she had better rethink her dreams.

Chapter Forty

1868 Late Summer
Carson Valley, Nevada

Will Toal sat in the main room of the Johnson Ranch house. The Johnson Ranch was one of the finest in the middle of the Valley. In the room were ten men. They represented every rancher of significance in the Carson Valley. None were happy. Martin Johnson spoke first.

"Men. Will Toal just returned from running a small herd of horses up to Fort Churchill. We all know and have done business with Captain Stewart. We know him to be an upstanding man of his word. He has dealt with all of us fairly over the years."

There were murmurs of agreement. Johnson continued.

"We all have come to know Will Toal. I will say that I have found that he, too, is a man of his word. He has come back from that trip to Churchill with news, bad news. That is why we called you all here tonight.

"Captain Stewart told Will that Fort Churchill is closing. The army has decommissioned it. The war in the East is over, and they do not need as many soldiers or forts around the country. The government is cutting back on what they are going to pay for."

There was general shock. Some looked at the man sitting directly next to them as if to ask if they had heard the words correctly. From the back of the group came a question.

"You mean the fort is shut down?" The comment came from Asa Wilson. He had one of the smaller spreads at the north end of the Carson Valley.

Johnson shook his head. "Yes, Asa, closed means shut down. I am speakin' English, am I not?"

The room collectively exhaled in a misplaced point of humor as each person present felt nothing like laughing.

"Will, you want to add anything?"

Will stood up. He looked around the room and saw men with far more ranching experience than himself. He saw men with wives and families. He saw men who depended on the sale of their beef, their source of livelihood.

"Gentlemen, every man in this room has been ranching far longer than me. You have all seen beef sales go up and down. But without the steady purchases from Fort Churchill, each one of us stands to be in deep trouble. Sales in Carson City cannot support us all. Sales in Virginia City might."

"They say there is going to be a bonanza in silver. Virginia City is going to be bigger by far than Carson City." It was Joe Schmidt who spoke.

Heinrich Dangberg took up the response. In his thick German accent, he said, "You might be right, Joe, but growth in Virginia City is going to take time. Can we all wait? Are we going to risk our futures on something we don't even know will happen? How many times have we heard some old mule driver with a long beard claim that he has struck the mother lode only to go bust the next month?"

Heads nodded, acknowledging the truth in what Dangberg said. Heinrich Dangberg had been ranching in the Valley longer than any of them. He had been the first to ranch in the Carson Valley. His voice carried more weight than any of the owners.

Dangberg continued. "Will has spoken to both myself and Martin Johnson. He has an idea; I think we should all think about it."

Heads now turned to Will.

"My idea is to collect the beef between all our ranches and plan the sales equally out of each herd to Carson City and then Virginia City. But the bulk of our herds are going to have to be driven down to Sacramento for sale to brokers who will buy for San Francisco."

"That's a long drive with risks," said Schmidt.

"That's true," said Will. "But if we don't collect together, it will be every man for himself. What will happen if we all compete for a price? The price will continue to drop because, here in the Valley, there will be too much beef. We'll all go broke."

"There is some truth in that," said Jed King. King had one of the larger ranches. "Same thing happened in 1857. We all had a great year with new yearlings, and there was too much beef. Don't you remember how we all tried to sell, and the buyers kept driving down the price? We all lost money that year, yet it was one of the best for our herds."

Again, heads nodded.

Will sensed the time had come to drive the point home.

"I have entered into a deal on the Purcell Ranch with Henry Millard of the Millard Luce Cattle Co. The beef from that ranch will be going to Sacramento and the brokers I told you about. I think if we were to make the right approach, we could use his company structure to sell all the beef in the Valley through his brokers for distribution into San Francisco. San Francisco is the unlimited market."

"I hear Millard is a snake. He is out to buy every ranch from here to Oregon. Hell, he's already bought half of them. If we start in business with him, we are letting the snake feast on the eggs." These words came from Jed King again.

Will shrugged.

"I found the man to be fair and straightforward. If you cross him, he will take any and all steps to see what he believes as right wins. But he told me about all the things he has done to improve ranching and towns south in California. He said he would be willing to do the same here. But the best reason to consider this is we really have no other choice. I don't have the money to pay my mortgage this month. This is the first month I have ever missed. I don't like the feeling, and I can't see any other way around the problem but to collect our beef and find a market. Mr. Dangberg and Mr. Johnson say they are in the same position."

Silence.

It was Heinrich Dangberg who broke the uncomfortable quiet.

"This is a big step. We should each go home, talk to our wives and families, and think it over. Let's be back here at Martin's house in two weeks to see if we can come to an agreement."

By the movement of heads and offhanded grunts, the group agreed with Dangberg's suggestion.

"Then back here in two weeks," said Martin Johnson. "I'll have Sue bake some pies."

Chapter Forty-One

1868 Late Summer
Placerville, California

Charles Crocker sat across a simple wooden table from Dale Paris. The summer heat swelled within the closed confines, grabbing clothing so close it became a second skin. The collar on both men's shirts showed a wetness where it met the neck. Though they wore jackets, their underarms would show the same moisture had it been visible. The heat, the sweat, the unwanted travel to get here all worked to fuel the tension of the meeting.

They were in Placerville, a location halfway between Sacramento and the Donner Summit. It was their second such visit in the same place. The last visit ended with Crocker telling Paris he had better come up with some idea on the Purcell Ranch problem, or he would find someone who could. Paris knew the current state of affairs was not going to be well received. No one else was in the room.

"Paris, this is beyond disappointing. Up to now, you have been the most reliable agent on the railroad staff. We need to get that right of way. The snow sheds will be completely finished soon. It's almost October. We do not have the luxury of time, not that we ever did. We need a solution, and we need it now."

Paris unconsciously shifted in his seat. Though normally in command of his nerves, his nerves were strangely out of control, undoubtedly due to the reputation and persona of the man on the other side of the desk. It could also be due to the fact this might be his last day of employment in a very lucrative job.

"Mr. Crocker, I have been poring over this for weeks. When we last met, I had simply run out of options up in Carson City…"

Crocker interrupted. "I know where we ended the last conversation. I don't need to hear about what has passed. I need to hear where we are going."

The comments were uttered in a cold, hard, yet quiet tone as if a storm brewed, about to unleash its fury. Charles Crocker weighed over two hundred and fifty pounds. That could be a lot of fury if the storm erupted.

"I have an idea, but it involves money."

"Mr. Paris, if you haven't already noticed, everything we do on this railroad involves money," came Crocker's condescending response. "However, if it can solve our problem, we can find the money."

Paris continued, doing his best to get his idea out in the open before there were any other comments.

"Will Toal has a mortgage on his Carson Valley property. Fort Churchill has now closed. Toal's source of revenue is dead. More importantly, Toal is in default on his loan. He missed his last payment. My contact in the title office tells me that Toal's loan is secured by a deed of trust against his ranch in favor of the Bank of California."

Paris could tell by Crocker's body language he now had the man's attention and had it in a good way.

"My proposal is to buy the secured interest and foreclose. I think, since he is also now a part owner of the Purcell Ranch, we can assert the same debt against any property where he is on title. If true, then we can foreclose on the Purcell Ranch at the same time. By the way, the other ranchers in the Carson Valley are in the same position. The Martins and Dangbergs and the rest are all in default on their loans."

Paris had almost rushed to get the words and concept out. He wanted to beat the coming outburst. He held his breath, awaiting the response.

"Interesting."

Crocker looked out the window and then back to Paris.

"How much are we talking in terms of buying the trust deeds?" Crocker asked.

Paris checked the notes he'd gathered from reading the recorded deeds in Fallar's office. "Will Toal has a mortgage of five thousand dollars. The Martins and Dangbergs are each double that amount."

Crocker mused. CPRR had done its share of wheeling and dealing for credit. Huntington had spent half of 1863 drumming up loans and credit on the East Coast, which provided the capital for the first shipments of rails and locomotives. Crocker was very familiar with deeds of trust and personal guarantees.

"We might be able to work with this. Banks sell deeds of trust all the time. We can probably buy the notes for two thirds of the face value of the loan. If we buy up all three of the loans in default that you've mentioned and foreclose on them, we could resell the properties after the railroad goes in. We can probably quadruple the current market value. The proceeds could help pay for some of the extra charges we have incurred with the snow sheds." Crocker voiced the words out loud, but it appeared to Paris as if he was talking to himself.

Paris exhaled. He might be off the hook. Crocker looked truly interested.

Crocker turned to Paris again.

"Okay, I have to clear this with Huntington, but at these numbers, I think I can pay for the mortgages out of my current budget. Which bank holds the mortgages?"

"The Bank of California holds all three," said Paris.

"Good. Duane Bliss is the person to talk to there. I will bet he has the authority to sell these mortgages."

Crocker pulled out a piece of printed paper. At the top was the logo of CPRR.

"This is a note to Mr. Bliss. Make sure he knows it comes directly from me. He has met with us on behalf of a small railroad some investors from Virginia City want to build. They want to connect Virginia City to the railway we are building so they can establish shipping lines to San Francisco. Tell him if he wants our support for the connection, he'd better assist us here with this current problem. He will accept our representation that he can draw the funds for the purchase from our banks in Sacramento."

Paris now thought he might just survive the meeting.

"Paris, you have authority of fifteen thousand dollars to purchase all three of the mortgages on the ranches we discussed. If there are any others in the Carson Valley with the same prospects now that the beef market has evaporated, wire me, and we can think about purchasing all of them. The Carson Valley is not part of the U.S. government land disbursement program under the Pacific Railroad Act. But if we can buy these acres at a reduced rate, then we can sell those ranches through the same land agents who are selling the land the government gives us. We have the structure in place to treat them just the same as the government grants. Profits from resale of the ranches can help replenish our capital reserves as we head east into the desert."

"I will leave immediately. I'll be in contact by telegraph in Carson City."

Paris stood and walked to the door. He grabbed the knob and was turning it to pull the door open when Crocker stopped him in his tracks.

"Paris, make this happen."

Dale Paris knew he had one last chance, this one, and there would be no others.

Chapter Forty-Two

1868 Early Fall
Patten Ranch, California

His horse grazed in a large paddock, not a far walk but only if you had two fully functioning legs. Drake Sutton only had one fully functioning leg. Sutton stood outside the small cabin at the Patten Ranch. He watched his horse, wondering what kind of reaction Beth would have upon her return. In fact, he had thought about the possibilities Beth would not return at all.

His leg was healing. He could walk now without using the crutch. But he had to half-swing his right leg from the hip in order to take a step. He could not power normal leg movement with normal muscles. He had tried to mount his horse, but he had to catch it first. He couldn't run after the animal. Bribery was his only option.

So far, his horse had responded well to offered carrots. Lifting into the saddle presented other challenges. His left leg was fine. Holding himself up by the horn and putting his left leg in a stirrup was manageable. But after lifting up, swinging his right leg over the back of the cantle caused new sharp pains deep in his right hip different from those experienced right after the wound. The more he bent the joint, the more pain it caused. However, if he could get up into the saddle, he thought that if he had to, he could ride.

Sutton thought of trying to make another run at catching his horse and practicing lifting into his saddle when he saw a rider approaching from the west. It took only a few more seconds for him to realize it was Beth. He watched as she walked her horse the entire way up to the house. She dismounted awkwardly, leaning away from the saddle farther than normal. She touched down extra gently.

"Stomach now really getting in the way is it?" Sutton said.

Beth looked at him with a hint of despair. Her protruding belly must be becoming even more noticeable. The ride home had taken almost six days because she had to walk her horse the entire way. She found trotting caused discomfort around her mid-section. It was the beginning of October, about seven months after her evening by the river with Will. Her energy had diminished. Her motivation had diminished. Her general outlook on life had diminished. She did not like the fact that Sutton could so readily see her difficulty in dismounting.

"Is it so obvious?" came her reply.

"It is to me," said Sutton. "How long do you think it will be before you give birth?"

"I have no idea," Beth said. "I have never had a child. I have no idea how this will work."

"Well, so you know, I will not be here when it happens."

"What do you mean you will not be here?" Beth blurted.

"Just what I said. Did you think I was going to stay here and be a nursemaid?"

"You were going to take me to San Francisco!" The words came out as a shriek.

"How do you think I am going to take a pregnant woman down the hill all the way to San Francisco? There is no way I would even think of doing that in your present condition."

"After I hauled you all the way from Carson, nursed you when you couldn't even walk? I cooked and provided all the while. You would just, what, leave?"

"That is precisely what I intend to do. Tomorrow." Sutton had not really planned to leave this early, but the conversation had headed in this direction on a path of its own.

Beth looked at him in utter disbelief.

"You are going tomorrow?"

"That's what I said, I'll be gone tomorrow. I'll leave you the wagon. I would recommend you consider using it should you insist on heading off to San Francisco. I will take my horse, and that's all."

The heat of her anger surprised Beth. Her body tensed, muscles in her legs locked. In such a state, Beth thought she would have problems formulating coherent sentences. But the opposite happened. She had no problem firing off words of rancor. She didn't have time to stop and think whether this was because of her pregnancy or the impending abandonment. But she was close to reaching for her gun.

Drake must have read her mind as he stood straighter and had his hand over his own holster. Beth had not realized he wore his holster, but she noticed now. Sutton's recovery had obviously progressed during her absence.

"Don't even think about it," said Sutton. "You draw, and I will kill you."

Beth stood her ground but did not move a muscle.

"You know you cannot outdraw me. Don't force me to do it. I could just kill you here and now if I wanted. I will let you live because of what you did after I got shot. But don't push your luck."

Beth hung frozen in space from a combination of both anger and fear. She knew Sutton could easily outdraw her. She had no advantage.

"Why don't you just go right now?" said Beth. Her words were spoken more out of anger than rational decision.

"Maybe I should. Seein' as how you might try your best to shoot me in my sleep, I probably should take my leave sooner rather than later."

The small satisfaction Beth took from his agreement to leave came balanced by the fact that she was now going to be alone, really alone.

Sutton, without taking his eyes off Beth, then suggested, "Why don't we take a step back and both unhook our gun belts. I will get my things, get mounted, and leave. We can then strap them back on and say good-bye."

"Any way you want to do this is fine with me. I just don't ever want to lay eyes on you again."

Sutton then walked to a tree stump in front of the house. He waived Beth forward to do the same thing. He reached down to his leg strap and untied it. He waited to undo his buckle until he saw Beth do the same thing.

Beth approached but was more than just tentative. She had no reason to trust this man now if she ever did.

"How do I know you don't have another gun in the house and, while these two are sitting here on the stump, you just go grab your second?"

Sutton chuckled, "You don't. But you were the one who packed me all the way from Carson City. Did you see a second gun?"

"I suppose I didn't," replied Beth.

"Look, I told you I would leave you, and I will. I have no desire to kill you. I am heading back up over the summit."

Then it dawned on Beth what Sutton's real intentions were.

"You are going back to kill Will Toal."

Sutton grinned. "The thought had crossed my mind."

Beth wanted Sutton gone. She wanted to be relieved of any further fear. She knew Sutton was serious about his anger with Will. She had seen Sutton at his worst. She could tell from the deep throated answer he had given her he would follow through on his threat to kill Will. In that one moment, she knew what she had to do next. She had to warn Will. Though unintentional, she had been the cause for Sutton coming into

Will's life. She couldn't let Sutton be the cause of his death. It would almost be like she had caused it herself.

Ten minutes later, Sutton emerged from the cabin. He had a small bag. He dropped the bag near the stump with the guns and walked over to the large corral holding his horse. He held out a carrot, and the animal trotted over. Sutton put on a saddle and bridle. He turned to Beth.

"Now is your chance. If you were going to shoot me, you are standing right next to both your gun and mine." A malicious grin lifted the side of his mouth. More a look of scorn and belittlement than a challenge.

Beth considered going for her gun. She had seen the future and could stop it here. But she couldn't force herself to do it.

Sutton walked over to the stump, holding the reins of his horse.

"I knew you couldn't do it," he said.

"Desmond might disagree with you."

"But I am different than Desmond. Better you didn't try for it. I have a feeling you will run to your little rancher friend to tell him to watch out for me. Who knows, you might even tell him he's a daddy."

Beth had kept a pretty good front on her face until now. Hearing Sutton's words, she crumbled inside. No matter how she tried not to show it, Sutton's words hit home. He saw it.

"Ah, I was right. You have a big soft spot for the rancher. Well, when you get there, tell him I'm comin'. That rancher interfered with me and you. He's the reason you would never have stayed with me. Not only did he take my leg, he took you. He will pay."

With that, he picked up his holster and strapped it on. He then moved back beside his saddle. He stumbled over to his left stirrup, hitched up his left leg and half stood, half pulled himself up. Beth could see how much pain the movement caused.

There was no goodbye. Sutton said nothing. Beth said nothing. Sutton rode off heading east just as he said he would.

Beth sat down on the stump. Her life continued to go opposite of anything she planned. Her destiny was disappointment. Maybe she had set those wheels in motion with her first decision to leave the Purcell Ranch. She had to get to Will.

*****

Beth had collected what few belongings she had and put them in the back of the wagon. She had no illusion about riding a horse back up over the Donner Crest. Her stomach felt like it was getting bigger and bigger each day. Riding a horse even at a walk required a flow and rock of the rider's hips. There was no way her hips could rock at this stage of her condition.

The trip would take just as long as the one she had taken with Sutton coming west. On that trip, she had to go slow to avoid bumps that caused *Sutton* pain. This time, she had to go slow to avoid bumps which would cause *her* pain.

She had to get back to Will and tell him Sutton was coming.

But to deliver the warning, she would have to talk to Will. At this point, she had no idea how she would even start such a conversation. She'd have plenty of time on the way back to think of something.

Chapter Forty-Three

Paris rode out to Toal Ranch. He found it hard to contain his satisfaction. It had taken almost a full month, but he had finally convinced Duane Bliss to sell the mortgages he sought. Not only was he able to buy the mortgage of Will Toal, but he also bought the mortgages on the Johnson's, Dangberg's, and other ranches, though it took some extra money from Crocker. When the foreclosures were completed, CPRR would own virtually all the decent land in the Carson Valley. He had to pay almost full value for the mortgages. Bliss sensed CPRR wanted them badly and held out for top dollar. The normal discount evaporated. But even at the price CPRR paid to buy the mortgages, once the railroad went through Reno, they could sell the land at four to five times what they had paid. More importantly, the railroad now had imminent pending access to the right of way. All he had to do was complete the foreclosure process. Crocker was pleased.

Completing the process began by giving the ranchers notice of the pending foreclosure. Legally, they were entitled to a chance to pay the full amount of the debt owed. As holders of the mortgages now in default, CPRR had the option to call the debt due in full. That is exactly what Paris intended to do. Both he and Crocker figured none of the ranchers had that amount of cash lying around, or they would not have taken out the loans in the first place. If they could not pay in the allotted thirty days after being notified, CPRR could take possession.

Paris had gone to S. Samuel Grande to have the appropriate paperwork drawn up, but he had refused. He said something about a conflict of interest. Paris had been forced to hire another lawyer in Carson City to draft up the necessary paperwork for each of the foreclosures. One good thing about working out of the town doubling as the Territorial Seat was there were plenty of lawyers in the immediate vicinity.

Paris had gotten an early start. The brisk cold of late October morning air normally would cause him discomfort but not today. Summer had passed. It had taken more time than he'd estimated to put this plan into action. But he'd finally lined things up.

The days might still be warm, but the nights and the mornings were definitely colder. Trees were beginning to turn colors. For land here in the West, the Carson Valley had trees passing through the change of colors during the fall months. Most land west of the great Utah desert was dry and arid. There were no trees which changed in the fall. But the Carson Valley had plenty of trees that went through the change, making it a beautiful time of year. For a man like Paris who came from the East, looking out across the Valley right now reminded him of his family's home in Illinois. This might even be a good place to buy land.

Maybe he could get land cheap from the railroad after they took possession. He would keep that in mind. But now, he rode to deliver the notices of foreclosure. He prepared himself for an angry reception at each location. Because of the anticipated reactions, he had insisted on doing this job himself. He wanted to see each of their faces when he delivered the news. He wanted to drive home the fact that their plight was hopeless.

The wind blew to the east. The cold air from around Lake Tahoe elevations was again streaming down the side of the Sierras and heading out toward the warmer air in the lower desert east of the Valley, driving the morning chill deep inside his suit. The wind had returned as it always did in the Valley. It would probably stay steady day after day until January.

As he rode south from Carson City, the dust from his horse blew to his left. At the rise and fall of each hoof, the dust that was kicked up was immediately blown off low and hard. At least he did not have to breathe any billowing clouds of dirt as might happen in the summer. Anyone who saw him approaching with his duster on and the powdery earth blowing sideways would have thought he looked like a specter. He felt like one. He felt he had power over people's lives. And he did.

Paris walked his horse into the central area of the Toal Ranch out in front of the main house. He kept scanning the field of vision 180 degrees in front of him. He did not dismount and had already flipped the leather safety off his revolver. Careful on his approach, he knew where the regular hands of the ranch were. None were behind him.

"Will Toal," Paris shouted. "I am here on court business to deliver a notice."

Will walked out from the front of his house.

"I thought I told you before; you are not welcome here."

"Yes, that you did. But I am here to serve you with papers. By order of the circuit court of the Territory of Nevada, you are being served with notices of foreclosure. Here are the papers. Read them."

Will squinted up at the man. He took the papers from Paris' left hand and noticed that his right hand hovered over his revolver. Will was unarmed, so he held no thought of gunplay. He grasped the papers without ever breaking eye contact with Paris.

"And what is it you think these papers say? Seein' as you took it up-on yourself to deliver them personally, I wager you know what's here," said Will.

"They tell you that your mortgage is in default. The debt is being called due and payable in full. You have thirty days to pay, or the owner of the loan can take possession of your ranch."

"Duane Bliss never said this was coming. I don't believe a word you are saying."

Paris smiled. "That's because Duane Bliss doesn't own the rights to your mortgage anymore. The Central Pacific Railroad does. Your loan has been purchased. And they are calling the note due as you are in default."

The news struck home hard. Will had counted on Duane Bliss working with him foregoing payments on the mortgage until he could arrange the cattle drive down to Sacramento. If the CPRR did own the mortgage, there would be no grace period if Paris had anything to do with it. That realization drove worry deep down into his gut.

"What would the railroad want with land so far from the tracks?" Will threw out the question, groping to come up with a way out of this. "The actual track is supposed to go through Lake Crossing, not the Carson Valley."

"Toal, your name is also on the title of the Purcell Ranch. As your creditor, CPRR can assert their rights for repayment as against any piece of property you own. We intend to pursue any unpaid amount as against your interest in the Purcell Ranch, too. The CPRR intends to have its right of way."

Now the intent and motive were clear. The railroad planned to take his property just to make sure they had the rights to lay track over the Purcell Ranch. The railroad had a public mandate: lay track all the way across America. Anyone, small or large, standing in their way had to move over.

Paris continued. "We have bought the mortgages on other ranches here in the Valley. I will be riding straight on to each delivering the same notices."

Paris paused to revel in the impact this news was obviously having on Toal. It was hard not to gloat.

"After the railroad goes through up to the North, these properties will be worth more than what we had to pay, and the profit will go toward funding further construction heading east."

Though unquestionably reeling from the news, Will tried to catch himself and steady his resolve. "You try to kick every man in this Valley off his ranch, and you will have a range war on your hands." Will's anger was only thinly veiled.

Paris returned with an equal amount of venom. "I have been authorized to hire as many men as necessary to take possession. If we have the rights to the property, I can assure you we will take possession."

Again, Paris paused for emphasis.

"However, you can make this easy. You can sell your property to the CPRR right now. Even though we are going to obtain the rights to it eventually anyway, the railroad would like to make this simple. I am prepared to offer you twenty-five cents per acre."

If not already incensed, the offer added a new level of anger in Will's current state of mind. He took the offer as an additional insult. He tried to work out the math in his head but knew he had paid four times that amount when he bought the ranch in the first place.

"That is not even close to what the ranch is worth, and you know it."

With an air of utter superiority, Paris replied, "You are right; it is not. But in thirty days, we stand to take your property without any further payment. The offer is very generous considering we have already paid to obtain the mortgages."

"Get off my ranch. If you think you can, then you can come and try to push me off," was all Will could find in himself to say.

"Be careful, Toal. You are going to lose. Don't get yourself killed in the process."

With that, Paris turned his horse and rode off.

Will's knees buckled. He had to grab for the side of his house to steady himself. The years of work. The risk of starting to raise a herd. First, Fort Churchill closes. Now this.

Will knew he didn't have the money. The railroad probably figured that, too. But he wasn't going to let them just walk in and take his ranch. He would fight. He was a Scot. He had to get to the other ranchers. They needed to talk.

Chapter Forty-Four

1868 Fall
Carson Valley, Nevada

The deafening noise in the Johnson house came from shouts, threats, and swearing. The meeting had no order. The men in the room were afraid. They were the same ten ranchers who had originally met to discuss driving their herds collectively to Sacramento. Now, their conversation was much more serious. Their families and homes were at risk. That risk generated a myriad of emotional responses.

Paris had delivered six notices to different ranches. Each of those stood to be taken in foreclosure. But the other four men in the room held out no illusion as to what would take place if the railroad did take control of the six ranches foreclosed upon. They would come after their property later, and they would be relentless.

"This is the same thing those railroad bastards did in Mussel Slough out in California." The speaker was Joe Schmidt.

Dangberg spoke up. "Joe, no sense in using that language. We need to keep our heads about us."

"Heinrich, I know I should watch what I say, but I'm mad. These men aim to take what's mine, what I have worked fifteen years to build. I have no intention of simply walking off my property."

Every man in the room nodded their agreement.

"Then what do you intend to do?" asked Dangberg. "Will told us Paris had the authority to hire men to help him kick us off our land. You know as well as I do, he's going to hire gun hands."

Joe Schmidt looked hard at Dangberg.

"Then we should hire gun hands, too," said Schmidt.

"That's a big step, Joe."

The words came from Asa Wilson.

"I know it sounds simple, but I intend to fight. If the other side plans on bringing more men to the fight, then we should, too. Paris cannot kick us off by himself. We are too many. But if he hires gun hands, then we need to do the same." Schmidt hoped to collect agreement amongst the rest. There was a pause. No one spoke. Then Will offered his thoughts.

"If this were a battle in the war, we would have advanced scouts. If we saw the approaching force, we would have snipers and other smaller forces try to pick at them as they made their way to the battlefield. We know these men will be coming from Carson City. We should have scouts on watch and think of a way to alert the rest of us. Then we should pick a place for the battle we want and guide them there. The place we select should be a spot where we have a lot of protection and they don't."

"Sounds like you spent time fighting in the war," said Martin Johnson.

Will hesitated but then responded truthfully.

"I did. I was a sniper for the South. That may not sit well with some of you, but I saw several engagements during Sherman's March to the Sea. I may have been on the losing side, but I saw how wars were fought. I saw good commanders, and I saw bad ones. If both sides have the same weapons, then the side who has the best plans and determination to succeed will win."

Joe Schmidt spoke.

"I don't care which side you fought for. You just offered us a very solid plan, and I think we should all agree to follow it."

"If Paris is hiring gun men, then we are going into battle. But who is going to be our army?" asked Wilson. "Are we going to hire gun hands, too? Are we going to sink to the level of Paris and his ilk?"

Schmidt was firm but collected in his response.

"If they hire guns, then we should, too. I intend to keep my ranch. If I can get my beef to market, I can pay my debt. I may be short of living expenses for a few years, but if I pay off my loans, I don't lose my ranch. If we must drive the steers to Sacramento in order to sell, then so be it. But I will say it again: I don't intend to walk away from everything I've worked for. If I must fight now to keep a hold until I can get the beef to market, then I will."

The men in this room had each created their ranches using their own hands, their own backs, and their own know-how. They respected and responded to a man like Joe Schmidt who was self-reliant.

Martin Johnson spoke next.

"I like Will's plan. I like Joe's spirit. I don't intend to walk away from my ranch, either. If forced to, then I will also fight. But I have one suggestion to make before we take the step of hiring gun hands ourselves."

"What's your suggestion?" said Jed King. As the owner of the largest spread in the Valley, he had listened but obviously looked for an option other than steps leading to a range war.

"Jed," said Martin, "my suggestion would be to try and set a meeting with Paris and the railroad to see if they will agree to hold off on trying to kick us off our property. Give us time to sell our beef. If the object is to collect money owed on the loans, then why would they not at least wait for us to get that money?"

Asa Wilson interjected. "That sounds real reasonable to me. We could ask, and they might say yes. If they said no, then we know what we have to do."

"And who is going to walk up and ask for this meeting to take place?" The speaker was Joe Schmidt again.

Will had an idea.

"I don't think any one of us should do that. I would suggest that, if we are going to seek a meeting, we have someone else do it. I have had S. Samuel Grande, the lawyer, review things for me. I suggest we have him do the asking."

No one objected. Will looked around the room and continued.

"I think we should make plans in case they refuse the meeting. It might just buy us a little time to get ready. But we should try and have friends in town let us know if and when they see men who look like gun hands begin to collect in the saloons and hotels. Once we hear Paris is collecting men, then we figure out a rotation for each of us to watch the north road into the Valley from Carson City. I will ride out and scout for spots where we want the fight to take place. We should not wait just on the hope they might meet with us."

Joe Schmidt now stood.

"I think we have an overall plan. I will agree to Martin's suggestion to ask for a meeting, but I also agree with Will's plan to get ready for a fight. Are we all agreed?"

Everyone's head nodded in agreement.

Dangberg spoke. "Will, why don't you talk to this lawyer and, on your way back from town, look for favorable spots for a gunfight. Martin and I will organize a rotation for scouting. Joe, why don't you get a count of both owners and ranch hands that can commit to a fight and then look for others we can hire."

Will looked around and said, "I think that all works. If they want to talk, we will talk. If they want to fight, then we will give them something they aren't counting on."

Chapter Forty-Five

1868 Fall
Carson City, Nevada

"Anyone in?"

Will had just entered the office of S. Samuel Grande, almost a regular event for him. He had never been in any lawyer's office until he came to the Carson Valley. Now it seemed he was here every other month.

"In the back."

Will recognized the lawyer's voice.

"I'll be out in a minute."

Will looked around and again marveled at the stacks and stacks of books. Books had been moved since his last visit. The stacks were different. But the volume of stacks still surrounded Grande's desk and filled the floor. There might have been movement, but the overall picture remained the same. Will wondered how this man could ever hope to read all this stuff. He must stay here day and night.

"Well, my young client, what can I do for you?"

"I am here to ask you to do something for the ranchers in the Valley."

"Lawyers are not usually accustomed to doing *favors*." The word *favors* had a sarcastic ring to it. "We are hired and paid a fee for our services."

"We are willing to pay. The ranchers and I want you to ask Dale Paris and the CPRR for a meeting."

"A meeting about what?"

"Fort Churchill is closing. They will no longer buy any beef from the ranchers in the Carson Valley. None of the ranchers have any cash to pay their mortgages. The CPRR found out about it and decided to buy up all our mortgages from the Bank of California."

Grande frowned.

"This has to do with getting their precious right of way, doesn't it?"

Will nodded, again amazed at how quick Grande could analyze the situation even without seeing all the cards in the deck.

"How did you figure that out so quick?" was all he said.

"The whole Purcell Ranch problem is well known and obvious. If the CPRR has purchased your mortgage, it is undoubtedly because your name is on the Purcell Ranch title now. The timing of their behavior from the recordation of your interest to this action is pretty transparent."

Grande lifted a finger to his cheek as if another thought had just struck.

"If they found out about the Fort closure, it would have been an easy ploy to check for defaults on the mortgages. Have you failed to make any of your payments to the bank?"

Will looked down at his feet. Grande could see the embarrassment, the feeling of failure.

"How many months?"

Will looked up. "Only one. I thought Duane Bliss would give me a little leeway while I drove my stock down to Sacramento to sell on the markets there."

"But do you have a guarantee anyone will buy?" said Grande.

"No, but there are brokers in Sacramento also buying for San Francisco, and that market is huge. Even Mr. Millard said so."

Grande sat again in thought. As he did, Will asked, "But why did they decide to buy up the mortgages of the rest of the ranchers?"

Grande mused, "The railroad is going in. Land will double or triple in value after it is finished. If they are going to buy up one, they might as well buy up all they can. The railroad construction is eating up lots of money, and they can use all the cash they can lay their hands on. You just fell into a trap which provides them with more capital in addition to solving their right of way problem."

"The ranchers want to ask the railroad to give us time to drive the combined herds to Sacramento. If we can sell, then we can pay off the mortgages. We just need time. If they refuse, then we are going to fight," said Will.

"Fight? That won't do much good. The railroad has resources. They can hire guns," said Grande.

"So can we," responded Will.

Grande shook his head.

"Gunplay will not solve the fundamental problem. People will just get hurt."

"The general fear among the owners is we could lose our ranches. I feel the same way. I don't like not being able to pay my debts. I have the beef, and I have the horses. I just need to get them to a place where people can buy them."

Grande looked directly at Will. For the first time, Will could see a look of puzzlement on Grande's face. The man always seemed to have answers, control of the conversation. He now looked less confident.

"So, what can I say to convince them to hold off? They want the right of way. The railroad probably doesn't want to have you pay off the loan. They want control."

Will answered, "That's why we need you. We couldn't think up something to say, and we were hoping you could."

Grande returned his gaze to Will.

"How long would it take you to collect up the herds and drive them to Sacramento?"

Will thought for a moment. "Probably take two weeks to round them up here in the Valley. That's what it's called: a round up, by the way, not collect."

For the first time in this conversation, Will let a small smile spread across his face and then continued.

"The drive to Sacramento would take another two weeks. We could probably make ten to twelve miles a day, and we are talking roughly one hundred miles from here."

"That would mean you want me to ask them to delay for one whole month? Could be a tall order. I can't imagine why they would wait, unless we sued them."

Will brightened. "Could we sue? Could we stop the foreclosures?"

"Probably not," said Grande. "But we could delay the process. Maybe up to four or five months depending on what the judge feels like on the day the hearing takes place."

"Do whatever you have to. We just want to meet and see if we can get them to give us some time."

Grande sighed. "I might be able to get them to meet but agreeing to the delay is going to be tough."

"Get the meeting," said Will, offering his hand in thanks.

"You'll get my bill."

"Always knew I would."

Grande now cracked his own wistful smile.

"I suppose I have to be successful here, otherwise you won't be able to pay me."

Chapter Forty-Six

The smoke was so thick you could barely see across the room. The smell of tobacco was everywhere. If the saloon's patrons were not smoking rolled cigarettes or cheroots, they were spitting chewing tobacco on the wooden floor. On top of the various tobacco smells, there was a pervasive aroma of beer mixed with other spirits. The overall combination spewed forth a musty, earthy scent. Dale Paris loved these kinds of places. He had been in many saloons from Chicago to San Francisco. Many were different, but almost all had the same scent.

Paris stood at the bar of the saloon in the Ormsby Hotel in downtown Carson City. William Ormsby might have been a poor commander leading those soldiers and volunteers while losing the battle of the First Paiute War, but he gave his life in the process, and the folks in town wanted to show their appreciation by naming a hotel after him. It was a good hotel, too. It had an even better saloon. The Ormsby attracted men from every walk of life, rich or poor, successful or busted. You found someone from each category here on a weekend night.

Paris tried to keep an eye on his new employees. He had hired three men in the last four days. Each could handle a gun. He had made sure by running them through some paces under his personal observation just outside of town. However, even though someone could handle a gun, one could never know how a man would react when under fire until you were in a confrontation and could see them respond. Paris had no history with these men other than an ex-soldier named McCormack. But so far, he felt good about their qualities.

To make sure he could get all six of the ranchers to move off their property, he probably needed two to three more such men. The ranches in the Carson Valley were small compared to those in Texas or Oklahoma. Ranches in Texas could have twenty to thirty hands working for the owner. Here, the most would be five or six hands working any one ranch. If Paris had a total of six good gun hands other than himself, he felt confident he could handle any situation with the ranches in default.

"I hear you are looking for men who are experienced either in law enforcement or from the war."

Paris turned to see a tall lanky man who must have been in the back of the saloon as he did not come through the front door. The man already stood only a couple of feet away, and Paris' first thought was to wonder how he got there without Paris noticing. The man wore grayish looking trousers and a long jacket of the same material. The outfit looked tailored. A gun was strapped to his right leg at a level providing a signal to those who knew what to look for.

"I am looking for a few *special* employees," said Paris.

"Well, I have never been in law enforcement, and I was in the war for only a short time, but I think I could be of assistance in whatever task you have before you."

Paris was not used to men speaking in flowery language, especially gun hands. Whatever the man's capabilities, he was obviously educated.

"Sounds to me that you have spent some time in school," said Paris.

"That I have, but I would wager education is not the most important capability you are looking for in your upcoming endeavors," said the man in gray.

"No. While I certainly need men who can use their heads, I am looking for men who can handle a gun."

In a voice oozing confidence and with a small hint of a smile, the man in gray looked directly at Paris. "I have exceptional qualities with a handgun."

Just then a miner on the other side of the gray suit shoved his shoulder into the gray suit's back. In a drunken, spittle laden voice, the miner said, "Ah, yore nothin' but a dandy, all gussied up in a purdy suit but probably turn tail and run scared o' yore wits if you'd been on a battlefield durin' the war."

The gray suited man turned immediately to face the offending miner, and Paris saw the flash of barely controlled anger and the ever so slight movement of his right hand toward his gun. In that instant, Paris knew this man was not one to be trifled with. But the anger disappeared, returning to some internal well within this man as quickly as it arose. With a sardonic smile, he addressed the miner.

"Well, good sir, it appears you have had quite a bit to drink. I will take that into consideration and excuse your lack of breeding and manners."

The miner was a well-muscled man of good size even if he was eight to ten inches shorter than the lanky gunman. Paris thought if there was going to be a bare-knuckled event, the miner would probably win.

But the man in the suit, in an overly dramatic calm voice, said, "Let me see if I can convince you that I can actually use the weapon strapped to my leg. I see you have a silver dollar sitting on the bar top. Flip it high in the air above your head. I'll draw and hit the coin without ever taking my eyes off you."

"Can't be done. How you goin' to hit the coin if yore lookin' at me?" laughed the miner.

"Let's just say that if I hit the coin, then you pay me two more just like it; if I miss, then I pay you two dollars."

"Sure, you ain't ever goin' to hit it, so I stand to make good money."

The saloon's din hushed. As the conversation moved through the talk of wager, more people in the immediate vicinity began to listen. At this point, no one was even moving. Everyone wanted to see if the man in the gray suit was just talk.

"Go ahead, toss the coin."

The miner slowly slid his hand across the top of the bar. He used two fingers to pick up the coin but held it just above its original resting place. The man in the gray suit stared directly into the miner's eyes without flinching. His right hand was hovering above his holster. The miner smiled a big smile, albeit one showing several missing teeth. The smile displayed a look of superiority. He obviously thought he would double his wages from the day. In a sudden jerk, the miner flipped the dollar in the air.

The speed with which the gray suited man drew his gun astonished Paris. The shooter's arm extended only slightly toward the flying coin. Without moving his head at all, the gun roared, and the bullet hit the coin. The shooter had never taken his eyes off the miner. The saloon erupted with shouts of amazement. Smoke billowed out toward the ceiling. Now, in addition to tobacco and beer, there was the pungent smell of gunpowder.

But then, just as fast as the original draw, the shooter pulled his gun back in front of him, cocked the hammer, and pointed the barrel right between the miner's eyes and pressed it into his forehead. The saloon became hushed almost as fast as it had erupted.

Holding the gun aimed at his opposition's head, there came a sneer of pure venom on the face of the man in the suit.

"And if you ever push me in the back again, I will put the next bullet through the middle of your oversized head, which will be a much easier shot than the one I just made. Am I understood?"

No one moved. Not the man in the suit, not the miner, not anyone. The entire bar could see the miner's discomfort. He was obviously both mad and embarrassed, but he did not say a word.

Paris broke the uncomfortable silence.

"I think you have made your point," he said to the shooter.

The man in the suit slowly eased the hammer back. He then slowly lowered the gun but still had it pointed at the miner. "Why don't you find another place to stand," he said.

The miner moved slowly away from the bar to a corner of the saloon near the front. Others also moved away from the bar.

Paris said, "Looks like you won't have to worry about a bump in the back again this evening. That was a fine piece of shooting. Could you see the coin?"

"Peripheral vision," came the reply. "If you are going to shoot guns at people, you have to have good peripheral vision."

"What's your name?" asked Paris.

"Jake. Jake Palmer," came the reply.

Paris said, "Mr. Palmer, I'd like to offer you a position with my group. Pay is $15 per day starting now."

"Not to appear ungrateful, but what is the nature of the work?" asked Palmer.

"We must evict several ranchers off the land soon to be owned by the railroad."

"What ranchers?"

"Dangberg, Johnson, and Toal to start. There will be others after that."

With another ever so slight grin, the man who called himself Palmer said, "I will accept your offer of employment. When do we start with the evictions?"

"In three more days after the judge signs the final eviction papers."

"I'll be ready. I am staying at a boarding house down the street run by a lady named Larson."

Paris nodded.

Palmer started walking to the front door. Paris saw a noticeable limp in his right leg. Paris thought he almost had to swing it forward from the hip.

Chapter Forty-Seven

Grande walked away from the Ormsby's lobby desk. He had left a note for a Mr. Dale Paris, a patron of the hotel. The letter asked for time today when the two could talk. He let the attendant know they could deliver the response to him at his office.

Later the same day, there was a knock at his office door.

"Come in."

"Mr. Paris, there was no need for you to come here. I told the attendant at the hotel that he could deliver the response here, and I would return to the hotel."

"I thought it was better if we had the conversation here in your office. Fewer chances of being overheard."

"Understood," said Grande. "I need to ask if you'd be interested in meeting with the ranchers you seem bound and determined to evict from their homes and livelihood."

"And why would I want to meet with them?" responded Paris.

Grande stood. He towered over the smaller Paris. Grande felt more comfortable making the most important point of his current meeting while standing, as he would in court when making a key argument.

"Well, the best answer is if you meet, then I will not file suit on behalf of the ranchers to block or delay your foreclosure procedure."

"There is no way to do that," blurted Paris.

"Actually, there is a way, and I have already drafted the lawsuit. If you care to take a look, I can provide you with a copy. It may or may not work, but in either event, the court will take time to consider it, and you will be delayed for almost thirty days just waiting for a ruling. If we are successful, it could take up to four months for a full trial."

Paris was taken aback. He had not anticipated this. He couldn't afford thirty more days, much less four months.

Grande saw his advantage and pressed his cause. He had heard about Paris hiring his hands around town and figured he would not be pleased at the prospect of having to pay them for months while they did nothing.

"So, meet with the ranchers. Hear what they have to say. There is a good chance you can come to an agreement, saving everyone a great deal of concern."

Paris was quiet. He could not go back to Crocker with another delay like thirty days and certainly not one of four months.

"Where do they want to meet?"

Grande turned to a map on his side wall. "I have arranged to use the park just outside of town to the south. I have asked the ranchers to bring their wives and families. I don't want this to be a pretense for some gun battle. I thought in bringing their families, then they would be more subdued and focus on talking. You should do the same."

"When?" came the simple response.

"In three days," said Grande.

"I'll agree," said Paris. "I am agreeing to talk, but that doesn't mean I will agree with what they have to say."

"Understood," said Grande. "At least talking is a start."

Paris left Grande's office. Grande immediately sat down to draft a letter addressed to Henry Millard. Millard Luce Cattle Co. needed to know of the mounting tensions which could involve their property, too, in case the meeting went badly.

Chapter Forty-Eight

1868 Fall
Toal Ranch, Nevada

Beth drove the wagon into the main compound of Will Toal's ranch on a late afternoon in early November. It had taken her three weeks to return from the Patten Ranch over Donner Pass back to the Carson Valley. She was tired, sore, and anxious. She had no idea how Will would react to her return . . . in her condition.

The day was cold even though the sun was at its highest in the sky. At this time of year, the weather in the Valley required a daytime jacket or warmer clothing. Beth wore only the dress she had purchased in Sacramento and the light jacket she'd used when she had originally left Carson City. A short jacket, it provided little warmth and certainly did not cover the protrusion of her abdomen.

She had spent many a night in the open air under blankets, shivering. This late in the afternoon, Beth would not have time to return to Carson City, and she desperately hoped that Will would at least allow her to spend one night in his barn under a roof. She would probably have to find a place to stay until the baby came if Will would not take her in.

She had been thinking of returning to Carson City or going to Genoa. Maybe Miss Larson still had rooms to rent. Thank goodness she still had money on deposit. Those funds would be more than sufficient to pay for costs of room and board over several years. But did she want to stay in Carson City? Right now, she had no idea what she should or would do.

Beth pulled up on the reins and was about to climb off the wagon when she saw Juan walking from the corral. He had a saddle in his hands and looked like he had been working a new horse and had just finished.

"*Señorita Beth*!" he exclaimed. "It is good to see you, no?" Juan had a big smile on his face. He dropped the saddle by the corral gate and hurried over to the wagon.

"*Señorita*, let me help you down from the wagon."

"Hello, Juan. It is good to see you, too." The comment came out with an overriding sound of relief at the welcome in Juan's voice. At least Juan had not been told to send her away should she ever return. Beth edged bit by bit, sliding sideways on the bench until she was at the side of the wagon. She had to turn around and carefully place her feet on sections of the wagon siding and wheel to negotiate the distance down from the seat on the bench. It was a slow process. Juan reached out to assist where he could.

"Ah, *Señorita*, are you with child?"

"Yes, Juan. I am with child."

"Mister Will, he will be interested you are with child?"

"Oh, I am sure he will be very interested. Right now, I cannot imagine what he is going to think. Is Will here?"

"No, but Mister Will, he should be here soon. He say he go into Carson City to talk to a lawyer but will return right away."

"Juan, do you think it would be okay if I were to have a seat on Will's front porch and wait for his return? I need to talk to him, but it is hard to stand right now."

María then came up, after hearing the conversation outside.

"*Señorita* Beth, I am *so* happy to see you." María had elongated the word *so* which added to the obvious welcome in her voice just as it had been in Juan's.

"Hello, María, it is good to be able to take a seat for a moment on something not bumping around. How have you been? How are things going here on the ranch?"

"Ah, *Señorita*," said Juan. "Things are not good. The fort up north has closed and will not buy our beef or horses. Many of the ranchers in the Valley cannot sell their steers. Mister Will, he not able to sell our beef. Money is hard right now. *Señor* Will, he is worried all of the time. He says we might have to fight for the ranch." Juan looked down. "Not good, *Señorita*, not good."

María looked at the immediate concern in Beth's face.

"I think he also misses you, *Señorita*, but he no wants anyone to know."

Beth's heart lifted at this news but, as she sat, she forced herself back to reality. The brace of the chair felt wonderful after days and days atop the wagon without much support for her lower back. Her legs were spread to the limit her dress would allow.

After getting situated, Beth looked up to Juan and María now standing in front of her. It dawned on her that they might not have any idea what actually happened. Will was such a tight-lipped man, maybe he had never told his crew what had taken place that day almost eight months ago ending in her hitting him over the head. Beth stopped to consider; yes, it was almost eight months since the shoot-out at the Reynolds camp. Eight months since her walk to the river with Will. She decided to be frank with these good people in front of her.

"I was not nice to Will," she said. "He will have every right to be mad at me and tell me to leave."

A sadness immediately came over María.

"No, *Señorita*, you must stay. *Señor* Will was very happy when you were here."

"It is so nice to hear you say that, María, but I was very bad to Will, very bad. He will probably ask me to leave. I just need to talk to him. I need to warn him he could be in danger. Then, if he wants me to leave, I will."

María was about to say something, but just then Will trotted into the compound on Powder. He pulled up looking at the wagon and then turned to see the trio of people out in front of the house. He dismounted and let Powder drink. He could see Juan and María talking to someone, but the person was obscured by María, who was standing in his line of sight. From what he could see, it looked like a woman in a dress, but he had only a limited view. After letting Powder take a few good gulps, he loosened the cinch and tied him off to the hitching rail in front of the barn. He started walking back to the house.

It was about halfway across the compound that María moved, turning to look back at him approaching. He could see who was sitting in his rocker. It was Beth. He stopped.

Her hair was no longer tucked up under a hat. She was not wearing the jeans, jacket, and holster rig as when he'd last seen her. She was in a dress. Her blonde hair was windblown and spread out around her face. But she looked almost the same as the days she had been wandering around the ranch before they left to the shoot-out.

His mind was moving quickly. *The shoot-out. She hit me in the head. Why? Why is she here? Never thought I would ever see her again. Do I want to see her?* While it was the same Beth, she looked different somehow. Her face was fuller. *She has been out in the sun. Where has she been all these months? What could she want with me now? What did she ever really want with me?*

He started to walk again. No words were spoken as he strode up to the porch. He could see that Beth was watching his every move. There was anticipation in her look. But there was also a softness, or was he imagining that, too?

"Why are you here?" Not particularly nice in his tone, Will surprised himself at his lack of welcome. He was confused. He had been angry at this woman for so long, he did not believe he could ever think of her in any other way. Seeing her on his porch evaporated some of the anger but not all of it.

"Will, there is so much I want to say to you. I know you probably don't want to listen or have me here. But I came back to warn you. After that, I would hope you might let me spend a night in your barn, but then I'll leave if you want me to."

Will was stern. "What's the warning?"

Beth sighed. *He is mad. He has every right to be. He was never going to want me to stay here. Might as well just tell him what I came to say and be on my way.*

"Drake Sutton is coming back to Carson City. He is mad. Mad at you. Your shot damaged his hip. He now walks with a bad limp, almost swinging his right leg from his waist. He blames you and says he wants you to pay. He also thinks you took me away from him."

Will listened to the first of her comments with stoic defiance. He'd not be easily shaken with threats. Will wouldn't run from anyone. But the last of her words left him incredulous.

"I took you away from him?" his voice raised up at least an octave. "How the hell does he think that happened? You slugged me in the head and left. How is he so twisted to think I took you away? That's just flat ridiculous."

Beth sighed. "I know it's ridiculous. But Will, he is a very dangerous man. I did not bring you to the camp that first day. But when I first saw you, I was desperate for help. I was in trouble, and you saved me from that. I feel responsible. I drew you into a bad situation. You were nothing but good to me. You don't deserve Drake Sutton. I probably should not have come, but I felt I owed it to you to at least warn you he is coming back."

Beth placed both of her hands on the rocker's arm rests and, with the extra effort required of women in her condition, pushed herself to a standing position.

"I'll leave. I'll head back to Carson City and try to get a room there."

As she stood, it became obvious to Will the reason for her extra effort. At first, he thought she was injured. But then he saw her full figure.

"You're pregnant."

Beth looked up. "Yes, I am pregnant."

Will was now seriously indignant. "And how does that play into Mr. Sutton's feeling about me *taking* you away from him? You leave with the man and get pregnant. Obviously, he is not logical, but I already figured he was twisted up."

Beth had now given up any hope of remaining, so she had no reason to hold anything back.

"The baby is yours, Will. I never had any relations with Drake Sutton. He was too injured before he left me, not that I ever thought of having any relations with him anyway."

Beth noticed the broad smile spreading across María's face. It was a look of joy.

"Do you really expect me to believe that?" asked Will.

"No, I suppose I don't. After what I did to you, I am not sure I would react any differently if I were in your shoes. But Will, I hadn't been with Josiah for months before the massacre, and there has been no one else. It has been about eight months since our walk to the river. The baby is yours."

María's face changed from a look of joy to one of concern. She could see the cloud in Will's face. But as Beth tried to move off toward her wagon, Will reached out and touched Beth's shoulder.

"You cannot leave now. It is too late for you to head back to Carson City in your condition. You can stay here for now."

Will's demeanor softened. There had been a clear lack of pretense when Beth spoke. He was not sure he could ever trust her again, but she did not look like she was making her story up. She looked tired. She looked almost helpless.

María, seeing there was going to be an issue as to sleeping arrangements, said, "*Señorita*, you can stay out in our rooms. We have a new bunkhouse. It is not being used. Juan and I will go to the bunkhouse."

Will shook his head.

"No, María, she goes into my room. Just like the old days. At least until I can figure out what we need to do. I will sleep in the bunkhouse."

There was a small tear that welled up in each corner of Beth's eyes. She said nothing, but María could see that her look conveyed everything she needed to know that Beth really did have true feelings for Will.

"*Señorita*, let me help you to get your things from the wagon, and then María will make us all some dinner."

Chapter Forty-Nine

1868 Fall
Carson City, Nevada

Dale Paris was looking at four men. They were seated in his hotel room at the Ormsby.

"Gentlemen, tomorrow we ride out to attend this *meeting* with the ranchers." There was a sarcastic inflection when he uttered the word *meeting*.

"I am told these people will be bringing women and children. I want to approach this as nothing more than an appeasement. I have no intention of agreeing to anything they propose. I don't care what they want to talk about or what they might suggest."

Paris could see that he had the attention of each man. A good sign.

"I want this group to act professionally but look menacing. I don't want any of you to say a thing. I will do all the talking. But I want these folks to see we have armed men, and we mean business. We intend to proceed with the foreclosures and evict them from their ranches. If they cannot pay off the loans, then that is the end of the discussion."

"Are these owners going to bring their ranch hands with guns?" The question came from Ansel McCormick. McCormick had worked with Paris before. A solid soldier who had fought for the Union during the war in cavalry operations, McCormick knew how to follow orders. He was also a rock under fire, having been in multiple battles.

"Ansel, a good question," said Paris. "I don't know. But it don't matter. Nothing is going to happen tomorrow other than wasted words. If they do show up with their hands, we can see what numbers we are up against and take a good look at them."

That comment got some nods around the room.

"Also," continued Paris, "I have arranged for U.S. Marshal Alonzo Poole to ride with us and attend the meeting. Marshal Poole will have the official eviction orders signed by the court. He will also give our group the clear look of an official body. So, are there any questions?"

"When do we start with the evictions?" This question came from Jake Palmer.

In the days since they met in the saloon, Paris had watched Palmer, finding him to be cool and quietly confident. Almost too quiet. But something else lurked beneath the surface of the man's demeanor, making Paris uneasy in the way he handled himself. Maybe he was just an unknown. But he seemed awful anxious to move ahead with the evictions.

"We will start the evictions the day after the meeting," said Paris.

"Who do we start with?" pressed Palmer.

"Not sure yet," said Paris. "Why?"

"Just thought we might start with the Toal Ranch. From what I hear from people in the saloon, Will Toal sounds to be the one collecting the other ranchers to put up the resistance. Maybe we should deal with him first."

"Maybe. It depends on which of the ranches the court issues notices on first and which one Marshal Poole serves," replied Paris.

Paris thought to himself that Palmer seemed far too interested in the Toal Ranch. He made a note. There had to be a reason. It was cause for Paris to keep a close watch on Palmer.

"So, are there any more questions?"

Hearing nothing further, Paris decided to break up the meeting.

"Be in the lobby downstairs here in the Ormsby tomorrow at ten o'clock sharp. We will ride out to the park together."

The men began to leave the room. Paris paid particular attention to Palmer. The man had a serious limp, he hoped would not hinder his ability to function. But he had seen Palmer handle a gun. He was exceptional there. You didn't need to run to fire a gun. Still, he bore watching.

Chapter Fifty

1868 Fall
Toal Ranch, Nevada

It had been two days since Beth's arrival. Will had spent lots of time away from the house. But whether riding out collecting horses or working around the corrals, his mind was thoroughly preoccupied with Beth and the news she brought. She claimed he was the father of her child. Right now, he relaxed in his rocker on his porch, looking out over his grazing land.

It was evening. The perpetual breezes were relatively calm. The air had a crisp fresh scent. Tomorrow would bring the meeting with Paris. Will used the rhythmical rock of the chair to try and clear his head and think of things which needed to be said and the arguments to be made at tomorrow's gathering. Success would be an agreement to delay any evictions. Success would be obtaining time to get the beef down to Sacramento.

Then, as had happened in frequent occurrences over the last couple of days, his mind wandered back to Beth.

How could this be? Was he a father? Could he ever trust Beth? Should he even think about trusting her? Should he take any responsibility for the child just on her word? How would that work? As the mother, Beth would have to be with the baby. But did that mean she had to live here at the ranch?

"Would you allow some company? It is a beautiful night and a good one to sit and view the horizon."

The words had come from Beth, who stood in the doorway. Along with Raúl, Juan, and María, the group had eaten dinner together as they had done for two days. But there were few words spoken at the dinner table. In fact, there had been few words between Beth and Will since she arrived. It was not that he had avoided her, but he just didn't have a good grip on anything he should say.

"It is a perfect evening," said Will. "Have a seat."

Beth sat on the bench just to the side of Will's rocker. They both gazed out over the range.

"I would like to tell you why I did what I did if you'll listen," said Beth.

She looked ever so slightly at Will, who kept rocking with his gaze fixed outward. He said nothing.

"I don't think I can ever properly explain. That's probably because there is no good explanation. But I would like to tell you why I did what I did and how I thought I was protecting you."

Again, Beth paused in the hopes that she would get some positive response, at least something to indicate she should continue. But Will was silent, unmoving. She waited. Still nothing other than an extended, uncomfortable silence. At last, she thought maybe this was his way of saying she should go ahead. At least he had not told her to stop.

"When these men first came to the house, I saw a way to get away from a marriage I had no hand in creating. It was awful, both for me as well as Josiah Purcell. He wanted a son. He didn't get one. First Wife tried to be nice in the beginning, but I was an intrusion into their life."

Will kept rocking in silence. Seeing as she had started down this path, Beth continued.

"I never thought I'd be staying with Drake Sutton. I had no feelings for him at all. I just thought he could get me away. That was all I wanted. Maybe I was foolish. I *was* foolish. I couldn't see running away with a grown man would lead him to think I intended to be with him. I was both naive and stupid."

Beth now looked at the ground in front of her, too embarrassed to look at Will, who was still rocking.

"I had no idea there would ever be any shooting. I had no intention of taking any deeds or the script until after it all blew up. And the fire. That was horrific."

Will was not looking at her, but he was acting almost like a priest hearing a confession. However, he had no intention of providing any absolution. At least, not now.

Hearing no indication to stop, Beth continued. "After all the killing, I couldn't stay. I admit I wanted to go all along. But at that point, I had no time to really think. I just reacted in the moment, thinking I could figure out later how I could get away from these men as soon as I could. I just wanted Drake to take me to San Francisco or someplace away from here. He said he would. He didn't."

Again, Beth paused. She had not moved. Her eyes were still fixed on a space of the porch about ten inches in front of her shoes. At this point, she couldn't imagine what Will was thinking, but she had to get the story out once and for all.

"What about the slug to the head?" His first comment. He didn't sound sympathetic.

"You were wonderful to me. Everything I told you the evening before we left for the camp was true. But I thought at some point, you would finally wonder about me as a woman you could marry. After what I'd done, I thought you deserved better."

Beth hoped he would at least respond to her words. But he didn't. More silence.

"I knew Drake and Desmond would not give up. After I took the script and the deed, I knew they would want them. Then Drake left. Reynolds was truly a monster. He did everything just as I told you before. I really thought he was going to kill me when you rode up."

Without turning his head or altering the steady, slow rocking back and forth, Will said, "I am still unsure why I got hit in the head."

"I knew if Drake Sutton showed up, I was going to have to leave with him so he would leave you alone. I just had a feeling he and Desmond were somehow waiting for me to get back to the camp. I thought I could get the script, and then I'd leave. That's why I left the letter with María. But then the shooting started. I knew Drake was fast, and I was amazed you beat him. But he wasn't dead. You were either going to have to kill him, or he would keep trying to kill you.

"You are not the kind of person who could just walk up and put a bullet in a wounded man. If Sutton lived, you would have a lifelong enemy. I had put you in this position. I thought it was up to me to get you out of it. I had to get Drake away. It may have been crazy, but in that flash of a moment, I thought if I hit you and took Drake away, you would be safe."

Beth raised her eyes and looked up at Will.

"There, you have the story. I make no excuses. I have done what I have done. I cannot change it. But Will, I hope that someday, you can come to at least not hate me. I just hope that you won't hate me."

Her voice quivered. She had hoped he would look at her, give her some indication of a reaction. She watched for any body language, any movement that would give a clue. But he gave up no sign.

"And Will, what I said is true. The baby is yours. It had been months since I had any relations with Josiah. And I swear to you, I never lay with Drake, ever. He couldn't even move until almost the day he left me. Not long after he figured I was really going to have a baby, he left. He wanted nothing to do with any babies or pregnant women."

Her voice had now lost any quiver. It had the resonance of firm conviction.

256

There was another extended silence. Will turned to look at Beth. He saw the face he remembered when she had stayed with him. He saw an innocence lost which had followed a misplaced trail. He turned back to looking out over the range.

"I will think on it."

He kept rocking slowly back and forth.

*****

The next day, Will rose early. He ate sparingly. Nerves. He had asked Juan to saddle Powder for him. He rarely asked anyone to do his tack. He liked to saddle his own horse. There was a kind of comfort knowing you strapped your saddle on as both you and your horse liked it. But Juan was good. Today, Will had other things on his mind.

Will stood up from the table. Beth and María were still seated.

"I'm riding out to meet the other ranchers. They are bringing their wives and families. S. Samuel Grande thought having family members might make the men keep their heads. He might be right. But then, he might be wrong, too."

Will had started out looking at María but now turned to Beth.

"Stay here. I am not sure how this day will go. In your condition, you should rest and avoid any travel if you can, anyway. All in all, it is better if you stay here."

Beth simply looked at him and said, "Be safe." There was an ardent concern in her voice.

She had hoped he would give her some reaction to their conversation last night. But he had not raised the topic. Beth felt it best to let him do his thinking and let him answer in his own time. That is, if he ever gave her any answers.

Will turned to go. "I'll be back before dark."

Chapter Fifty-One

1868 Fall
Carson City, Nevada

The park had a green grass floor covered by large spreading oaks. Will had never seen a stand of trees quite so amazing. The oaks were old and branches were knarled overhead throughout the space in between the ring of trunks. Some of the branches along the outer rim lowered to the ground and rose back up into the air. But underneath, there was a wide central expanse of open shaded space all covered by the tree branches.

However, whereas most oaks fill in the total space around the trunk, for some reason, this section had a ring of the largest oaks which had branches full of green on the outer rim, but the underneath central portion was not cluttered by branches or other trunks at all. In fact, the umbrella covering of branches rose to a sixty-foot ceiling as one would find in a large building or a church. There was something spiritual about it.

The locals even called it the Cowboy Cathedral.

Today, the Cathedral was full of people. Husbands, wives, and children were spread everywhere. People sat on the grass, chatting. Children were running all around as children do. The green umbrella protected the community beneath, shielding them from the sun and, to a great extent, blocking the wind.

"Why, Will Toal, I have not seen you in ages. What have you been doing with yourself?"

The question came from Katerina Schmidt, Joe Schmidt's wife. A joyful lady, she had a stout figure, as did many a woman who survived on a country homestead. She had undoubtedly helped her husband over the years with calving, bringing in hay, growing the family vegetables, and the like. *Country women are a solid bunch*, thought Will.

"Well, I have been busy trying to figure out how all of the ranches can get their beef sold."

"I do hear from Joe that you have come up with some fine ideas. Joe thinks highly of you, young man." This was a high compliment from a lady who, along with her husband, had built everything they had with their bare hands and simple tools. Folks like these were careful with their compliments.

"I appreciate the kind words, ma'am. Very nice of you to say so," Will replied, trying to remember his mother's instructions on how to respond in proper conversation. Conversation in general did not come easy for Will, and conversations with ladies were even more difficult. He always felt self-conscious. He did his best to make sure he did not say anything that would offend, but in the process, he never felt natural. His conversations seemed forced in a way.

"You can stop with the ma'am business. Everyone calls me Kat. You should, too."

"Yes, ma…" catching himself, he instead said "Kat." She chuckled at the fact he had to catch himself from repeating his earlier response.

"I am going to move over and talk to the men before the railroad people get here," said Will, anxious to some degree in ending a conversation with this nice lady.

"Yes, you run along and join the males over there and make sure you get your stories straight. We need those railroad people to give us some time."

"We are sure gonna try." Will then headed toward the group of ranchers.

"Gentlemen," Will started. "Are we ready?"

"Can't say we're ready," said Asa Wilson. "Ready means we have an agreement to hold off any evictions until we can drive the herds to Sacramento. We won't know how we are doing until the railroad men agree."

"I'm not expecting any agreements on the part of the railroad," said Joe Schmidt. "Those crooks have nothing on their minds but track and profit. We are obstacles, not neighbors."

Will looked at the group in a sweeping glance. "Men, we have to keep this meeting calm and collected. We must keep control of our emotions. You have your families here. This is not the time nor the place for gunplay. So, no matter what they say or do, let's just agree right now to walk away and talk about it, and then we can plan what we want to do later."

"Will's right," said Martin Johnson. "We keep a straight face, and we decide what to do later. We don't tell them what we have in mind today. Keep them guessing."

"Here they come," said Joe Schmidt.

There were essentially two large openings in the oak umbrella of the Cathedral. The ranchers were standing next to one, and about fifty to a hundred yards across the grass was the other. Six men walked through the opposite opening. There were two in front and four behind.

"Well, well," said Joe Schmidt. "Look at all the gun hands Paris has brought with him. If he doesn't want any gunplay, why has he brought those gun hawks with him? And he brought Marshal Poole. Wonder why he's here."

Will didn't say so, but he, too, could see that other men besides Paris and Poole had guns strapped low and very visible. Their jackets were tucked behind their weapons as if ready to use. The look was obviously to intimidate. But, with these independently minded ranchers, the visual presented would be taken as more of a challenge. *That could be a problem*, thought Will.

The railroad group strode to a point about thirty feet away from the ranchers. Paris and Marshal Poole stood side by side in front and the four gunmen stood behind. Paris spoke first.

"I understand from attorney Grande you want to talk. What is it you want to say?"

As the most respected and successful in the community, the ranchers had agreed Heinrich Dangberg would be the one to present their idea. Dangberg's reputation as a levelheaded, keen businessman was known throughout the Valley. If the railroad people were going to listen to anyone, it would be Dangberg.

"We understand the railroad has purchased the mortgages on several of our ranches. We have the beef to sell, which can be used to pay off those loans. But we need time to drive out cattle to new markets in Sacramento because Fort Churchill is closing." Dangberg was simple, direct, and to the point.

"How long will that take?" said Paris.

"Two months from today," replied Dangberg.

"We haven't got two months," said Paris. "The railroad is going through here in less than one month, one way or the other. You are in default. I personally delivered the notices of default to each of you, giving you thirty days to pay off the full amount of the loans or risk forfeit. No one has paid their loans. Time is up."

"You know damn good and well we don't have the cash until we sell the beef," interjected Joe Schmidt.

"You should have figured damn good and well to get your beef to market before the thirty days ran," retorted Paris. "Why should the railroad wait another two months to be paid what they are owed now?"

Martin Johnson suggested, "But if all you want is to get the money you are owed, why don't you give us the time to sell the beef so we can pay you?"

Paris turned his gaze to Johnson. "Because we can get more money for your property after we take possession and the railroad goes through. We have the right to take possession, and we intend to do that as soon as it's legal. Marshal Poole is here to formally deliver the notices to leave your property, now. Your lawyer Grande tried to delay things, but the court just ruled that the notices for eviction can be delivered."

Poole spoke. "Gentlemen, I am an officer of the court duly sworn to serve you with notices that the foreclosures have been ordered, and you must leave your homes immediately. That's the law." Poole extended his hand, holding several pieces of paper for full view.

"You never had any intention of negotiating with us, did you? You just wanted to get us all in one place so you could serve us with your useless little pieces of papers," sneered Joe Schmidt. "You just brought your gun hawks with you to make sure you could serve us all together."

Paris grinned. "You might be right. But it's *legal*."

At the mention of the word *legal*, as if on cue, the four men who had been standing behind the front two fanned out to either side of Paris and Poole. Two went to one side, and two went to the other. The railroad group now presented itself as a carefully separated single row strung out to the left and right of Paris.

"Gentlemen let's do this cool and calm. Please take the notices, and then head home." Marshal Poole sounded as if he still had hope of keeping a lid on the rising emotions. But the effort was lost in the obvious move to intimidate as the gun hands fanned out.

"Cool and calm, is that why the gun hawks are fanning out with their jackets tucked?" Again, it was Joe Schmidt.

One of the men who had been directly behind Dale Paris took some extra time walking out to his position to the end of the now single row of railroad men. He walked to a position directly across from Will. Will saw the pronounced limp. He saw that the man almost had to swing his leg from his waist. He did not recognize the clothes. He did not recognize the walk. But he did recognize the man's stance and silhouette.

Every man who faces another in a gunfight has his own particular stance in readiness to draw. Will had seen that same stance before. But earlier, the man had been wearing black. Will and this same man had faced off; he knew it. It was Drake Sutton. Right then, Will knew there was going to be trouble. He also knew he was going to be directly involved. Drake Sutton was here for a purpose. That purpose was Will.

"Who will come forward to take delivery of the notices to vacate?" asked Marshal Poole.

"Why don't you just drop them at your feet? None of us has any intention to take your notices." The challenge came from Joe Schmidt, obviously the man with the largest chip on his shoulder.

Joe Schmidt's hand moved closer to his holster. He readied to draw. But the rest of the ranchers had not. Other than Will and Joe, they were bunched in a tight group and not spread out as the railroad men were. They were almost a bunched target. None of them had unhooked the safeties on their holsters. Most had simple handguns without any leg straps tying the holsters down. At that moment, it dawned on Will none of the ranchers present were experienced in any serious gunplay. In short, they were outgunned and outmanned. The odds didn't look good.

"If you are so brave, then why don't you just go for your gun?" The comment came from the man with the limp. The voice confirmed it. This man had the same low baritone. He had the same sinister confidence. On hearing the voice, any lingering doubt was erased. The man in gray was Drake Sutton.

"Shut up, Palmer," said Paris. "You've no place but to back the Marshal."

The voices could now be heard throughout the Cathedral. The women began frantically collecting the young kids and heading for an exit. Movement behind the railroad men became frenetic, all aimed at getting out of the way of an escalating standoff. A few said hushed prayers the confrontation would not get out of hand.

"This is just like what you railroad men did at Mussel Slough." The comment came from Asa Wilson. His voice lifted an octave as he finished, revealing an increased level of anxiety. "You intend to just gun us all down with women and children present?"

"Your side is the one who appears to be intent on elevating this to a fight." Again, this came from the man Paris called Palmer who looked directly at Joe Schmidt in a clear challenge.

To Will, Palmer obviously pushed the proceedings, trying to bait the ranchers. But he appeared uncomfortable. Maybe he did not like the Cathedral's surroundings and wanted to generate chaos and leave.

"Jake Palmer, I told you to shut up!" This time, Paris outright yelled the comment.

Will grinned. "That is not Jake Palmer, Paris. Any doubt as to your intentions faded real quick when you brought this man here as support. You went out and hired a flat-out killer. That man is not Jake Palmer; his name is Drake Sutton. He's the man who killed Josiah Purcell and his wife, then burned them to ash. The only reason he's here is to do some more killing."

Paris looked down the line at Palmer. At the same moment, Joe Schmidt flinched his right hand above his holster. Under Paris' direct gaze, in a lightning movement, Sutton drew and shot Joe Schmidt, who stumbled backward. Sutton then immediately turned his gun toward Will. Will dove to his right, and Sutton's second shot barely missed. The

264

other gun hands standing next to Paris and Poole all drew and started firing at the ranchers. The ranchers were all slow and nowhere near ready for the fast-evolving action but were still going for their guns.

Martin Johnson got off some shots. Jed King did, too. Heinrich Dangberg was winged in the shoulder and hit the ground before he could clear leather, but after he was on the ground, he tried to start firing. Will hit one of the gun hawks, who went down immediately. Will rolled and came up to one knee, firing and looking for Sutton, but the spot where Sutton had stood was empty. He saw the man half running, half limping toward the opening at the other end of the Cathedral. He was shooting at the women and children running the other way. Will saw Kat Schmidt get hit and fall heavily.

Paris raised his hand, calling for a halt. "Stop! No one is here to shoot anyone!"

But no one heard.

Even Marshal Poole drew his gun and fired at Asa Wilson, who dropped in a heap. Asa had his gun in his hand but had never gotten a shot off.

"Cease-fire!" yelled Paris. There was a lull. Gun smoke filled the lower levels of the Cathedral. There were screams and crying from where the women stood. Will aimed directly at Paris, but Paris looked directly at him with his hand raised.

"Don't do it, Toal. This was not supposed to happen. I knew that man as Jake Palmer. He's the one who pushed this, not me. I was deceived."

"Oh, you got exactly what you wanted," sneered Will. "You brought a killer to a picnic, a place of peace."

"We were here to deliver lawful notices. Not shoot people," said Paris.

Will looked around. He saw the cluster of women kneeling around Kat Schmidt. Her husband, Joe, lay on the ground bleeding badly from his gut. Asa Wilson was on his back with a death stare lifted upward to the ceiling of the Cathedral. Heinrich Dangberg had been on his stomach but now rolled onto his back in obvious pain. In one of those instantaneous battlefield judgements, he knew that Asa was gone, Heinrich would survive, and Joe Schmidt was questionable.

Will knelt beside Dangberg. Heinrich clutched his shoulder, looked up at Will and in a weak voice said, "Railroaded. Will, we've been railroaded."

Will reached out and touched the man's leg. "Hang on Henry, help's comin'."

Poor Asa was right. It was just like Mussel Slough. At Mussel Slough, the railroad had tried to evict settlers who had homesteaded their ranches in California with the same result. A meeting to hear a politician speaker turned into an ugly gun battle with people killed. Ranchers throughout the California and Nevada area had heard of what had been done. The scene here looked just as what one would imagine after hearing the story of that California incident.

*****

Just then, Will heard a scream. It came from outside the green umbrella of the Cathedral beyond the opening which had been used by the railroad men. Recognition of the scream stabbed Will. It was Beth.

"You better do what you can to help these people, Paris, or you will be a hunted man the rest of your life." The words came from Will as he jumped up from his kneeling position and headed to the Cathedral opening.

The screams continued but were becoming fainter. Will reached the opening. He could see a wagon about one hundred yards out on the road away from the park. The wagon was driven by Beth. In another of those instantaneous assessments a soldier becomes accustomed to making, Will figured Beth had driven to the park, albeit against his wishes, and arrived just about the time Sutton exited.

She was heading the opposite way now, so she must have turned around. She had the horse and wagon moving as fast as she could leaving no doubt at her attempt to escape. Sutton galloped his horse in pursuit and had his revolver stretched out in front of him. Will was about ten yards from where he had tied Powder. He ran to the gray gelding and reached over the saddle to pull his Enfield rifle out of its scabbard.

Just about the time Will grabbed his rifle, he heard a shot. Sutton had closed the distance to the wagon and taken a shot at Beth. Will ran to a flat spot in the road with a clear view of the wagon and Sutton. He hit the ground elbows first and immediately took aim. Just like in the war. Also, just like in war, the Enfield was always loaded.

Beth ducked after the shot. Will could not tell from his vantage if she had been hit. But she screamed again, so if she was hit, it was not immediately fatal. But she leaned drastically to her right, pulling the reins with her. The horse responded as trained and turned sharply to the right. While the horse could change direction in a tight turn, the wagon could not. It began to tilt upward onto two wheels and flipped, throwing Beth off the rig to the left. Will thought Beth had tumbled, but the wagon rolled once more in his direction, and he could not tell if it struck her.

Will needed a clear shot at Sutton. He had taken shots at many a riding Union officer. But the best shots were of a stationary target. It was extremely difficult to hit a rider moving at speed. He needed Sutton to stop. He had only one shot in the Enfield, and he had to make it count.

Sutton slowed his horse, approaching the overturned wagon. He was some three hundred yards out and probably thought he was too far for anyone to accurately get off a shot from the Cathedral. He walked his horse around to where Beth lay. He stood up in his stirrups and raised his right arm, extending his revolver in an accentuated aim for the final shot at Beth.

He looked back at the Cathedral almost as if he hoped Will watched. His lower canines protruded in an even more demonic grin. But that was his mistake. Will was watching. Three hundred yards was far but not for an experienced sniper. Will squeezed off his shot. Sutton's head exploded. His body was thrown violently off the side of his mount. He hit dirt.

"That was an incredible shot." The voice was Martin Johnson's. Will did not know how much Martin had seen, but he obviously had seen the final shot.

Martin continued. "I saw you lying there and figured you didn't have a prayer's chance in hell of hitting that man."

Will glared. "Maybe Hell's where he belongs."

Martin looked down at Will, who was still prone on the ground. "I was horrified to think we had to watch that embodiment of evil kill the girl. But you got him. You got him good. How'd you learn to shoot like that?"

Will did not have the time nor the inclination to tell Martin he had done similar things during the war. All he wanted to do was get Beth.

"Martin, I have to go get Beth. She's pregnant and hurt, maybe dying. She just got thrown off a wagon behind a galloping horse. Can you send someone with a wagon out to me so I can get her to the doctor?"

"Sure, go on, son. I was unaware that you even knew the lady. Go quickly. We have plenty of people here with wagons. There are going to be lots of people hauled off to the doctor. I will make sure one of them moves out to pick up you and the lady."

"Thanks, Martin," said Will.

Will was already moving toward Powder. He threw the Enfield back into its scabbard and swung up onto the horse's back. A quick squeeze of his spurs, and he was off.

As he raced out to get to Beth, Will's thoughts moved almost as fast as Powder.

Is she going to die? She's taken a terrible fall. The wagon could have hit her as it flipped. And then there was the baby. There had to be a tremendous risk of injury to an unborn at this late stage who had been thrown so violently off a moving wagon.

He told himself to look for broken bones. He had often seen battle-field medics look for gunshot injuries but miss terribly broken limbs in the process. He pulled up Powder in a sliding stop with the horse's back haunches lowering down as if Will had just roped a calf and needed to tighten the riata. At the same time, Will slid out of the saddle before Powder came to a full stop.

"Beth, can you hear me?"

Will saw Beth try to raise herself up on her elbow. A good sign.

"Don't move, wait until I can get there," said Will, hurrying to her side.

"Oh, Will, I hurt." Beth had collapsed back on the ground and was looking up at Will.

"Hold on, I'm here." Will quickly looked Beth over, hoping not to see something serious. There was no blood, no open wound. Sutton's shot must have missed. Another good sign. Beth's eyes had been closed but then opened.

"You really have to stop this habit of looking a girl over head to toe every time we meet. Especially when I am in this condition laying in a dust heap." Beth winced in obvious pain.

Will kept looking for apparent signs of injury. As he did, he smiled and said, "At least you have kept your sense of humor. Did Sutton hit you with his shot?"

Beth couldn't answer right away. Then she opened her eyes again.

"I wasn't hit by any bullets. The crack shot ended up missing me. Not that he wasn't trying."

Will moved on to other types of potential injuries. "Do you think anything is broken?"

"No, I don't think so. I know my backside is skinned up as I feel it burning. But I don't think anything is broken. My arms, knees, legs, and backside are going to be real sore. I rolled a couple of times after hitting the ground, and I think it created just enough separation from the wagon and myself. Thank goodness I did because when the wagon fell after tipping, the side of the wagon crashed just shy of my legs and feet. It was close. Had it taken one more roll, it would have landed right on top of me."

Will was relieved. He saw small circles of blood seeping through her dress around the top of her knees, but there still was no evidence of a serious loss of blood. He couldn't deny that his heart had been racing all the way out to Beth's side. The old feelings welled up from deep down. No sense in trying to cover those up.

"But Will, my stomach hurts bad."

Will's newfound relief evaporated. "How bad? How does it hurt?"

"It hurts bad. It came in a wave and then eased off. My back and legs hurt, but they are nothing compared to my stomach. Here it comes again." She winced again as the pain increased, her eyes closing as it crested.

"Could it be that the baby is coming?"

Beth's eyes reopened. "I don't know, maybe. I don't know how having a baby works. First Wife never had one and neither have I, so I just don't know."

One of the young sons of the Johnson family then came up with their family wagon. "Pa said I should come out and let you have the wagon. If you need me to drive you somewhere, he said that I should do that for ya'll, too." The towheaded teenager tried to act much older than he appeared, having been placed in a position of authority and assistance. Will was impressed.

"Help me get her into the wagon, and I will sit in the back with her and you can drive us to the doctor in Carson City."

"Will, I don't want to go to any doctor in Carson City. Please just take me back to the ranch."

"But if there is something wrong, if the baby is injured, you need a doctor."

"No, if the baby comes, then the baby comes. I don't want to be in Carson City for that. Please just take me home."

Will considered. He had heard the word *home*, but it didn't register as being out of place. Her voice told him how badly she wanted to go back to the ranch. He did not have a good grasp as to why Beth was so stubborn about not going to Carson City. But right now, he wanted to get her some place where she could be cleaned up and made comfortable. With María's help, they could do that at the ranch.

"Okay, we will take you to the ranch. Let's get you loaded. I'll tie Powder to the back of the wagon, and you can lay your head on my lap as we go."

Beth sighed. "Thank you, Will."

Chapter Fifty-Two

1868 Fall
Sacramento, California

"I think we should do the deal," said Collis Huntington.

Crocker found Huntington in his Sacramento office. Construction had reached a point that Huntington was in Sacramento only for infrequent stays. He was spending more and more time either in San Francisco or on the East Coast raising money. Crocker thought Huntington might as well buy a house back there. For all Crocker knew, Huntington had done just that.

"I'm glad you agree," replied Crocker.

"Glad?" inquired Huntington.

"Yes, because I have already agreed to the deal. We need the right of way, and we need it now. The snow sheds are just about done, and the track has now been completed through Tunnel #6 at Donner Pass. We have also finished tunnels #7 and #8 further east from Donner along with grading two steep crevasses. We will be ready to start the fifty-five-mile run of track from the Donner Tunnel along the Truckee River to Lake Crossing in a matter of weeks. We could not afford any further delays."

"Nice of you to keep me informed, even if it is after the fact." Huntington smiled ever so slightly to correspond to the sarcastic tone of his response. But Huntington knew the close personal relationship with Crocker would lead him to take his comment the right way.

Crocker had not seen Huntington's face to fully catch the humor from a man rarely humorous. Crocker was looking down at his notes. He continued outlining the deal, effectively ignoring the sarcasm.

"We get a permanent easement over the Purcell Ranch in return for an agreement that all the beef from Millard Luce Cattle Co., and his affiliate ranches in the Carson Valley, will be shipped west to Sacramento at a reduced freight charge. Millard will pay the ranchers for their beef at the railhead in Lake Crossing, and then he will pay us in a single fee for the shipping. He then owns the beef and will sell it through his Sacramento brokerage network already in place. Ultimately, the beef will reach the markets in San Francisco, which has always been Millard's main source of business. The deal works for us, and the deal works for Millard."

"It will be nice to have a steady client for the commercial shipping. Do we have estimates for annual revenue under the deal?"

Crocker looked up at Huntington to see the full nature of his reaction when he answered the question. He knew this would be one of the rare pieces of good news since they'd started this gargantuan project, and he wanted to at least obtain a measure of congratulations for it. "We have only the beginnings of commitments on freight shipments. This deal will double our current annual contracts."

"And that revenue can be used to help finance the construction as it heads further east from Lake Crossing?" asked Huntington.

"Absolutely," said Crocker. "That's why the deal makes such good sense. We get our right of way, which we desperately need to follow the government's specified route, and we get a commitment to double our freight shipments. Further, we end this madness of trying to force the ranchers off their land."

Huntington looked very pleased, as Crocker knew he would be.

"That *is* good news. Well done, Charles."

"We have been getting a huge amount of bad press in San Francisco on the gunfight outside of Carson City. It's good we ended that situation. The bad press is the last thing we needed. All those articles are finding their way Back East to the politicians. We need to keep the land swap subsidies coming. We have just started receiving regular approvals on the government bond allotments coming with the land subsidies which we later have to sell to repay our lenders.

"And right now, as you well know, we have lots of lenders. We cannot go back to seeing delays and interruptions in those land allocations like we did during the beginning of construction. All four of us almost went broke in those days." Huntington now reverted to his stern business look.

"No," said Crocker. "I cannot survive another cash crunch like that one."

Huntington made sure he had Crocker's attention. He waited until Crocker looked up from his notes as he wanted to be certain all the remaining obstacles of this massive undertaking had been surmounted. "So, who put this deal together?"

Crocker smiled. "A lawyer in Carson City named S. Samuel Grande came up with the idea of the easement in return for beef shipment cost reductions. He approached Henry Millard who then approached me."

"Must be a sharp man," said Huntington.

"Before you get too complimentary, my connections in the press tell me Grande was also the source of the story about the gunfight in Carson City, which has led to all the bad press."

"Well, Charles, you have to admire a man who figures out how to soften up his opposition before he opens negotiations with them. I am not keen he made a target of CPRR, but you must admire his methods. Maybe we should hire the man. Would he accept a general counsel position?"

"I can ask," replied Crocker.

Chapter Fifty-Three

1868 Late Fall
Carson City, Nevada

"How is Beth?"

The question came from S. Samuel Grande. Will was seated in his office once again. Grande had sent a message for him to come into town and talk. Will did not want to leave Beth, but the note from Grande sounded insistent.

"She is having what the doctor said are preliminary contractions. It's been three days since the battle at the Cathedral, and the contractions still come, sometimes close together and sometimes not for hours. Doc looked her over pretty good and said she is one lucky lady to have fallen out of a wagon and not been hurt bad. She has plenty of scrapes and bruises, but it could have been a lot worse." Will delivered the assessment in a way and in a detail which told Grande how truly concerned he was.

"I'm glad she wasn't hurt any more seriously and appears to be on the mend."

"So, what is it you wanted to talk to me about?" asked Will.

Grande reached for some papers in one of the many stacks on his desk, pulling them closer so he could read them.

"We reached a deal with the Central Pacific Railroad to end this entire mess surrounding the attempted evictions of the Carson Valley ranchers."

"Who agreed to the deal?" asked Will in a skeptical voice. "Those guys are responsible for two people being dead and several wounded. Asa Wilson is dead as is poor Joe Schmidt's wife, Katerina. Joe barely survived being shot himself, although he has said he would give any-thing, including his own life, to have his wife back alive. He's devastat-ed. Why would we ever negotiate with them now?"

"To prevent any more killing," came the simple direct response by Grande. "It never should have happened in the first place. I should have thought of the solution earlier, and this all would not have happened." Grande evidenced no small amount of Catholic guilt, something Will had seen a lot of over the years.

"It was not your fault, Sam," said Will. "Sutton triggered it all. He went out of his way to start the shooting. I don't even think Dale Paris wanted people shot out there in the Cathedral. He just wanted to intimi-date."

"Well, I came up with the idea of giving the CPRR a permanent easement for their track over the Purcell property. In return, they will ship all the beef the ranchers want to sell down to Sacramento at a reduced fee. I spoke to Henry Millard about the idea. He said he knew Charles Crocker and would approach him with the concept. Henry came up with the idea that he would buy all the beef when delivered at the railhead in Lake Crossing and would pay for the shipping. He would then sell it through his brokerage operation which is already set up in Sacramento. The ranchers will have to enter what's called an *affiliation* with the Millard Luce Cattle Co. as the railroad wants to deal with only one company and not a bunch of individual ranchers."

"What's an affiliation?" asked Will.

"A simple agreement to work together. Millard Luce Cattle Co. will have no financial interest in any of the ranches."

Grande watched Will's face for evidence of a reaction. He seemed satisfied to an extent, but Grande could see he still had questions. He had come to know the young rancher to the point he thought could read his face like he could read a book. Grande knew the idea of an association was going to be the problematic concept. The ranchers, Will included, would hesitate at anything they thought could lead to someone trying to take their ranches. Especially after the recent gunplay.

Grande continued. "Anyway, the railroad gets its right of way and a regular source of freight fees. The ranchers can sell all the beef they can produce. Millard Luce Cattle Co. gets even wider access to another source of beef for sales to the markets in San Francisco. Seems like a win-win all the way around."

Will remained silent as he thought.

"And no one is going to foreclose on our loans?"

"No, the foreclosure cases against all the ranchers here in the Valley are being dismissed. The ranchers will have to pay off their loans as they normally would have. But they will still make their payments to the Bank of California who will continue to handle the deeds of trust as an agent for the railroad as the railroad now owns all those secured interests."

"I can't think of any reason not to do the deal, can you?"

Grande looked at the young man across from him. "No, I think this works out the problems and issues to everyone's benefit."

"Then let's do it," said Will.

"The paperwork is being drafted as we speak. The ranchers can sign in the next day or so, and then Henry Millard will sign. After everyone has signed it at this end, we will send it off to the railroad. They have already dismissed the foreclosure cases as a sign of good faith."

"That's a switch."

"Well, they have been getting a lot of bad press about the shooting lately. We agreed to make sure the press heard that CPRR is dismissing the suits in return for an overall agreement regarding the right of way and sale of beef. We kept the details confidential, just telling the press that everyone, including the ranchers, are pleased with the deal. That will take the CPRR off the hook with all their current bad publicity."

"Sam, I cannot thank you enough. For three days, I have been worrying about Beth but, at the same time, thinking about how we must gear up for further gunplay. Now, I can go home and relax."

"Glad it's working out," said Grande. "I am sorry that I didn't come up with the solution before the guns started shooting."

Just then, there was a commotion out on Grande's porch. His door opened, and Juan stepped inside.

"Jefe, you must come now. It is *Señorita* Beth. It is bad."

"I'll head out to the ranch right away. Go get the doctor and meet me out there."

Chapter Fifty-Four

Will arrived and tied up Powder. He didn't even loosen the horse's cinch. He just rushed into the house.

"Beth!" he yelled.

"*Señor* Will," it was María. "You do not come in your room. You stay out there. It is not good for you to come right now."

"Juan went to get the doctor. He should be here soon."

María was still behind the door to his room and out of sight.

"You stay out there and wait for the doctor. Is a good thing he is coming. I think we need the doctor soon."

"María, how bad is it?" asked Will.

"I do not know. There is a lot of blood. More blood than I ever see in any birth of babies."

Will heard horses out front. He went out the door to make sure it was Juan and the doctor. The doctor dismounted and gave his reins to Juan, who took the horses. The doctor strode directly to the front door and Will.

"Where is she?" There were no wasted words.

"She's in the back bedroom. María is with her. Just let me know if I can do anything."

"I will go to her right now, but I can tell you for sure I will need hot water and lots of it."

"I will get it right away."

The doctor watched him go. He would probably need the water, but it was best if a prospective father had something to do to keep him busy.

The physician turned and headed into the house.

*****

It had been six long hours since Will had last seen the doctor. He spent most of the time by the barn as he could not stand to hear the screams. They just kept coming and coming regularly. But the screams had stopped about thirty minutes ago. Will had no idea what to expect. He had no idea whether the screams stopping was good or bad. He had no idea if things were still as terrible as María had made them out to be or if things had turned around.

The doctor came out of the front door. He looked haggard. He motioned for Will to come over to the house.

"You are the father of two boys. They seem to be fine. They came early but seem well formed and in good shape."

Will felt his whole being lifted. Two sons. Not one but two. He was about to let his mind run at what he could see in a future with two sons when the doctor interrupted.

"But Will, Beth is in a bad way."

"Bad way? How? What are you telling me?"

The euphoria of the moment completely evaporated. Instead of walking one or two feet in the air, the world felt like it had crashed on his chest. Try as he might to deny it, mad as he might be at her, she was someone special in his life.

"Will, she is bleeding badly. Now most women lose a lot of blood in childbirth. Beth's births were not easy; they never are. But the births went as one usually expects."

The doctor now paused. He was trying to figure out how to put this. The longer he held off, the greater the concern grew in Will.

"After a birth, there are physical parts of the birthing process that come out. Once that is done, we compress the stomach and, within a few minutes, a mother should stop bleeding. Beth has not stopped. I have compressed the stomach as much as I feel I can without causing more injury. I have tried to plug the areas that are bleeding. Nothing seems to stop it."

Will absorbed what he could. He couldn't even think of words, couldn't even think of a question to ask. There was a knot of dread in his throat. He wasn't sure he could talk if he tried.

The doctor saw Will's discomfort. He reached out and put his hand on his shoulder.

"Son, I have to give this to you as straight as I can. I am in this practice to help people live. I will surely do everything in my power for Beth. But I have always felt it is best to give folks the best assessment I can. Will, I have never seen a mother bleed as much following a birth. If this doesn't stop soon, we are going to lose her."

"You mean she is going to die?" His voice had a slight quiver.

"Yes. I hope I am wrong. Maybe the compresses and plugs will work. But it is out of my hands at this point. There is nothing more I can do except to keep her out of pain. Whether she lives or dies is in the Lord's hands."

"Can I see her?"

"I thought you would ask. She is in bad shape. She is extremely weak. I am not sure how long she will remain awake with the tremendous blood loss. I know you want to talk to her. It may be the last time you can."

The doctor hesitated as if weighing what might be advisable to say as a doctor versus what he would say to a man who obviously cared for a woman.

"So, I am going to let you go in. But you must be quick. Say only what you feel you should say and try to be positive. We must keep her spirits up. As soon as she quits and gives up, it will be over for certain."

Will couldn't believe what he was hearing. The rapid fire of information swung from the highest of highs to the lowest of lows. His head swirled with a cauldron of emotions. But there was no one he could express it to, except Beth. He felt drawn into the room as if pulled. He had to see her. "Can I go in now?"

"Yes, but be prepared to see a lot of blood. Don't be shocked. Don't let her see that. Tell her she looks good. Tell her what you have to but be gentle and be positive."

*****

Will walked into the room. There was an overpowering smell. The only other time he had come across the same oppressive smell was in the war with lots of wounded men laying around. It was the smell of blood. That smell was never good.

Beth lay on his bed on her back with her eyes closed and completely covered with sheets. The sheets covering the lower half of her body were soaked in blood. There were other sheets on the floor near the walls. Blood soaked all of them. Will could not believe one person could generate so much blood. There couldn't be any left inside her.

Will walked slowly to the bed. Beth opened her eyes just as he got near. Her face was near white, a pale removed of color, and her smile was weak. She tried to reach her hand up to touch him.

"The doctor tells me I gave you twin boys."

"Yep." Will looked over towards Maria who was tending to two baskets. "They are here near you in two baskets by the wall. I intend to spend a great deal of time with them."

Pain registered all over Beth's face.

"Are you okay? I can get the doctor."

"No, I really don't feel much. Just very weak. The reason for the look is what you said."

Remembering the doctor's orders to stay positive, Will tried to cover anything he might have said to upset Beth.

"Beth, the doctor says they are fine boys. You have to pull through this for your boys."

"Will, I worry I am going to die. I know it. I can feel it. I am trying to hold on, but I am slipping."

Another wince. Uttering words became more difficult.

"Will, they are *your* boys." She placed heavy emphasis on the word *your*. "I have already said you were the father. I had not been with Josiah for some time before I left him and never had any relations with Sutton."

She again had to pause. "Those boys will have blue eyes. That will be the final proof."

Will tilted his head in question. "How will blue eyes prove that they are mine?"

"I'm not sure I have energy right now to explain, but you need to know. Will, our eyes are blue. The Mormons watch these things."

Beth paused as if a wave of pain came over her.

"They know if a blue-eyed mother AND a blue-eyed father have children, then all those babies will have blue eyes. If both of those boys have blue eyes, then they are yours. If the boys have anything other than blue eyes, then I am wrong. But I know I am not. Ask the doctor. Purcell and Sutton had brown eyes. My eyes are blue. Yours are blue. Ask the Mormons."

It was true Will had expressed doubts about being the father. At first, it seemed like he should be talking to Beth about other more important things than the color of the children's eyes. But now he realized that

Beth was doing what she could even in her present condition to protect her boys. Even if she couldn't hold them, she was their mother. She was doing what she could to make sure they would be cared for.

"Will, in a short amount of time, I made some very bad decisions. But being with you was not one of them. Having those two boys was not one of them. They are yours. Take them and raise them. Be good to them. They are yours. Wait and see. If both of the boys have blue eyes, then you will know I have told you the truth."

If this was true, then they would be his. The euphoria he'd felt when the doctor first came out started to build again. But the only woman he had ever really cared about was here on a bed, dying.

"Beth, I will take them. I will raise them. But don't you leave. You have to get well."

Beth still had a hold of Will's hand. She pulled on it. There was little or no strength, but Will could tell she was pulling.

"Come here," she said.

Will leaned in close. She kissed him softly on the mouth. Her lips were dry, almost flaking. Her hand went to the side of his face in a gentle caress.

"I did love you, Will…I hope you know that…I was such an idiot not to know what that meant until it was too late. I did go and speak with Father Cecconi as you suggested. He talked of penance. Maybe what is happening is my penance for what I've done."

Her speech was becoming halting, short, and spaced.

"Now go out and let me sleep…Start thinking of…of how you will raise those boys on the ranch and…and what a wonderful life you will have with them."

She pushed his hand away from her and turned her head facing up again. Her eyes closed. Her breathing labored. He took another look at her face. In this condition, she was not the same as the girl on their walk. But then again, she was.

Will left the room. He walked out and looked at the doctor.

The doctor could see the shock and concern in Will's face. "Now you know why I was so worried. She hasn't got much left. Frankly, I am amazed she is still with us. Hold on a second and let me check on her and the boys. I will be right back, and we can talk about what we are going to do with the twins."

The doctor went back into Beth's room. Will sat down. A flood of emotion clogged his regular thought patterns. There were so many questions, so many things to consider. *Twins. Mine? How do I raise them? Should I even think about the color of their eyes? Why would Beth lie to me now, here on her deathbed? She must be right.* He was swimming in one thought after the next when the doctor walked back in the room.

"I don't think she is going to make it."

Chapter Fifty-Five

June 1869
Toal Ranch

Beth arrived late morning with the boys. She pulled up in the wagon, and the boys were in two baskets strapped down in the back just behind her seat. The twins, Luke and Sean, were now about seven months old. Summer approached, and the weather had begun to warm up. As a result, the boys wore light clothes without any blankets or jackets.

Will tried to set aside at least one day each week he could devote to just being with the twins. Even though they were young, he felt drawn to have them around. He could already tell the pull to have them near would only get stronger as they got older. It wasn't something he could readily explain, but the feeling pushed him to make sure his ranch duties were open for one day a week if possible.

Will grabbed the bridle on the single horse in harness. He pulled the animal across the yard and tied it off on the corral rail attached to the barn. In this position, the horse would get some shade if Beth decided to stay for a couple of hours. He would make sure it got some water before long. As soon as he had the horse secured, he turned to Beth to see how she wanted to get the boys down.

Beth swung over the side of the wagon in a smooth, easy motion. She did not wait for him to help her down. That was not her way. He noticed she moved again with the quick agility and graceful control she had before the births. It might have not been the most feminine way to step down, but it was Beth. It did not offend Will in the least. In fact, he kind of liked it.

It had been real close. The doctor said he did not think Beth would survive the births. She lost a tremendous amount of blood. But she held on. Slowly, she began to stabilize and then, ever more slowly, to recover. She did not get out of bed for two weeks. The doctor said that María had to feed the twins as Beth was too weak to nurse. She needed all the strength she could muster just to survive. Those days were not easy. Feeding and caring for the boys created a constant wave of demands. Between the two, someone always needed something. María had been great.

But Beth finally got back on her feet. Will looked at her now, organizing what normally should have been the simple process of taking a walk but which demanded all manner of planning to get the two babies ready to go. He thought to himself that she had become a wonderful mother.

Today, Beth wore a simple dress with a high collar and long skirt. But the simplicity of the dress molded to the form of her upper body, enhancing its effect. The dress had a line of buttons from her collar to her waist. Her waist had not yet returned to the trim line of the day she wore Raúl's old belt with the extra holes, but it was getting close. The thought struck him that it must be a new outfit, maybe one being worn with a purpose.

"You're getting back to your trim self," he commented.

"Will Toal, a girl could get real self-conscious about the fact she is always going to have to pass inspection upon meeting you."

While she threw the words at him as something of a rebuke, he was glad to see she had an impish smile on her face. When Beth first returned pregnant and in need of shelter, he felt more than just conflicted. He was absolutely mystified she would have the audacity to even return. She had hit him on the head. Damn near broke his skull. She had run off with a guy dressed in black, then showed back up saying she was pregnant with his children. He had missed her terribly.

Everyone on the ranch could see it. He knew it and would have to admit if anyone should put the question to him directly. But he was also angry. While he still harbored deep feelings for this woman, he hesitated to let himself be tricked again. Other wounds may have healed, but the wound to his pride and trust in this woman had yet to fully mend. It left him hesitant to expose the feelings he had for Beth. He just didn't feel as natural around her as he did before. But today had started off in a much more lighthearted way. He almost felt comfortable.

"Any trouble on the ride out of town?" he asked.

"No, it is a wonderful morning. Cool right now but not cold. The heat will come soon enough. Can you grab one of the boys, and I will get the other?"

"Sure," said Will. "I'll get Luke, and you can get Sean."

Will leaned over the top of the side railing and cupped his hands underneath the child, once again marveling at how small he was. While they each had doubled in size in their first seven months of life, they were still so, so small. He no longer felt a self-conscious concern he might hurt them each time he held one, but he still was overly careful in handling the tykes. At some point, that would change. But right now, they were still very, very vulnerable little beings.

"Have you thought about our conversation of last week?" asked Beth.

Last week, Beth had asked if he would consider her moving to the ranch along with the boys. She worked on a part-time basis in the Carson City land office for Mr. Fallar. The small room she rented would eventually be too small when the boys started crawling and later walking. It was also upstairs in the boarding house. She needed the job as she was trying not to draw on the funds she had on deposit, but she could ride into town easily enough from the ranch on the days she had to work. She had not pressed him about marriage. That question always lingered in the background, but Beth had not pushed marriage, knowing Will would have to make that decision, if he ever did.

"I have." He did not elaborate.

"You still question whether the boys are yours?"

"Beth, you know I question whether they are mine. I think it's a reasonable thing to question if you were standing in my boots."

They had been down this path before. On those earlier occasions, Beth had not pressed the issue. But today, she was prepared to do just that.

"Will Toal, look at my eyes. What color are they?"

"They are blue. But you know that. You talked about this same thing right after the boys were born. I never really understood what you were trying to tell me."

He didn't say it, but he had always thought she had the deepest bright blue eyes he had ever seen. Before the shoot-out at the Reynolds camp, he had told her how much he admired her eyes many a time.

"Okay, next. What are the color of your own eyes?"

Will was uncomfortable with the topic. Beth had suggested that he talk to others about her assertion, but he'd never done so. It may have been lack of motivation, or if he was truthful with himself, it may have been out of fear Beth could be right. His knew his face probably betrayed his personal hesitation, and while he'd have preferred to end the conversation, he answered.

"My eyes are blue, I think."

"Yes, your eyes are blue, too," said Beth.

Will knew where this was leading, but he had not yet fully come to grips with the reality that the boys were his. He still had his doubts but had not figured out a way to express those doubts without creating an emotional upheaval. He tried to think of a way to quickly end the conversation but could not come up with the words to do so. Beth must have sensed an opportunity because she pressed the issue, only making him even more uncomfortable.

"Josiah Purcell had brown eyes. Drake Sutton had brown eyes."

"What does the color of their eyes have to do with our discussion here?"

"As I told you before, Mormons are very conscious, almost reverent about every new birth. New persons on the Earth are special to Mormons maybe even more so than in standard human nature. They study births and families. They search records of origin for families, identifying where the Church's members came from. They study the combination of husbands and wives. And they have found that if a husband and wife both have blue eyes, then all of their babies will have blue eyes but if one of the parents has brown eyes, then the children more often than not will have brown eyes."

Will had been walking to the ranch house, but he stopped and turned to face Beth. They were right in the middle of the central open expanse between the barn, house, and bunk house.

"Okay, so what are you trying to tell me?"

"You have to be the father of both Sean and Luke. They both have blue eyes. Neither Josiah Purcell nor Drake Sutton could have been the father. I have told you that neither of those men were the father, but you still have doubt. But the proof of the fact that the twins are your sons is staring you right in the face. Look at their eyes."

Will looked down at Luke, cradled in the crook of his right arm. The boy's eyes were definitely blue. So were Sean's. Beth had Sean cradled in her left arm.

"You want to come back to the ranch, to live here, right?"

Beth looked unblinking at Will's eyes with the thought this could be the final time Will would ever consider the question. She had pushed, and now she would get an answer. But the answer was not necessarily going to be the one she hoped for.

"I have thought about it. I have thought about it a lot." Will now stopped and turned to Beth. He wanted her to know he had given this a good deal of thought, and he knew this moment was an important one for both.

"I believe I am the father of the boys. I intend to provide for them in every way I can. I look forward to seeing them each and every day. The fact you are with them in town away from me is something I wish could be different."

Beth found herself allowing hope to well up from deep within. Was he going to allow her to come back? She would do so even if he didn't want to marry her. Just to be here on the ranch with Will and the boys together would lift her to a place of peace she had never experienced.

"But I don't think it would be a good idea for you to come back to live on the ranch."

All hope vanished.

"Beth, I just can't bring myself back to a point where I leave my heart that open, that exposed."

Beth felt a lump clog her throat. She did not think she could speak. She couldn't think of a response now, anyway.

Will could see the sorrow in her face. He could see what he was doing to her. He felt so deeply for this woman but had not arrived back to a place where he could see them as husband and wife. But he did not want to crush her. She was the mother of his sons. Even more, he *did* feel deeply about her. He had just lost the ability to gauge what that deep feeling meant and what he should do about it. Nonetheless, he knew he couldn't leave the conversation hanging as it was now.

"I have seen how you moved on with your life. You have a job in the land office with Mr. Fallar. You have a lady watch the boys, but you still push on to earn your way. You have not asked me for anything though I have offered and stand ready to pay for their needs and yours."

The effects of the emotional blow were still hard, and Beth could not find it in herself to speak. He was trying to ease the impact, but the answer and blunt truth had already been delivered.

"Beth, I also see how you have begun helping at the church with Fr. Cecconi. He has told me after the masses I have been able to attend how impressed he is with what you do for the other parishioners. He has even told me that you have had conversations about converting."

Beth nodded her head in a mighty effort to appear still engaged in the dialogue even though her mind and heart were buried deep below her feet.

"I know it would be easy to just say 'come stay at the ranch,' and we can work things out as we go. But I just don't think two people who are not married should be in that position. The temptation would eat at both of us. Maybe someday I can get past what happened at the camp, but I am not there now, and that's the honest truth. I want to be with you, Beth, but I just cannot do it now."

Beth was doing her utmost not to cry right in front of Will. She held her stomach as tight as she could, praying everything would not come gushing out. Finally, she outstretched her arms with Sean in her hands, offering him to Will.

"Here, you take both of the boys down to the river. I will be along in a minute. I need to get something out of the wagon."

Will knew it was probably an excuse. Beth needed time, a moment. He had hurt her. It was not his intention. He cared about her. He had avoided the conversation up to now because he knew it would hurt her.

But she had asked and deserved his answer. He took hold of Sean, turned, and headed down the path to the river.

*****

As soon as Will left the compound, Beth walked over to the front porch and sat down on Will's rocker, the rocker she had hoped to use each day in a life on the ranch with Will and the boys. She looked one more time to make sure Will was out of sight. She then dropped her head into her hands and sobbed.

It took about five minutes. The tears flowed. But they finally stopped. Beth used her dress to wipe the watery tracks from her face. She looked out toward the river, knowing the only men she cared about were all there and she should join them soon.

Fr. Cecconi had, indeed, talked to her about becoming Catholic. She did not want to do this if it were going to look like a contrived ploy. Fr. Cecconi said if her actions came as the true expression of her heart, she should not worry how things might appear to others. People would eventually see her motives were sincere, even Will. When he said this, Beth was a bit shocked the priest could see what she was thinking without revealing her full thoughts. Then he had talked to her about penance.

Maybe what was happening was just that: penance. Maybe one did have to pay for the consequences of one's own actions, either here on Earth or later. Maybe it was better to do one's penance here on Earth as opposed to the afterlife. Maybe Will would see she did love him and would someday forgive her. Beth could see and sense he did love her, he just had to come to terms with it. Maybe, if he could ever forgive, then he could let that love show.

Hope.

Beth placed her hands at the ends of the handrails on the rocker. She had to consciously push with force to lift herself up. Her body felt heavier than she knew it was. Maybe emotion carried a physical weight. The last time she had to force her way out of this chair, she had just returned to Toal Ranch. On that day, she also had to lift up with effort and was about to leave when Will stopped her, saying she could stay. Different from today. She stood and faced the path to the river. Maybe someday.

Hope.

Epilogue

June 1871
Toal Ranch

Will sat on the riverbank marveling at the differences between Luke and Sean. The boys were now nearly three years old.. How could boys born at the same time from the same mother and father be so different? These two were inseparable. They always wanted to know where the other was. They would play together like the best of friends and in a flash tackle one another to the ground, gouging and swinging. Some of the play was dominated by Luke. Some of the play was dominated by Sean. They always figured it out, often to the amazement of watching adults. They were a mystery yet so often predictable.

"Hey, you two, come over here," said Will.

The boys had been looking at some crawling critter. It was most likely a common lizard, but to them, it was one of the seven wonders of the world.

They both ran up, one behind the other.

"Da . . . ad . . . dy," said Sean, who had developed a mild stammer when he got excited.

"There's a lizard!"

The words were almost shouted. He couldn't be more excited if he had just been told he was going to get a new horse. They both loved to ride. As often as he could, Will and Beth would saddle up, put the boys in front of them, and walk out on short trips. They always cried when they were pulled off by either Juan or Raúl. They couldn't get enough.

Luke came up holding the lizard upside down.

"I got the lizard!"

It was more a statement of fact than a statement of accomplishment.

Will knew he couldn't replace these moments. Both boys looked up wide-eyed at him as a person in a position of authority, asking with their facial expressions what they should do or think about this new development.

At that moment, Will again saw both pairs of deep bright blue eyes. He knew then if not before, these boys would always be in his life.

FROM THE AUTHOR

FACT FROM FICTION

I have always admired the books of Steve Berry. He picks wonderful historical events themselves possessed of a bit of mystery, and then he weaves lustrous tales, adding more mystery to the real events. He always includes a section at the end of each of his books acknowledging his fictional additions but also points out the often-surprising facts. So, here is my attempt to identify some of the events in the Carson Valley story which are nonfiction.

PROLOGUE

The Big Four—Huntington, Hopkins, Crocker, and Stanford—did take over the financing and building of the western portion of the Transcontinental Railroad. The original concept and path was promoted by Theodore Judah. A visionary bordering on obsessed, Judah was a civil engineer who had helped build smaller connecting rail systems in California after working on several railroad lines in the East. Judah was the first to generate a legitimate engineering plan for a route over the Sierras. A brilliant railroad man who had multiple engineering break-throughs in the East, he originally came out West to Sacramento before the Civil War started, about the same time as General William T. Sherman arrived in that same town. It is a little-known fact that, before the Civil War, Sherman was assigned by the army to explore the possibility of connecting the country by rail. Sherman spent time in Sacramento, met Judah, and supported his efforts. But it was Judah who generated the original plan and became fixated on building a railroad across the country. He tirelessly promoted the Transcontinental Railroad both on the West and East Coast. He traveled to Washington to promote the idea beginning in the late 1850s. Altogether, he traveled to Washington over the Isthmus of Panama three times with his wife, Anna, to lobby both Congress and President Buchanan. Later, he also petitioned Lincoln to fund the effort. Time and time again, he met with defeat.

While the country in general wanted the railroad built, the Northern legislators wanted the road to be at the forty-first parallel while the Southern legislators, led by then Secretary of War Jefferson Davis, wanted the route to pass through the South from New Orleans to Santa Fe to Los Angeles. Washington was in a stalemate until the Civil War and the defection of the Southern legislators. On his second trip East after war broke out, Judah again tried to get his plan approved. On this trip he was joined by Huntington, who was a master at engendering support with politicians (a feat generally believed to have been supplemented with cash). Together, they pushed the Pacific Railroad Act through Congress. After congressional approval, Judah returned to Sacramento and, along with the Big Four, was a founding principal of the Central Pacific Railroad.

In continuing efforts to find the best route over the Sierras, Judah met storekeeper Dr. Daniel Strong. It was "Doc" Strong who showed Judah the path through the Sierras to Dutch Flat over what is now close to the route used by US Interstate 80. While part of CPRR at the start of the project, the Big Four ultimately forced Judah out of company management following differences on how to finance initial purchases. Judah contracted yellow fever on his third and final trip over the Isthmus. He was headed to New York for meetings with Eastern railroad tycoon Cornelius Vanderbilt. Judah's intention was to ask Vanderbilt to buy out the Big Four, but he died two weeks after arriving on the East Coast, before he could attend the meeting with Vanderbilt. He never saw the railroad built. (For further details on this topic, see *Nothing Like It in the World* by Stephen Ambrose).

General Grenville Dodge was an engineer and surveyor by training prior to the Civil War. It was Dodge who ultimately plotted out the route for the Transcontinental Railroad from the Missouri River to the Rockies. Prior to the Civil War, he traveled all over the plains as a part of various troops involved in Indian Wars. But he always looked at the terrain as an engineer, too. Dodge even met Abraham Lincoln in Council Bluffs while Lincoln campaigned for the presidency. Before the first meeting between the two men, Lincoln had been told that Dodge had the best knowledge and experience to plot out a route west for the railroad. When they actually met, Lincoln asked Dodge which route to take to the Rockies. Dodge told him to hug the North Platte. Lincoln would later order the route follow those early suggestions by Dodge.

When the Civil War started, Dodge wanted to command troops in combat. He was initially a successful battle commander in the western frontier of the Civil War. However, he then went into intelligence, as indicated in my story. Dodge originated the first army group specifically tasked to obtain military intelligence. His information gathered from ex-slaves and others was invaluable to Grant in the Battle of Vicksburg. He was then assigned to Sherman's corps during the March to the Sea to work on rebuilding railroad track destroyed by the retreating Confederate Army. Sherman marveled at how quickly Dodge could repair what looked like a hopeless mess of tangled iron and destroyed bridges. All the while, Dodge continued to manage the intelligence group. Both Grant and Sherman came to rely on his sources and information throughout the rest of the war.

Following the war, Dodge signed on with the Union Pacific and once again connected with Grant, who relied on him for expert advice during the building of the railroad. In return, Grant supported Dodge in his almost constant corporate battles with Union Pacific Vice President Thomas Durant. Durant had tried to remove Dodge as the main authority for construction but based on Grant's experience with Dodge throughout the war, Grant saw to it that Durant never removed Dodge. (Again, see *Nothing Like It in the World* by Stephen Ambrose). While Dodge had gone into business with Durant at the onset of work on the railroad in the East, the two battled throughout the construction of the UP portion over control of both finances and, more often, route for the track. While Dodge remained with the UP until the Transcontinental Railroad was built, he would leave the UP when the Crédit Mobilier scandal hit. Upon his departure from the UP, Dodge ran for Congress and was elected. Known for his involvement with the railroad at its inception, he was tasked by his fellow congressmen to follow through with the completion of the Transcontinental Railroad and monitor the re-payment of bonds which were issued.

At the start of the railroad project, Dodge was the main conduit of contact between Huntington and the government. However, there is no record of any meeting between Dodge and Huntington with Lincoln. The timing of the meeting in my story is at least two years before Dodge even left the military. I have obviously altered the timing to fit my story. But Dodge was a remarkable man whose record and impact on this immense project is little-known. I thought he should be in the story. Dodge City is named for him. Modern military intelligence of today and its use in combat owes its legacy to this man.

The Transcontinental Railroad would never have been built had it not been for Theodore Judah and Grenville Dodge, two critical and capable personalities.

Abraham Lincoln was indeed predisposed to a transcontinental railroad. He had represented the Illinois Central and Chicago and Rock Island Railroad companies in multiple significant lawsuits. Lincoln appeared before the Illinois Supreme Court over 175 times, many for railroad clients. If there had been a meeting between Lincoln and Huntington, I do believe the two would have had similar agendas.

While there is no documented meeting between Huntington and President Lincoln as represented in Chapter 6 that I could confirm, there are several sources that indicate Huntington negotiated the land sale/bond concept with Grenville Dodge, who acted both on behalf of the government and himself. Huntington spent almost six months in 1861 traveling between Washington, D.C. and New York lobbying for the passage of the Pacific Railroad Act and could have been at the White House during those negotiations.

The original concept of a "land swap" was proposed by Asa Whitney in 1841. Whitney had seen the same plan used by the state of Illinois during the building of various spurs throughout the state by the Illinois Central Railroad and later the Chicago and Rock Island Railroad. Whitney even went to multiple different states along his proposed route from Milwaukee to San Francisco lobbying for the deal. Amazingly, he got twenty state legislatures to approve the plan. However, the concept died on the floor of the U.S. Congress due to opposition from Southern states (who presumably had some trouble visualizing how it would help them). Whitney died broke and working a milk run in Washington, D.C. (See *The Railroad Photographs of Alfred A. Hart, Artist* by Mead B. Kibbey along with accompanying history).

The Pacific Railroad Act was signed by Lincoln in 1861 utilizing a series of bond acts that functioned as the plan for financing the railroad as outlined in Chapter 6. The checkerboard of America was a fact. You can find several versions throughout the internet.

There were many stories of range wars throughout the Old West. But if you look carefully, many of those range wars were rooted in battles over railroad property that had been sold for pennies only to have a buyback or lump sum payment later, after the ranchers who had worked to improve the land could not pay.

Many critics at the time, and ever since (including a 2017 documentary series about the building of the West produced by Robert Redford), claimed incorrectly that the land-for-railroad capitalization plan was a boondoggle for the railroads or an outright gift. This was not the case. According to respected historian Stephen Ambrose, in his book *Nothing Like It in the World*, the U.S. government issued $64,623,512 in bonds, or loans as some call it, for the approved grades and construction of track laid (p. 377). By 1899, in final settlement with the government when the bonds came due, the railroads had paid back the U.S. government $63,023,512 in principal plus $104,722,978 in interest. This did not even take into account the monumental savings in cost and time for troop movements the railroad provided. Before the railroad was built, General Sherman, during his time in Sacramento, argued that it could save the military huge dollars. After the war, he went out of his way to document those savings. The principal savings for the U.S. Army came in both cost and time for movements of troops and material. In short, the U.S. government was paid in full for the land issued to the railroads and later sold for the generation of capital that neither government, banks, nor individuals possessed at the close of the Civil War. The additional value for the connection of both the East and West to settlement and commercial Pacific trade was incalculable.

CHAPTER 6

Henry Millard is a thinly disguised play on the Miller Lux Cattle Company. Henry Miller was trained as a meat processor in Germany who traveled over the Isthmus of Panama from his native Germany by way of New York to land in San Francisco. He started work there as a butcher's apprentice. He ended up quickly buying the business. He noticed the need for beef in the growing San Francisco city and began buying up cattle property within easy reach. His interests expanded, and by the end of his life, Henry Miller and the Miller Lux Cattle Co. owned over a million acres of ranch land. Miller was personally responsible for quality land management, reservoir construction, and administration of ranch operations from Oregon to Bakersfield. The Company's script was known throughout California, Oregon, and Nevada as just as good as cash money. (See "*The Cattle King*" by Edward F. Treadwell). Almost all banks would honor the script. The Miller Lux Cattle Company would reimburse the bank.

CHAPTER 8

It would have been next to impossible for Huntington and Leland Stanford to have had the conversation as represented in Chapter 8. For the most part, Corliss Huntington resided in New York during the construction of the Transcontinental Railroad. He traveled back and forth to Washington, D.C. as the partnership's front man for governmental relations. I brought him back to Sacramento onto the front lines of the construction effort purely for purposes of the story.

However, it is a fact that Huntington and Stanford had a falling out and Huntington played a part in ousting Stanford from the company. But the split was not until some years after the Transcontinental Railroad was built and the CPRR merged into the Southern Pacific RR. Stanford was ousted as president of the now main holding company, the Southern Pacific RR, but remained president of CPRR. (See "The Builders of the Central Pacific Railroad," by John Debo Galloway, C.E., on CPRR.org).

Charles Crocker did effectively act as CPRR's superintendent for construction. Samuel Montague and, later, Lewis Clement were the chief engineers, and James Strobridge was his field superintendent. Crocker made the day-to-day decisions on getting the track laid. His efforts in hiring Chinese laborers have been documented by dozens of writers. The need for that labor was indeed caused by the lack of interest in ex-Civil War soldiers who were distracted by the mining success in Virginia City. At the time, some felt there was an issue of abuse, but in *Nothing Like It in the World*, Ambrose documents the efforts of CPRR to accommodate the special diets and habits of cleanliness the Chinese laborers demanded. The bottom line is that the CPRR portion of the railroad was built, and it would not have happened without the Chinese labor force.

The contracting operation for the CPRR was consolidated under Charles Crocker's construction company as represented. This made things eminently more efficient. It was also eminently more profitable for the Big Four. Crocker did leave the board of CPRR to maintain an appearance of propriety and separation, yet all the while the Big Four owned the construction entity as well. The corporate structure was very similar to the one used by the Union Pacific Railroad with Crédit Mobilier being the construction arm where profits were skimmed from government payments. Following the well-known Crédit Mobilier scandal, there were multiple congressional hearings into CPRR's corporate structure. However, before the hearings and investigation could be completed, the accounting books for Crocker's construction company were burned in a fire. Despite some cries by politicians voicing suspicion as to the origin of the fire, CPRR was never sanctioned by Congress as was the UP. (See *Nothing Like It in the World* by Stephen Ambrose).

The passage about Crocker losing his employees to the mines also comes from Ambrose. In fact, the representation by Ambrose is that 1,900 of the two thousand men hired by Crocker on the East Coast and transported at CPRR cost arrived in Sacramento and, within a matter of weeks, left their jobs and headed up the hill to Virginia City. This Irish flight is what ultimately led Crocker to begin hiring Chinese laborers.

CHAPTER 9

The small village of Genoa was the first real settlement in Nevada, albeit when the Carson Valley was still part of the Utah Territory. It was settled by Mormons who established a trading post called Mormon Station in 1851 located adjacent to what was then called the California Trail. The original Mormon Station was burned in a fire in 1910, but a replica has been rebuilt and is now part of the Mormon Station State Park in Genoa, Nevada.

CHAPTER 10

The Lake Crossing toll bridge was real. One can see a historical marker of this at the Virginia Street overcrossing of the Truckee River.

Present day Reno, Nevada, was originally known as Lake Crossing, just as described in this chapter. Charles Crocker ultimately influenced the naming of the new town and depot after Major General Jesse Lee Reno who was, indeed, killed in the Battle of South Mountain. This writer could never uncover the reason Crocker wanted to use that name, but it stuck. There is documentation confirming that Charles Crocker spoke with Myron Lake (for whom the original crossing was named) about renaming the city and putting a depot in the town several years before the railroad construction made it over the Sierras.

CHAPTER 12

The Homestead Act was amended in 1867 to allow ex-Confederate Soldiers to participate. Before that, anyone who had fought for the South was denied the ability to stake a Homestead claim. The discussion about the limitations on how much land you could homestead and signing the affidavit of allegiance is accurate as represented by my fictional lawyer, Mr. Grande.

The Dangbergs were one of the original ranching families in the Carson Valley. The founder of the family ranch, Heinrich Dangberg, was born in Minden, Germany. He became one of the most successful ranchers in the Valley and eventually worked to establish the present town of Minden, NV, obviously named for his birthplace. His ranch holdings at one time approached thirty thousand acres.

Sue and Martin Johnson were ranchers in the Carson Valley during the 1980s. Their ranch was adjacent to present day Johnson Lane right off Highway 395. My wife and I bought our first horse from Sue and Martin Johnson. We enjoyed riding that horse for many years. We last saw Sue and Martin just after they sold their ranch. I hope they are doing well.

CHAPTER 13

The Mustang was not indigenous to North America. The Spanish brought the horse to the West in their first travels to Mexico and the southern parts of the U.S. and also from their original settlement of St. Louis. The Spanish traveled up the Mississippi to St. Louis long before it was taken by the French and made part of the Louisiana Purchase. There were other horses which had escaped in the East, but the Indians of the Eastern Seaboard were still traveling on foot long after the Sioux and Western Plains Indians were riding horses to hunt buffalo. Those horses came from the South as escapees from Spanish groups who had come to explore. The early horses were of exceptional stock brought by officers as their personal mounts. They were descendants of the Andalusian. The Andalusian breed was established by a group of Cistercian monks outside the Spanish town of Jerez in the 1300s. The breed is now highly protected and prized in Spain under the name of Pura Raza Española (PRE). Each year, there is an annual festival at the Royal Andalusian School of Equestrian Art in Jerez put on by the Fundación

Real Escuela Andaluza. The Spanish riding school presents regular shows in their wonderful arena in Jerez throughout the year once or twice a week. The arena and shows will remind one of the Spanish riding school in Vienna. It is something to behold. One of these presentations involves a horse trained in the old school manner to work the bulls as described in the story. Despite centuries of evolution both in breed and function, if you see this portion of the show, you will notice right away the similarity between the working Andalusian and any modern-day roping horse in any rodeo arena.

CHAPTER 16

There was a gun manufactured by Colt Patent Firearms Manufacturing Company in 1862 which bore the nickname "Pocket Navy." It was as described in Chapter 18. There were only about nineteen thousand made as compared to the standard Colt Navy, which saw over two hundred thousand produced in 1861. The Pocket Navy was described by some as elegant. I thought its use by a woman might fit the story line.

CHAPTER 20

The premise of the book is CPRR's 'difficulty' in obtaining the title to land along the right of way beyond Tunnel #6 and east to Reno. In reality, during 1866-1867 the CPRR dragged three locomotive, forty railcars, rail iron and ties for over forty miles of track that was built "as an island railroad" east of Tunnel #6. This was done with oxen, sleds and a lot of sweat hauling the material over the dirt road known as Dutch Flat Road to then link with the Donner Lake Wagon Road. (See "The Builders of the Central Pacific Railroad," by John Debo Galloway, C.E., on CPRR.org). In this way, the CPRR was far more prepared for the push east to the desert when the tunnels had been completed. This forty mile stretch would have been right where the fictional Purcell Ranch would have been. There were no problems with title to right of way in that stretch.

The CPRR offices in Sacramento were, indeed, very nondescript. In his book *Nothing Like It in the World*, Ambrose documents that one of the first battles Theodore Judah lost to Collis Huntington was the location of CPRR's main office. Judah wanted a large impressive structure and had one picked out. The ever-cost-conscious Huntington said they had to be mindful of the appearance of extravagance to the Eastern investors, and the office should be considerably more modest. Huntington won as was common in the battles between the Big Four and Judah.

Crocker and James Strobridge were the driving forces behind the construction of the CPRR portion of the Transcontinental Railroad. Their engineering, material logistics, and manpower management were unprecedented in this country. The railroad had to deal with hundreds of issues each day which had never before been addressed by any business in America. Analysts have said the tools used to manage labor and material on the railroad provided examples for later management to expand big business in America during the 20th century. Crocker was the consummate overseer. He took care of problems before they became issues. A prime example was how he dealt with Native Americans. Whereas the Union Pacific had continuous and serious conflicts with the Native American tribes they encountered, the CPRR avoided any problems with Native Americans largely because Crocker personally negotiated a peace with the Paiute Indians. He would later do the same with the Apaches when building the Southern Pacific Railroad. Those agreements were never broken by the CPRR, the Southern Pacific RR, or the Native American partners. (See *The Railroad Photographs of Alfred A. Hart, Artist* by Mead B. Kibbey along with accompanying history).

James Strobridge is another fascinating but relatively unknown figure in American history. His talents were discovered by Crocker early in the building process for the railroad. His abilities for organizing men and solving problems quickly led to his rise. Crocker ultimately came to rely on him exclusively for field supervision. Early on during the construction over the Donner Crest, the Union Pacific people came west to inspect their competitor's challenges and went back, telling Durant that CPRR would take three years to completely bore the Donner Tunnel. If true, then the UP would have the prospect of laying more track on level grade further through the flat Utah desert and would receive more government bond (land) allocations than the CPRR. After hearing the reports from his spies, Durant counted on that extra reimbursement. But Strobridge had other ideas. Without revealing anything to the Union Pacific people when they came to inspect, as soon as they left, Strobridge had a completely new construction road built and two locomotives and rail transported up the hill using oxen and horses in some places to pull the sleds over the snow. He then attacked the Donner Tunnel from four different entry points, completing the work in one year. This allowed the CPRR to lay miles and miles of track over the Utah desert, obtaining land swap sections the Union Pacific thought they would get.

Strobridge would later head the Big Four's operations on the Southern Pacific Railroad from Sacramento to Los Angeles and then on to Texas. Strobridge was renowned for his aversion to alcohol. He had little problem in this regard on the western portion of the Transcontinental Railroad as his primary labor force was Chinese, whose main libation was tea. This differed from the UP which was made up of a largely Irish workforce, leading to multiple and constant alcohol issues. Strobridge would routinely destroy any attempted building of saloons along the route, using legal authority when he could. He often destroyed these mobile saloons, such as those that followed the UP construction crews, doing so even without legal authority. He thought alcohol was the single greatest impediment to productivity. (See "The Builders of the Central Pacific Railroad," by John Debo Galloway, C.E., on CPRR.org). Any reading of the UP construction discusses a movable town kept at the far reach of construction and moved forward as the construction progressed. That town was referred to as the End of Tracks or, more commonly, Hell on Wheels. The staggering lawlessness that followed would tend to strongly support Strobridge's claim about the adverse effects of alcohol on productivity.

I have tried to be faithful to the construction details for tunnels and bridges from the Donner Summit to Reno. (See *The First Transcontinental Railroad* by John Debo Galloway, citing contributions made by John R. Gilliss, the engineer in charge under L.M. Clement).

The winter of 1867 was as represented. It was cause for huge concern as no one had apparently planned for such a snowfall. The ultimate cost for the snow sheds and galleries came to over $2,000,000 in 1868 dollars. That would translate to about $50,000,000 in today's currency. It is true that snowplow locomotives could not break through the 1867 drifts. It is also true that CPRR employed 2,500 laborers to hand shovel snow over that winter in what had to be brutal conditions. (See again *The First Transcontinental Railroad* by John Debo Galloway).

CHAPTER 32

Fiddletown, CA, located in Amador County, does exist. However, it is about forty-five miles from Sacramento and more on the route of Highway 89 over the Sierras than on the road from Donner Pass. It was founded around 1849-1850 by placer miners. The water source the miners worked was called Dry Creek as it would run dry in the summer.

It was said that the miners would then fiddle around during those dry months, leading to the town's name.

CHAPTER 36

There were multiple confrontations between settlers in the Truckee-Carson Valley and the Paiute Indians. Fort Churchill was indeed built on the old site of Fort Haven to provide protection. In fact, there were so many confrontations that some termed the period the "Paiute Wars."

There was a Paiute uprising in 1860 and a massacre at the Williams Station near the current city of Dayton, NV. The differing accounts of the reason for the attack are as stated in the chapter. William Ormsby did lead the first group of thoroughly disorganized volunteers into battle. About eighty men died, including Ormsby. I have no idea if there was an Ormsby Hotel in 1865, but there has been a hotel and casino of that name in Carson City for the past thirty years.

The history of Fort Churchill and Captain Joseph Stewart is real. Fort Churchill served as a Pony Express Station and depot until October 1861 as represented in the chapter. The fort was decommissioned due to budgetary cuts following the Civil War; however, in reality, that happened in 1869. I had to move the decommissioning date up a little bit to fit the timeline of the story.

CHAPTER 41

Duane Bliss came to the Virginia City area from the California gold fields at the age of twenty-seven. He worked in a mill, processing silver ore, and rose to become the manager. He saved his money and started a local bank near Virginia City in an area known as Gold Hill. His bank was called the Gold Hill Bank. Bliss eventually sold that small bank to William Sharon and other partners, all San Francisco investors, and it became the Bank of California. Bliss stayed on for a time after the sale and at the direction of the bank's owner, William Sharon. During the time Bliss worked for the Bank of California, he coordinated land purchases for the Bank so that one of the bank's investments, the Virginia & Truckee Railroad, could obtain necessary right of ways. That railroad was the prize vision of Sharon, which led to the easy transportation of ore from the heights of Virginia City down to the Carson River where the stamp mills collected. These mills processed silver ore into bullion. This easy and mobile transportation led to the development of multiple new, more powerful mills that could process more ore. Sharon would then invest not only in the mines themselves but the mills to process the ore along with the railroad to transport it. Based on his position, Bliss would have been quite familiar with land purchases and railroad right of ways.

Bliss would have a falling out with Sharon, leave the bank and began work building a new company, The Carson and Tahoe Lumber and Fluming Co. Bliss saw the need for timber in supporting mine shafts in the booming silver bonanza of Virginia City and began buying property along the eastern shore of Lake Tahoe. Ultimately, he owned almost twenty-two continuous miles of Tahoe lakefront property used in lumber operations mainly out of the hamlet now known as Glenbrook, NV. His company purchased an ingenious flume which diverted the water from Clear Creek for the transport of large logs down from the crest of Spooner Summit, high above Lake Tahoe, to his lumber yard just outside Carson City. At one time, Bliss' Carson City lumber yard at the base of Clear Creek extended for over a mile stacked high with timbers ready to be used as supports by Comstock mining interests. But while Mr. Bliss would have known about land purchases for railroad rights of way, he never issued a loan to a Will Toal. (See *Duane L. Bliss: An Unusual Tahoe Visionary, Part II* by Mark McLaughlin).

CHAPTER 44

Mussel Slough was the location of a battle between representatives of the Southern Pacific Railroad and local ranchers. The confrontation happened in Hanford, CA, which is approximately halfway between Modesto, CA, to the north and Bakersfield, CA, to the south. The actual date of the incident was May 11, 1880, about twelve years after the incident here in my story. The Mussel Slough incident arose out of what was to be a meeting between landowners and the railroad to reach an agreement to stave off eviction from ranches. Homesteaders moved onto the government land with the anticipation (and pursuant to advertisement by the railroad) that the eventual price would be $2.50/acre less any improvements made by homesteaders. However, after years of toil and building, when the settlers went to formalize their stake and purchase the land, the railroad issued asking prices of two to three times that amount. If the amount was not paid, there was a threat of eviction. The meeting back then, as in our story here, was intended to reach an agreement, staving off those evictions. The Mussel Slough meeting, as in ours, took place at a park, albeit in Hanford, which the landowner's families attended to hear a speech by a former California jurist. The railroad group consisted of five people led by U.S. Marshal Alonzo W. Poole, who was in attendance to serve proper eviction notices to those land-owners who would not sell back to the railroad. The railroad had offered to purchase the ranches at exceptionally reduced prices just as in the story here. The meeting got out of hand when two men on opposite sides who'd had a longstanding grudge between them (as Will and Drake here) began shooting at each other. Both sides then erupted. Seven people were killed: two in the railroad's party and five of the owners. I have used the incident as a template here. However, the railroad in-volved in the Mussel Slough affair was the Southern Pacific RR, which was the successor company to the CPRR. The SPRR was started by our same Big Four of history, and our story here, but only later as they began building the Southern Pacific route from Sacramento to Los Angeles.

CHAPTER 51

The configuration of oak trees, dubbed the Cowboy Cathedral in this chapter, does exist. However, it is not in the Carson Valley but in Orange County, Southern California. It is in a regional park called Casper's. There are two trail heads leading into the park: the Bell Canyon Trail and the Nature Trail. If you take the Nature Trail either by foot or horseback, you will find it. There is a tremendous umbrella of oak branches under which you could likely fit almost an entire football field. The ceiling is at least forty to sixty feet tall. It is immediately impressive. I have ridden through this stand of oaks several times on horses I have owned over the years. Each time you enter, it feels spiritual. I will take responsibility for naming it the Cowboy Cathedral, for that name will not appear anywhere in the park directories.

About the Author

J.L. Crafts was raised on the outskirts of a very large city in Southern California. Thankfully, back in those days the very distant outskirts of that city still included open spaces and small ranches. As a young boy he worked wrangling horses on one of those ranches learning to rope, ride and train one of the most magnificent animals our planet has to offer. Those early years created a lifelong connection with, not only horses, but with the west of the 1800's. College led to law school followed by over thirty years of trying cases to juries up and down the state of California. Speaking to juries in a simple directness, he did what he could to elicit facts and arguments wherever possible through stories of life in the saddle and open spaces. He now spends his days creating those stories on the page and enjoys every minute of it.

Coming Soon!

J.L. CRAFTS
SILVER CITY RECKONING
A WILL TOAL NOVEL

Will Toal returns home to discover that his sons have been taken by a brutal desperado who wants revenge for the death of his brother. Will's foreman has been murdered, and his woman has already gone after the killer that has taken their boys. He heads out after them to set things straight. Just as things begin to look up for Will, he discovers that the woman he loves, the mother of his twin sons has been captured.

Can he find her before she's murdered? Will realizes he is not alone. He'll do whatever it takes to protect his family, starting with killing Sam Brown.

Hell is on the horizon.
There will be a SILVER CITY RECKONING...

For more information
visit: www.SpeakingVolumes.us

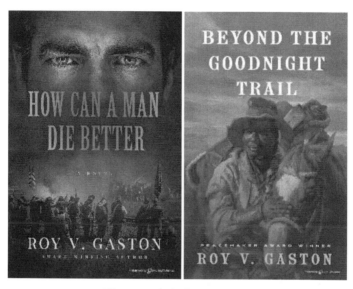

Now Available!

SPUR AWARD-WINNING AUTHOR
PATRICK DEAREN

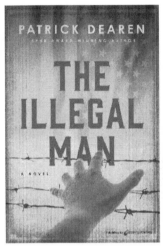
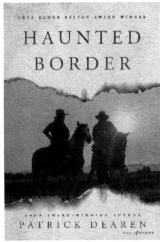
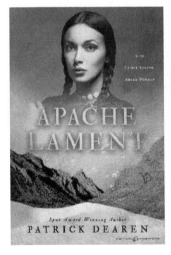
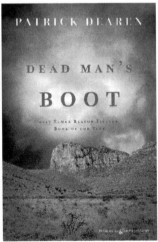

**For more information
visit: www.SpeakingVolumes.us**

Now Available!

SPUR AWARD-WINNING AUTHOR
ROD MILLER

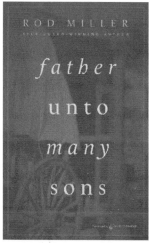
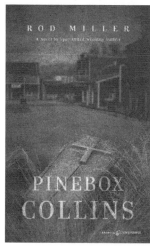
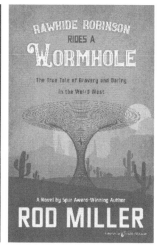

**For more information
visit: www.SpeakingVolumes.us**

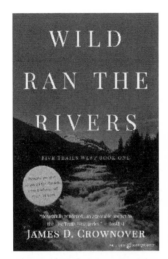
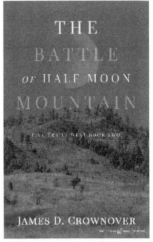
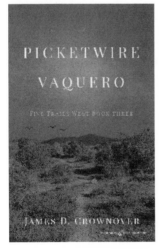
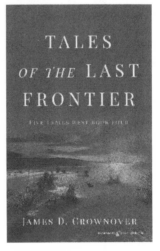